Who's Your Daddy

Dad Coms

Book 1

Brittanée Nicole

Jenni Bara

This is a work of fiction. Names, characters, places, and incidents either are the product of the author's imagination or are used fictitiously. Any resemblance to actual persons, living or dead, events, or locales is entirely coincidental.

Who's Your Daddy © 2025 by Brittanée Nicole and Jenni Bara

First Edition September 2025

Cover Art: elenbushe_art

Cover Design: Mel D Designs

Formatting by Sara of Sara PA's Services

Editing by Beth at VB Edits

Dedication

To all those who loved Beckett so much that we decided to do this again.

Contents

PLAYLIST

Whatever Lola Wants (Lola Gets) - Sarah Vaughan
Hey Daddy (Daddy's Home) - USHER
Monster Mash - Bobby "Boris" Pickett, The Crypt-Kickers
Make You Mine - PUBLIC
I've Got You Under My Skin - Michael Bublé
Don't Blame Me - Taylor Swift
I Think I'm in Love - Kat Dahlia
London Boy - Taylor Swift
Kiss Me - Ed Sheeran

Jersey Boys
Livin' On A Prayer -Bon Jovi
Glory Days - Bruce Springsteen

CHAPTER 1
Lola

"How could you hide this from me?"

My boss leans his forearms on his mahogany desk. He sighs as if exhausted by me, but I'm not the one trying to ruin our lives. "What good would it have done if you'd known, Lo?"

"I could have convinced him not to do this. He always cared about my opinion." Arms crossed over my black wrap dress, I glare.

"Obviously not about this, seeing as how he came to me, yet left you in the dark." Brian's tone isn't the least bit sympathetic as he talks about the man who was like a second dad to me.

I've worked at Murphy and Machon since I was twenty-two and Terance Murphy took me under his wing.

My heart sinks at the memory of the day I met him. I still can't believe he's dead.

His death is only part of the shock that's rocked through the firm recently. The rest came when Terry's will was read.

"It's not as bad as you're making it out to be." He laces his fingers on his desktop. "We only have to live and work there for a year. As long as we make that happen, nothing in the main office will change."

"*There?* That's what you're going to call it?" It's a rat-infested shit hole in Jersey. "Who lives in Jersey?"

"Billy Joel, Bruce Springsteen, Phil Simms, Bon Jovi, and all those—"

Annoyance flares hot in my veins. "I swear to God if you say desperate housewives—"

"It's actually real housewives."

Head tossed back, I scoff. "Why do you know that?"

"I live alone. I get bored sometimes." His smirk is far too mischievous for this ridiculously spotless office. The man keeps everything streamlined. There isn't even a paper on his desk.

If we end up in Jersey, that'll change very soon.

"Not anymore," I taunt.

Brian's smirk falls, and I swear he fights a wince. That little crack in Brian's normally perfect composure hints at just how unhappy he is about this massive change too. He's just good at hiding his emotions and playing his part.

Terry was damn near close to the most rational person on the planet, so it's impossible to wrap my head around why he would risk all he worked for over decades on some half-cocked whim.

"Apparently, you'll be living with dumb and dumber soon," I tease.

He sighs, his posture sagging slightly. "Sully is not that bad."

Sullivan Murphy is one of Terry's sons and a junior partner in the firm. Although I guess he and his brother are full partners now. Brian too. Terry's will, though chock-full of shocking terms, did stipulate that the three of them should have equal shares. *Conditionally.*

"Sully's almost worse than Cal lately. And that's saying something." Sully is a grumpy asshole on his best days, and since his wife Sloane left him, his bad attitude has grown exponentially. The vast majority of the staff are afraid of him. None of them even want to walk into his office.

He waves me off. "Cal's harmless."

"Cal's useless," I correct. "He spends more time on his hair than he does on his case files. You know he has highlights, right?"

"No, he doesn't."

I bite back a grin. "Being that pretty is not natural."

His lips tip up slowly. "You think he's pretty?"

"I didn't mean it that way." I toss my hands in the air, the annoyance in my veins building. "I can't talk to you when you're like this."

"Lo, enough with the drama." He runs a hand through his auburn hair, then laces his fingers on the dark wood desk again.

Yeah, he's drained. He's just better at containing his frustration. One look around this room tells me all I need to know. Brian won't walk away from this as easily as he's letting on. Every detail of his office screams his name. The perfect view of the Manhattan skyline through the floor-to-ceiling windows, the dark mahogany floors he requested during the last remodel, the open floor plan with the leather couches and oversized fish tank that he stops to stare at when he's deep in thought.

Rather than give in and admit that he finds this just as unappealing as I do, he sighs. "I'm dealing with this the best way I can. If we want the firm running, *and we all do*, then the trust dictates that Sullivan, Callahan, and I have to live and work at 100 West 3rd Street for three hundred and sixty-five days."

"*In Jersey*," I remind him, unable to keep from grimacing.

"Yes, it's in Jersey. And I get that you don't like that—"

"It's the armpit of America, what is there to like?"

Nothing. Absolutely nothing. And that small run-down building is the exact opposite of the office we work in now.

"How will I get to work? I live in New York."

"You could move in with us?" Sitting back in his leather chair, he chuckles.

I don't even acknowledge the ridiculous statement. There is no way in hell I'd live with the three stooges. I'd kill one of them within the first week. Probably Cal, he makes even the most reasonable person lose their mind.

"You'll have to lease an apartment for me in Jersey." The words taste bad leaving my mouth. Who in their right mind would willingly leave New York City? And for *Jersey*?

"Done."

"What?" My throat constricts.

"We're only allowed one paid staff member and you and I both know that you care too much about this firm and Terry's legacy to let us take anyone else along." He puts his hands behind his head, elbows out, and tips back in his chair, relaxed for the first time in this conversation.

Damn. He's got me. Of course, a lawyer as good as he is would talk me into arguing for something I don't even want. Because I definitely don't want to live or work in Jersey, and I definitely don't want to set foot in Terry's derelict starter office, let alone spend forty hours a week there for the next year. I visited the building a few years ago, and the spider-infested space is scary.

God, I hate bugs.

"Does it even have running water and electricity?"

"No clue." Brian huffs. "He told me about this plan after Sloane filed for divorce a couple of months ago. I thought I'd have plenty of time to talk him out of it. If I'd known he'd have a heart attack and drop dead at sixty-five, I would have pushed the subject earlier."

It wasn't so much of a drop. He was already on his back when it happened. In bed with a woman younger than I am. I close my eyes and shake away the images that plague me every time I think about where the man who was like a second father to me died.

My parents have always been entirely too open about their sex lives, so maybe it shouldn't bother me. But I'd give just about anything to erase the knowledge of how Terry spent his last few moments on earth.

And we aren't the only ones who know. Everyone does. The woman he was with hasn't stopped blabbing about it to anyone who will listen.

Everyone also assumed Terry would leave this place to Sully, Cal, and Brian when he retired. Although Brian isn't Terry's son by blood, he went to law school with Sully and was long ago virtually adopted into the Murphy family.

So their new status as full equity partners was expected. But leaving this massive office with its twenty non equity junior partners, fifty associates, and almost a hundred other employees, while they spent a year in another state has us all on edge.

The only other option would be to dissolve the firm, sell the building the trust now owns, and start over. Yes, some of the associates might move with the new firm, but we would need all new retainers, not to mention moving a firm our size would be entirely too much work. Also, Terry's money from the sale would be held in trust for ten years under this option which wouldn't help the guys at all.

Receiving the news less than two weeks after Terry's death has only added to the stress. They haven't even had a chance to grieve. None of us have.

"How long do I have to decide?" Guilt keeps me from meeting his eye. Instead, I focus on the collection of framed diplomas and certifications on the cream wall behind him.

He clears his throat and straightens. "We have one month from the date of his death to move into the apartment and get the office running. And ninety days to get Sloane and T. J. to move in with us."

Whoa. Lungs seizing up, I force my attention back to my boss.

His only response is an arched brow.

"Oh no." I splay a hand over my chest. "I'm not talking her into this plan. She and I may be friends, but that doesn't automatically mean I can convince her to move back in with her ex. I'll have enough to deal with just getting the place running on time."

A smirk spreads across his face. It says *got ya.* "Does that mean you're coming with us?"

Dammit. Once again, he almost had me agreeing.

"*Lola.*" Cal sticks his perfectly gorgeous head into the office without knocking, holding the stupid orange mini basketball he's almost always tossing against the wall, or at Sully's head, or in the air.

He's such a freaking child.

I choke back a huff. "I have no idea who you're talking to because that is *not* my name."

Besides my parents, he is the only person who calls me Lola. And he only does it to piss me off.

"Did I hear that right when I walked by before? Did you call me pretty?"

He's a master at pushing my buttons, and the asshole just *has* to speak with a sexy British accent. God, it kills me to have to listen to him. Why'd he have to grow up in England with his mother? If he'd lived here with his father, then he'd sound like every other New Yorker. Instead, his accent makes even the dumbest statements sound smart. It's incredibly infuriating.

Teeth grinding, I glare at him. The man is annoyingly aware of his attractiveness. "It wasn't a compliment."

With a hum, he breaks into a tease of a smile. "Sure. But it was definitely an offer to buy me lunch. I'm dying for a blue slushie and burger from that place on 8th." He tosses the ball back and forth from one hand to the other, blue eyes sparkling with delight. I swear he wears navy just to make the color pop. "We both know you adore their chips. And you're far more likely to get the order right. I always muck it up."

"It's fries, not chips. And you screw up the orders on purpose so we never ask you to do them."

He flashes me a smile so bright I have to fight the instinct to squint and look away. He must bleach his teeth. "Lies."

"Give us a minute," Brian says. "Then she'll get you your Slurpee."

Cal grins like he's won the lottery and shoots his ball into the net hanging on the door to the bathroom just off Brian's office. Cal has one too. They're freaking children. Every last one of them. How could I possibly be considering moving to a smaller office with these idiots?

As Cal disappears, I turn back to Brian, inhaling deeply to control my frustration.

"Calm down, Lo."

"Ever heard that you're not supposed to tell a woman to calm down?" I shake my head. "Brian, there is no way I can work directly with that man-child every day."

He pinches the bridge of his nose. "Look, none of us want this firm to disappear. And like it or not, this is the only way. Give me ninety days to show you that it won't be that bad. That'll give us time to settle and find a new routine. Besides, if Sully can't get Sloane to move in by then, it's over anyway."

A pit opens up in my stomach. The idea of losing this place, especially so soon after losing Terry, is unimaginable.

He's right. There's no other choice. Before I can put that thought into words, the door opens again, and Cal reappears. The basketball is still on the floor in here, and he's got one hand in the pocket of his dress pants, looking relaxed.

"I think the court dropped a kid off for us."

"What?" Brian's eyes flash to mine and back to the doorway.

I spin around to face Cal.

He lifts both shoulders nonchalantly, as if it's a common occurrence for kids to randomly show up at our office.

It's not.

"Some kid arrived with a note around his neck. Figured it was one of your emergency guardianships."

The strangled noise that comes from my throat is filled with both anger and shock. "He's joking, right?" I eye Brian, then glare at Cal. "You are joking, right?"

He takes a single step back and leans to one side. As he straightens, he pulls a small boy into view. Then he ushers him in a step and waves an arm. "Kid."

I blink at the little guy, then look back at the six-foot-something idiot standing beside him for a solid twenty seconds before I can speak. "You've worked here for ten years. You know that's not how this works."

"He's got a note." Cal flicks at the envelope dangling from the boy's neck. "It's your job to read that nonsense, right?"

Jaw locked, I slowly spin and face Brian.

"*Ninety days*," he pleads, his hands pressed together in front of him.

Summoning all the patience I can find, I take a deep breath, square my shoulders, and give the boy a comforting smile.

He stares back at me blankly as I pull the note from around his neck.

Unfortunately, no amount of breathing could have prepared me for the words written on that page.

CHAPTER 2
Cal

Do I really want a blue slushie, or is it more of a raspberry afternoon?

It sort of feels like a blue day. Though I don't know that I want to deal with an electric-blue stained tongue. Red's a bit more natural. It might be the way to go since there's a chance I'll have to stop by Judge Espadrilles' chambers today. She's always gawking at my mouth. It won't do me any good to give her more of a reason to stare.

I'd never go there, don't worry. Even I have my limits.

"What do you think?" I ask the boy by my side.

Kid's cute. Brown hair, blue eyes. Kind of looks like me when I was younger. He'll go far in life.

The little guy stares up at me like he doesn't have a clue what I'm talking about.

Oh. I chuckle to myself. Probably because I didn't say the first half aloud. "Should I go for a blue slushie or a red slushie today?"

He blinks up at me, his long lashes fanning over his cheeks.

Lola squeaks, pulling my attention to where she's looking at the note, eyes wide. Lola's got the greenest of eyes. When she's happy, they're light like the color of a football pitch when it's bathed in sunlight. When she's mad, like she so often is when I speak, they're more of a deep emerald.

Right now, they are definitely gem colored.

She shakes her head, making her pretty thick red braid sway, and tosses the note onto Brian's desk. "Ninety days," she practically hisses as she turns to me and the little guy.

She's glowering, like maybe she's angry, but I can't be certain, since that's how she always looks at me. I'm not terribly worried. There's a chance the expression is because, as it always is, her hair is secured in a braid, and the tightness of it pulls on her face.

Though when she looks down at the little boy, her expression softens, those green eyes warm and her lips tip up in a genuine smile. She's brilliant with kids. Really fucking brilliant. Sometimes I wish I were a kid so she'd look at me like that.

"Want to come with me to get slushies?" she asks in a soft tone.

The boy reaches for her in the same way I want to, both arms outstretched. She takes one hand, and then they disappear.

"Don't forget my blue slushie!" I holler after her, then think better of it. "Actually, a red one. And chips." I watch the two of them disappear into the corridor.

Lola's tiny, practically pocket-sized, which probably makes her seem more approachable to kids. Her shoulders are narrow, her waist is small, but she's still got an hourglass figure that makes my mouth water even now when I know she'd murder me with a serrated knife if she caught me looking.

She never does though. Lola Caruso has no idea of my little obsession and I'd like to keep it that way.

On the other side of his desk, Brian clears his throat, drawing my attention back to him. He's blinking rapidly at the paper in front of him. He looks stressed. He could definitely use a pick-me-up.

"Get Brian an ice cream soda, too," I call, gripping the doorframe and sticking my head into the hall. "But no whipped cream, he gets gassy."

Even-keeled Brian makes a weird, strangled sound deep in his throat.

Stunned by the sound, I haul myself back and whip around. "Did you just growl at me?"

Brian does that blinking thing again. "Have you ever slept with a woman named Brandy?"

Amusement courses through me. "Oh, that's where we're going this morning." I huff a laugh. "Did you have a snog with a Brandy last night?"

He scowls, one hand balled into a fist on his desk, the other crinkling the note a bit. "Do I look like I would sleep with a Brandy?"

I take a moment to study him, since that's what he's always asking me to do. Take his questions more seriously. Think before I speak. I'd tell him—my brother too—to maybe think a little less and live a little more, but then he'd probably growl again.

He leans forward in his leather chair and I can't stop staring at the vein in his forehead that's pulsing aggressively. With red hair that's a bit deeper in color than Lola's and that Irish skin tone, I'd say yeah, he looks like the kind of guy who'd shag a Brandy. If she had green eyes and freckles, they'd make cute kids.

Pinching the bridge of his nose, he tosses the paper onto his perfectly organized desk. "What are you doing?"

"I'm trying to decide if I think you'd shag a Brandy. And picturing your kids if you did." I scratch my head. "But in all these years, I've never seen you with a woman. Do you date men?"

He scoffs and straightens, his chair squeaking. "Focus, Cal." Finger tapping the paper, he zeroes in on me. "Seven years ago, did you sleep with a woman named Brandy?"

A hint of confusion worms its way in, but I hold tight to my humor. It's my go-to response and what he expects from me. "Jesus, take me out for dinner before you get so personal."

He presses on his temples and rubs aggressively. Then his amber eyes slide shut, a sure sign that he's trying to keep from yelling.

Fine. Let me think. I exhale and tilt my head. Have I ever

shagged a Brandy? Fuck, if I know. And *seven years ago.* I barely remember what I did last month, let alone who I slept with seven years ago. And why is he asking me such a ridiculous question? We have a new case to get started on. Normally, he and Lola take our emergency guardianship cases more seriously. This guy seems more concerned about my sex life than a poor kid whose world has been turned upside down. Looks like my dad was right. We need to get back to our roots.

He was a cute kid, too. Maybe five or six. Lips pressed together, I survey Brian's office while I replay the moment I spent with him. Wonder what happened to his parents.

I hope he orders a blue slushie. Then if he doesn't finish it—

"She's a model."

"Who's a model?"

"Brandy," he grits out, his face reddening.

I fight back a scoff. We're still hung up on her? "I thought you said you'd never sleep with a Brandy?"

"Fuck, Cal you make this difficult." He throws himself back in his chair.

Difficult? I avoid that kind of shit as much as I can, so honestly, I'm not trying to be.

I replay the last ten minutes again. I walked in here with a kid, handed the note to Lola, who acted like I'd done something wrong—nothing new there—and then Brian asked me if I'd ever slept with a Brandy. No, he asked if I'd slept with a Brandy seven years ago. Seven years?

Could it, no...that's not...

"According to this note"—he flicks the paper, causing it to move closer to the edge of his desk—"Brandy dropped Murphy Macallister here to be taken care of by his father. Apparently, she got a part in a movie and has to be in Bali for filming. And her opinion is that kids belong in school, not on film sets, so she needs Murphy's father to take over his care." Fingers steepled, he leans back in his chair. His focus is intent and fixed on me the entire time, his words slow, precise.

Macallister. Why is that name familiar? "Okay, so we need to search for his father?"

Brian nods, his eyes full of all kinds of unspoken words. I just have no fucking clue what they're saying.

"His name is Murphy," he eventually says.

My lips twitch. "It's a great name."

"Whose name is Murphy?" The question comes from the door behind me.

I spin and discover my brother Sullivan looming on the threshold.

Blueish silver eyes narrow, and the lines on his forehead bunch as he runs his hand through his salt and pepper hair. I used to tease him about going gray prematurely, but the joke's no longer funny. He's aged since Sloane left him. He's rarely smiled these last few years, but these last few months have been brutal.

"This cute kid who was dropped off at our office for an emergency guardianship."

Sully's eyes bore into me. "That's not how it works."

Brian shifts forward and rests his arms on his desk again. "I've been trying to explain how we've run our business for the last decade, but Cal doesn't seem to be picking up what I'm putting down." He nods at the paper on his desk.

My brother stalks into the room and snatches it from the mahogany surface.

As he reads, his expression, which is always stoic, grows more severe, his scowl so deep I can't help but comment on it.

"Still haven't tried the cream I left on your desk? You should. It really does wonders for wrinkles."

I wait for his reaction, Sully always gives me one. This is my fun. My fingers itch, the energy once again building up inside me needing release. I scan the room for the ball I tossed when I came in, but it's nowhere to be found. Dammit. I don't like just standing here while the two of them have a conversation with their eyes, leaving me out of the loop completely.

My brother squeezes the paper so tightly it crinkles in his hands. I wait with bated breath, anxious about what he'll say. Why, I have no fucking clue, but suddenly, the air in the room has gone thick, like a bomb is about to be dropped.

"You've got a fucking kid."

My heart stutters, and I blink. *Me?*

No. *He's* got a kid. I'm kid free.

He thrusts his hand out, shoving the note at me.

Instinctually, I reach for it. "We need that information to find the father. Don't you two know how this works?"

Sully makes a low, rumbling sound. "You *are* the father."

Breath held, I snap my head to the side, eyeing Brian, who is leaning forward, watching me like he's waiting for my response. He closes his eyes and exhales, clearly not impressed by the reaction.

"So very Star Wars of you," I say to Sully.

"Bloody Hell Cal, focus."

"Are you taking the piss?" I tease.

The only reaction my repartee garners is a glare. From both men. The two of them would be far more suited as brothers than Sully and me.

With a sigh, I admit defeat and give him my full attention.

"Seven years ago you had a one-night stand with a woman named Brandy," he starts, one brow cocked.

"Actually," I say, holding up a finger, "we haven't established that—"

His angry glare has me closing my mouth.

"And she gave the kid your surname as a first name."

"I'd remind you that Murphy is your name too. Are you sure you didn't have a romp with a woman named Brandy?"

Brian growls. "For fucks sake, Cal, your brother did not have an affair with a woman named Brandy."

"I never had a fucking affair." Sully's nostrils flare and I swear smoke billows from his ears. He's been quite defensive since his wife left him. From the beginning, he's claimed that he has no fucking idea what he did wrong.

"Maybe he's Brian's?" I suggest. "You always wanted to be a Murphy." I waggle my brows. "I could see you using our last name to ensure the woman couldn't track you down."

He gives me a flat look. "I assure you, I've never used your last name to get laid."

A bark of a laugh escapes me. "That's because you don't get laid, we've already established this."

"And he wonders why our father put the damn firm into a trust," my brother grumbles.

He steps up close to Brian's desk, and the two of them speak in whispered hisses and curses.

I stay where I am, running my hands through my hair. It takes a fuck ton of control to remain calm. I'm not an idiot—even if I'd rather play one right now. In a matter of seconds, I'll have to accept the fact that my life has just irrevocably changed.

When I'm certain I can't deny the truth any longer, I drop my hands. "I'm a father," I rasp.

My throat constricts violently.

Okay, that kind of hurt. Let's try it again.

"I'm a father." The words are a little bit firmer this time.

I clear my throat. "Okay."

They're still talking, ignoring me, though they do peer over at me every few seconds, matching annoyed expressions on their faces.

"Hello," I say louder.

They're still ignoring me.

"Gentlemen, please!"

That gets their attention. Both men straighten and blink at me.

"Did you just call us gentlemen?" If I thought he had it in him, I'd swear Sully almost smirks.

I shake my head. "Better than the wankers you're acting like."

"We're the wankers?" My brother says, a hint of amusement in his tone.

Shit. As terrifying as the conversation is, as hard as it's become to breathe with the truth pressing down on me, I'm determined to continue it. I haven't seen my brother smile in months, and if this is what it takes, then so be it.

Sucking in a ragged breath, I nod. "Talk *to* me, not about me."

Brian motions to the pair of chairs on the other side of his desk. "Take a seat and we'll tell you how this is going to go."

CHAPTER 3

Lola

"**A**m I staying in here while you go deal with the dad mess?" Murphy looks around my office, eyes wide. His lips are tinged blue from the Slurpee. The resemblance to his father is uncanny, but unlike Cal, this kid is sharp as a tack.

"It's not a mess," I assure him.

There's a good chance that's a lie. This could be the mess to end all messes. I have no idea how Cal will react when he finds out he has a six-year-old.

Murphy turns away from the bookcases he was inspecting and cocks his little brow. Although he doesn't say a word, the I'm not stupid is telegraphed clearly.

"We're just trying to get everything squared away," I say. "There is no issue."

"Unless you consider that my dad is an idiot." Murphy sighs, his little shoulders deflating.

God, this kid is far too perceptive.

"I wouldn't say that." Lies. I've called Cal an idiot more times than I can count. But this poor kid has been through more emotional turmoil than anyone should have to deal with. I don't want to add to it. "It's more like he looks at the world with childlike wonder." Murphy's lips pull into a tight line. As if it has a mind of its own my chin dips. I catch it quickly and shake my head instead. "How about you relax on the couch while I figure out the plan?"

"Fine." He drops his blue backpack on the hardwood floor with a thunk and settles onto the cushions. With his half-empty Slurpee cup balanced next to him, he digs a tablet from the bag. "What's the Wi-Fi password?"

"Oh." I stand. "I can connect it for you."

He shakes his head, his dark hair falling over his forehead. "I can do it. I just need the password."

I open the top drawer and pull out the card where I've typed out the information he's looking for. Then I scoot around the desk and hand it to him. At lunch, when he read the menu at Ruby's, I discovered that he reads at a level far higher than the average first-grader. I learned that he's going to start first grade this fall when I gently pried a few pieces of information from him.

"I'll be right back," I promise as I shuffle to the door.

He lifts a shoulder, his focus never leaving his tablet, like he couldn't care less whether I stayed or left. The reaction makes my chest squeeze.

How often is he left alone? For such a young kid who's been thrust into a situation that would be terrifying to even the most hardened adults, he's not the least bit fazed. Though it's probably a good thing he's self-sufficient, all things considered.

I slip out the door and rush back across the hall to Brian's office. When I step inside, I find Brian and Sully, but no Cal.

"Where is Cal?" I hiss as I scurry closer.

Sully, who's sitting in one of the guest chairs with one ankle resting on the other knee, scowls. "He needed a minute."

My stomach lurches. "He left? Don't we need a plan?"

My reaction is ridiculous, really. I shouldn't be surprised he ran away the moment responsibility called his name.

The men's gazes shift behind me, and a second later, a little throat clears. "Sorry. This was in my backpack. I was supposed to give it to you."

I turn and find Murphy holding out a manila envelope. Once I've taken it, he backs out of the room and disappears. I'm tempted to chase him, to assure him again everything is okay. But this kid is too smart to be placated. Most of the kids I deal with are all too aware of the nuances of their situations. So I fight the urge and peek inside the envelope. Finding what I assumed I would, I dump the birth certificate, social security card, and state health insurance card onto the desk.

"How helpful." I pick up the birth certificate and scan it. Sure enough, Callahan Murphy's name is printed on the line reserved for the child's father.

I shove it toward my boss, making sure he sees what I'm seeing.

"Yeah," Brian rubs a hand down his face. "We're aware. We already pulled a copy."

Sully lowers his head and gives it a shake.

"But having the original helps. I'll have to file it with the court so he can move to Jersey with us," Brian adds.

I wince. I'd all but forgotten about the hellhole since the bomb was dropped on us a couple of hours ago. Damn. This kid is going to have to live there right alongside us. Pursuant to the trust, it's not just the partners who have to live in the small apartment. Their spouses and children are required to as well.

Dread washes over me. What exactly was Terry thinking when he crafted the terms?

Brian sets the birth certificate down. "School doesn't start for another week or so. That means he'll have to be with you all day."

"Me?" I shift back and bump into the bookcase behind me. "What?"

"Emergency guardianship." Brian cocks a brow at me. "You're the only one with the credentials to hold him until the court grants the request."

I sigh. Right. That is my job. Normally I don't bat an eye at the long hours emergency guardianships require, but this is Cal's kid. Somehow that thought makes my stomach flip.

With a deep inhale, I shake off the sensation. I do this all the time. I need to get it together. The court should be ready to hear the emergent filing tomorrow. "Okay. I can keep him tonight."

"Three days," Sully all but growls.

Eyes narrowed, I shoot daggers at him. In this moment, I despise him almost as much as Sloane does. He could at least say please.

Sully must sense the angry energy flowing from me because his tone softens when he speaks again. "My brother will be in no position to take care of a child by tomorrow." His entire being sags. I can't blame him. So much of the responsibility is going to fall on him. I can already envision it.

I scoff. "But he'll be parent of the year by Thursday?"

"No. By Thursday we'll all be together." Brian frowns as if the words he's spoken have forced reality to finally set in.

Because, thanks to Terry, by Thursday, we will all be living in Jersey.

I'm not sure whether the idea seems better or worse than it did two hours ago.

"After the cleaning service and pest control get through the building, we can move in," he says, his tone full of false lightness, like he's working to convince himself as much as me.

"*Pest control?*" I shiver and blow out a rough breath.

Sully rubs at his forehead like he's trying to ease the headache he's suffered from for the entirety of his little brother's life. When he lifts his head, his blue eyes plead with me. It's a vulnerability I've never seen from this stoic man. "Please, Lola? We need you."

"Fine." I cross my arms and steel my spine. This is outrageous, yet once again I find myself signing up for the ridiculousness without much fight. "I'll keep him until Thursday. You two get the paperwork done, then you have to find me an apartment. ASAP."

Brian smirks. "Sure you don't want to live with us?"

"Oh, don't even try it, I am not going to be Cal's nanny."

CHAPTER 4
Cal

I pace back and forth in the conference room trying to wrap my head around this bloody situation. I have a son. I'm a father. No matter how many times I say it, the words don't make anymore sense than they did when Sully talked me through all of it.

And then they sent me in here while they did some research. Because their first instinct was to prove it wasn't true.

"We should require a blood test, make sure he's actually a Murphy," was my brother's suggestion.

"Definitely a DNA test, this isn't the first time someone has claimed you've fathered their child, I'm sure." That was Brian.

I scoffed at his assertion.

It absolutely was the first time anyone had suggested I was a father, and I didn't need a bloody test to tell me what I already knew. Murphy Macallister was my son. One look at him and it was clear as day.

And I could feel it. This strong unfamiliar need to comfort him. This overwhelming pull to race down the street after him and Lola. He was mine and I wasn't going to play their games. So waiting in here for Lola to return with Murphy seems like the best option. But it's been a while, and not only am I wondering what's taking them so long, I'm figuring the slushie will be melted by the time they return.

I shake my head. There's no way I could even contemplate eating or slurping right now.

I have a son.

A smile tilts my lips as I imagine how much fun we'll have. Unlike Sully, I'm going to be the fun dad. I'm already the fun uncle. I straighten my suit jacket, determined to stalk back into the office to tell my brother just that, and to tell Brian to forget all his silly concerns, when instead I find Murphy standing at the door, staring over at me.

All my grand plans go out the window when I see the uncertainty in his blue eyes. Eyes that are the exact shade of mine. Eyes that give off the impression that he's unaffected, just like I so often act, but I imagine beneath the exterior he's probably scared and nervous. Just like me.

"Murphy, right?" I say casually, trying not to rush at him and pull him to my chest. I've never so much as been introduced to my own son, let alone gotten the chance to hold him.

He nods and arches a brow. "Coming to terms with it all?"

His candor and delivery surprise me. My eyes widen, unable to hide my shock. "Yes." If he can be honest, so can I.

He nods like he appreciates that. "It's a lot. Don't worry, I heard they're figuring it all out in there." He thumbs over his shoulder toward Brian's office and I can't help my scowl.

"There's nothing to figure out. Can I—" Before I've even started speaking, I'm walking toward him and am about to drop to my knees to hug him when he seems to take a step back. I hold up a hand realizing he may seem older, but he's young, and despite the fact that I'm his father, he doesn't know me. "Sorry, I just wanted—" I shake my head. "Never mind."

What I want is to hug him, but what he apparently needs is space. For once in my life I'm worried about someone else's wants over my own, so I stay put.

He shrugs. "I'm sure Mom will be back in a few weeks. I know it will probably cramp your style, but I won't get in the way. I'm pretty good at taking care of myself. I can do a lot with twenty dollars a day." He holds out a hand like he's waiting for me to hand him some money.

I'm not sure what to make of any of it. He's only a boy but he's clearly not been given the chance to be a child. That ends today. I just don't exactly know how to accomplish that yet, so I reach into my wallet and pull out a twenty. Murphy seems to nod as I set it in his palm and then he slips it into his pocket. "Thanks."

"I know this is strange," I start, but I keep my hand held out. "But I'm Callahan. Most people call me Cal, but since you're my son, you can call me—"

"Cal." The kid gives me a placating nod. "I'll call you Cal."

Right.

He doesn't take my hand so I pull it back, slipping both into my pockets, and rock back and forth on the balls of my feet. "Well, you arrived at the perfect time. We'll be moving in with your Uncle Sully, your cousin T. J., and Brian."

"Do I get my own room?"

I don't actually know what the living situation is in the New Jersey office but I nod because he seems keen to move in with us if that's the case. "Of course."

"Great. Well, I can go hang out on the couch while everyone works out what happens next." The shrill sound of Lola's voice from the other room has both of us looking in that direction. "Seems like they might need some help."

I shrug. "Probably not from me."

He nods again. "Probably." Then he turns to leave, but I can't have us leaving it like this.

"Murphy?"

He looks up at me and I think maybe I took him by surprise because the mask he's been wearing the entire time slips and I see the smallest amount of vulnerability in his gaze. And maybe hope.

"I'm really happy to meet you."

He's quiet for a moment and I take the opportunity to take another step closer. "And I'm really excited to get to know you better. I know this is awkward, and I'm sure you're expecting that I've got no idea what I'm doing, but I'd really like us to be friends."

Murphy adjusts the backpack he's holding to one shoulder and nods. "Yeah, we could try that."

I can't stop the smile from moving across my face. Nor can I stop myself from kneeling down and reaching for him. This time, though, he doesn't step back, and though he doesn't hug me, he allows me to pull him into my chest and squeeze him tight. This feeling settles in my chest, making it hard to catch my breath.

"Oh, um, sorry for interrupting," I hear Lola say as I try like hell to get myself to release Murphy. With my head still on his shoulder, I catch the expression of surprise on her face. She's clutching a stack of papers but her head is tilted like she's trying to figure out what's happening.

I let Murphy go finally and smile at him, not wanting her interruption to mess up the little ground I've made with him. "Murphy and I were just acquainting ourselves."

I lean an arm against the conference table and stand up, then brush off my trousers. "What happens now?"

Lola seems to look back and forth between Murphy and me. "Well, um, Murphy, you'll be coming with me."

"What?"

The panic in my tone must be evident because Lola offers a tentative smile. "It's typical. I'm an emergency guardian," she explains to Murphy. He shrugs like it's no big deal. "So, until the court signs off on Cal's um—" She glances back and forth again like she's uncomfortable. "Paternity," She finally settles on the word.

"I'm Murphy's father," I grind out. "If they—"

She shakes her head. "We know you're Murphy's father. Murphy had the birth certificate with your name on it."

"We can do a test if you need," Murphy offers.

I glare at the question. "There will be no tests."

Lola sighs heavily. "I wasn't suggesting that."

"Good."

She straightens. "As I was saying, Murphy will come with me. Just give me a few hours to get it sorted with the court. Do you mind hanging here for a bit? There's a television in the other room. I could set you up in there?" she offers.

I hate how Murphy nods like he's completely comfortable with the idea and how Lola is the one taking charge. I should be doing something but the truth is I have no idea what to do.

"I could watch TV with you," I say right as Murphy is about to disappear.

"We need your help filling out some of these forms," Lola says, waving the papers in her hand like she wants us to see proof of the reason she's asking me to stay behind to spend time with her. *Obviously, she doesn't want to spend time with me, but this is her job*, is what her gesture clearly says.

"Right, well, I'll be here if you need me," I tell Murphy.

He nods. "Okay, Cal, I'll see you later."

And then my son disappears with Lola again, and even though I've only just met him, I feel like a piece of me is walking away.

CHAPTER 5

Cal

"Home sweet home," I mumble to myself as I walk around the disaster that is our new flat.

Brian and Sully look far more subdued than I feel. Can't imagine why they're not more excited about the move. How could anyone not be thrilled when they see the broken glass littering the kitchen from what appears to be an ancient baseball through the window, or the clumps of dust that have accumulated in every corner of the space?

The ceilings are ridiculously low. It'll be bad enough for Brian and me. But for Sully? It's a literal hazard. Already, he's hit his head on a doorframe. If he's concussion-free by the end of the day, I'll consider that a win.

Though we'll probably all need tetanus shots if we want to leave this place without lockjaw and painful muscle spasms. "I can't fathom Dad really setting this up. Are you sure this is the place?"

Brian must be pulling one over on us. Or maybe it's Lola. I've pissed her off enough over the years to warrant it. I could see her giving us the wrong address. Bloody hell, it's probably a ruse. Lips twitching, I turn to hit the men with another joke.

Before I can, Sully lets out a low curse and grips the back of his head.

Shit. That's the second time he's hit his head. The no-concussion thing is *not* looking promising.

"This is definitely the place," Brian says, his tone flat. "The office is downstairs. Your father brought me here when he signed the trust."

Sully gives him a murderous glare. Like me, my brother is upset about the way our father turned to Brian with the details of this situation, yet never brought it up to either of us.

There are so many questions we'll never get answers to. While Brian is stuck in this situation like we are, he at least had the opportunity to discuss it with Dad.

It feels an awful lot like everything in my life is tilting and twirling and I can't quite catch my bearings. It all started with the loss of my father. It's still hard to comprehend. The man was always so commanding. Always so in control.

I lived to push at those constraints, and now that he's gone, I have no one to push against. If he can see me now, I'm sure he's laughing. He truly did get the last word because if I don't do exactly what he has instructed, then I lose everything.

A bit ironic considering the way he died—while in bed with a woman who wasn't even half his age. Not sure he should be the one telling us how to live our lives.

As if his death and the stipulations of the trust haven't been hard enough on me, discovering that I have a kid, who I now have to drag into this mess, really has me lost. I want him here with me—it was nearly impossible watching Lola and him leave yesterday, but the rules are the rules, and until the court hears Brian's complaint, the law requires Murphy to stay with Lola as emergency guardian.

It's probably for the best considering the dump we've found ourselves in. At least I have another forty-eight hours to make it habitable.

"Knock, knock," a woman calls from the front of the flat. The three of us look from one to another, dumbstruck.

"You didn't set up appointments for today, did you?" Sully asks Brian.

Neither bothers to check with me. They know I avoid meeting with clients like it's my business. Avoidance should be my middle name.

But there's no avoiding the woman standing in the center of our living room, her dark black curls covered partially with a golden silk scarf. Beads jangle at her wrists with every step she takes. She's wearing layers of clothing draped loosely over her body, each a different color.

The lines on her face deepen as she smiles at us.

"You must be Terry's sons." She holds out her hand and a gold snake around her pinky finger grabs my attention as I return the greeting, its green eyes mesmerizing me in an almost trance-like way.

"We are," Sully says. "And who are you?"

Brian is less suspicious. He nods and gives her a professional smile, as if he recognizes her.

The air shifts, and my brother looks at me. Once again, Sully and I have been left in the dark.

"You must be Madame Esmeralda?" Brian shakes her hand, then darts a look at us over his shoulder. "Your father's psychic," he explains, his brows lifted.

"My father didn't have a psychic," Sully growls.

I have to hold back a laugh at the absurdity.

My father would never.

Me, on the other hand? I'm curious. So I take a step closer, once again transfixed by the snake.

"He did, and she's our third-floor tenant," Brian explains, using the even tone he perfected years ago when speaking to or in front of clients.

"Rent control," she singsongs, "it's a beautiful thing."

"There's no lift in this building." Sully narrows his eyes on the woman. "You climb three flights of stairs every day?"

The woman tilts her head, appraising him with a hint of a smirk. "Your energy is all off." Her words are knowing, her voice serious. "I fear you'll never get her to forgive you if you don't let go of all that anger."

My brother huffs and takes a step back, ducking an instant before he slams into a light fixture. "What is she talking about?"

"Seems like a pretty good psychic to me," I mumble, still studying the ring.

The older woman smiles. "Thank you. Your energy is much brighter. Though this apartment needs plants—lots of them—to really cleanse the atmosphere. Also, caring for plants will help you practice being a dad."

My heart stutters. "Someone get this woman a chair, she's bloody brilliant."

"Oh for fucks sake," Sully rumbles, gripping his forehead. Shit. It won't be long before he's complaining that I'm giving him a migraine.

"I was so sorry to hear about your father's passing," she says, her lips turned down in a sincere frown. "I told him to watch out for ginger."

A gasp works its way out of me. "Is that why he was always so weird when I brought sushi into the office?"

Brian shuts his eyes and groans.

She shrugs. "Probably."

"Lotta good you did him." Sully grunts. "He was with a woman named Ginger when he had the heart attack."

I clap a hand over my mouth and drag it down to keep my expression neutral. Yes, my father was having sex with a twenty-four-year-old named Ginger Days when he died. Doesn't get more cliché than that.

"Maybe be more specific next time."

She gives my brother a patronizing smile. "I only see what I see." Hips swaying and her bracelets jangling, she dances around the flat. She sweeps her hands through the air and flutters her fingers. "And what I see is a whole lot of good coming from this move." She spins around and holds up a finger. "But to be on the safe side, stay away from women named Ginger."

"Hell," Sully mutters.

"But sex wouldn't be such a bad thing for you." She gives him a wry look. "Might clean out your chakras." She turns that expression on Brian. "Same with you."

When she turns to me, I grin. I definitely don't need my chakras cleaned out, thank you very much. "You should probably abstain for a while." She waves a hand up and down my body. "At least until she's ready."

My head snaps. "Until *who's* ready?"

She's already heading to the door. "Welcome to the building, boys. Oh, and if you see a man with tattoos up and down his arms, just leave him be. His name is Sebastian and he's not here for you. He's here for me."

I'm still trying to decipher her comments when my brother curses behind me. "Is this the only bathroom?"

I turn and follow his voice. When I find him, he's standing in a locker room-style bathroom with three sinks lined up beneath a clouded, broken mirror. On one end of the room are two small stalls with doors and one larger stall with the door hanging half off its hinges, and on the other side is a plastic shower curtain that looks like it's seen better days.

"Maybe?" Brian answers. "At least there's more than one toilet." He pushes one door open with a creak and peers in. Quickly, though, he rears back, his entire body shuddering. "That needs to be cleaned."

"How many bedrooms?" I mutter as I come to terms with the reality of our situation.

I think it's finally sinking in. This is not a joke.

"Four," Brian says as he walks past me. I follow him to the living room. No way do I want to stay in the bathroom and see whatever he saw.

"I'll take this one." Sully peeks into a room with an oversized, rounded door. When he steps through it, he doesn't even have to duck.

"Murphy needs his own room." Brian points to two doors side by side. "These can be yours."

I frown. "What about Sloane and T. J.? Where will they sleep?"

Sully appears again, hands in his pockets, face etched with determination. "I can fit a queen and a bunk bed in my room."

Brian's lips turn down. "Only T. J. is required to stay. He and Murphy could probably share a room. They're close in age, and since they're both boys, I'm sure the court would be okay with that."

"No." My brother's tone leaves no room for objection.

I smirk. "No?"

"T. J. *and* Sloane are moving in. They'll stay with me."

Brian glances at me then back at Sully. "According to the trust, family is required to stay here. If Sloane signs the divorce papers, then she's not family."

I wince, my chest aching. It hurts to think of Sloane as anything but my sister. I can't even imagine how Sully feels since she left him. My normally grumpy brother has turned into an absolute bear, making me a little afraid to ask.

"She doesn't have to stay," Brian continues. "We just need to get her to agree to let T. J. move in."

Sully rocks back and forth on his feet. "*I'm* not signing them."

"You're not signing the papers I spent weeks working on so that she'd agree not to fight for interest in the firm? Your father's firm that you've sacrificed every good part of your life for?" Brian's words aren't harsh, despite the topic. His tone is one of pure confusion.

Sully shakes his head and hits us with his signature glare. "No. I'm getting my wife back. I'll convince her to move in with us. And neither of you will tell her another option even exists."

I run my hand over my face, trying to hide my smile. "Oh, that'll go over splendidly, I'm sure, considering that your wife hates you."

She truly does. I love my brother, obviously, and I adore Sloane, so I would love for them to work things out, but after the disaster their separation has been, I don't see that happening.

"You've got your own shit to worry about." With a scoff, he grabs his phone and stalks out of the flat, ending the conversation.

While Brian disappears into the last bedroom, muttering about how fucking miserable this next year will be, I take another step toward the bedroom they've delegated to Murphy.

The small space is sparse. It's empty of all furniture, and fuck, there isn't even a light fixture. I blow out a breath and rock on my feet, imagining what a little boy would like. Obviously, he needs a bed and a place to put his clothes. Does he even have clothes? If not, where do I get them? And what size should I buy? I glance down at my suit. Maybe my tailor could whip up a couple for him so we match. Shit, that makes me smile. Picturing the two of us in matching suits. Drinking our slushies. Smiling at Lola.

Lola.

What are she and Murphy doing right now?

Until now, I've never really thought about what an emergency guardianship entails. I've never considered how Lola knows what to provide, let alone what to say to kids when they're put in these situations.

I wish I remembered Murphy's mother, but try as I might, I can't conjure her.

Memory or not, the woman never contacted me about a child. That pisses me off. I've missed out on so much. I'd like to think I'd have done the right thing and been involved from day one if she'd told me. If that had happened, then my father would have gotten to know his other grandson. Fuck. He was always great with T. J.

But all these *would have, could have, should have's* don't change a thing. I didn't know, and now I do.

And I don't have a fuck ton of time to figure out how to be a father.

I slip my phone from my pocket and open the notes app. Then I start a list of things I'll need. Two beds, two dressers, two light fixtures. Clothes.

What else does a kid need?

The task is daunting, and regardless of the things I purchase for him, none of them will be what he really needs. He needs a parent.

I may play dumb, but I'm not. I need to get this right. More than I've ever needed to get anything right. This little boy's mother abandoned him with a father he doesn't know, and now we're moving him into a run-down joke of a home. I've got my work cut out for me.

"Bloody hell!" My brother booms from somewhere in the flat.

I peek out into the living room.

Sully lumbers through the doorway of his own room. "Rodents!"

Brian points at the phone he's got held to his ear and mouths, "On it."

"We need a housekeeper. Furniture and groceries too. And someone to fix the window."

As my brother rattles off one need after another, I add them to my list. We've only got forty-eight hours to get this place ready for Murphy and there's no bloody way I'm going to let him sleep in a place with mice.

I should be just as peeved about this situation as Brian and Sully are. I know I should find this entire debacle miserable, daunting even. But there's this part of me, a really large part if I'm honest, that is relieved my father forced this on us.

Not the whole living in a disastrous flat part. That's going to be miserable.

But the part where I have to live with these two men is more appealing than I ever thought it would be.

Because I have no idea what I'm going to do with a child.

And even if Sully isn't the perfect father, he loves his kid, and he's a hell of a lot more knowledgeable than I am.

Brian will help too. He may not be a dad, but he helped raise his nephew for most of his childhood. That alone means he's more qualified to be a parent than I am.

After they've had a few days to wrap their heads around the changes that are hitting us from all angles, I'm confident we'll figure this out together. We have to. For the first time in my life my only concern is for someone else: my son.

CHAPTER 6
Lola

I study Murphy where he sits beside me in the back of the town car. He looks so small on the black leather bench seat.

As the driver navigates through traffic, he stares out the window, focusing on the Hudson River below us. His eyes shift from the water to the George Washington Bridge, and then up to the New York skyline.

No fidgeting, no tension in his body, no sign of fear, nothing that would indicate the unease a child typically experiences when heading to a new place with virtual strangers.

"You nervous?"

"No." His words are flat.

Most kids in his situation would be, but in the days I've known him, he's been emotionless, almost numb. It's clear that being vulnerable makes him uncomfortable. So far, he's the opposite of Cal, who is all big feelings. Murphy presents as the kind of kid who's been let down, forgotten, and overlooked so many times that it has hardened him. It almost seems as if he's protecting himself by no longer allowing himself to feel.

I wish this wasn't normal for me. Witnessing this type of trauma. The kinds of walls kids build to hide behind. After eight years doing this job though, I understand. Pushing won't help, he needs time and unwavering support.

Hopefully, Cal can give him that.

Internally, I scoff at the thought. It'd be easier to believe in the Easter Bunny than it would be to believe the man-child will magically become the parent this little boy needs overnight.

Though Brian and Sully have experience, they also have to get the office up and running. The need to save the business will be the driving force for the workaholics, so I can't imagine they'll be a whole lot of help.

New office, new apartment, new kid.

I blow out a breath.

As irritating as Cal is, I feel for him.

The three of them will need a lot of help. So will the little boy next to me. Just the idea of leaving Murphy with them has created a knot in my stomach that tightens with every hour that passes. Cal is his father though. He needs to try. Like with any other guardianship, it's my job to give the parent the benefit of the doubt. It's my job to set them up so the situation works for them both. It's what's best for Murphy.

Which is why my fate is sealed. I'm moving to Jersey. Every time the thought hits me, it's accompanied by a shudder. But with six apartment showings this week, it has to be okay.

Yes, Jersey makes me think of chaos and clutter, but that doesn't mean it will be that way. My parents were the cause of most of the chaos. It's not fair to blame the entire state, and since I'm going to be a resident of New Jersey once more, I need to get rid of the idea that it's awful. *I can do this.*

Becoming a New Yorker nearly a decade ago was a point of pride for me. I jumped in with both feet, and made sure to always keep those feet in Valentino, Manolo and Jimmy Choos. Manolo's don't belong in Jersey.

I'm going to need new shoes.

Murphy shifts to sit back in his seat as we pull off the bridge and head toward the first exit.

Itching to perk him up, I say, "The views of the skyline are great here, especially at night."

At least I think they will be.

He gives me a clipped nod in response. That's it. This poor kid acts more like a surly old man.

I pat his leg. "It's going to be okay."

Slowly, he turns his head, his eyes telegraphing a response that looks an awful lot like *are you kidding me.*

Yeah, I get it.

Placating words are not going to cut it with him. He's too street smart.

I force myself to sit in the silence and watch the buildings go by. Each street we turn onto is more run-down than the last. Eventually, the car stops in front of a three-story building with a broken window. The flower beds out front are full of weeds, some so overgrown they've crawled out onto the cracked sidewalk. The entire façade is covered in a layer of grime. Like it needed a good power washing a decade ago. At this point, the sludge may be forever caked onto the surface.

"This is it." The non-question leaves Murphy's lips with a defeated sigh.

My shoulders slump with a similar sensation, but I keep my tone light. "They're still getting it together. I heard the inside's already done."

He turns to me in that slow way of his, never in a hurry, his eyes meeting mine. "Like we'll go through the door and find ourselves in another place?" The words drip with a sarcasm far too impressive for such a young person.

I bite back a breathy laugh. "Like we'd be that lucky."

Finally, his lips lift in a hint of a smile. The first I've seen from him since he showed up at the office.

Mental note: he responds better to snark.

My kind of kid.

"Let's go." I scoop up my purse and climb out. On the sidewalk, Murphy and I stand side by side and look up at the looming structure. The place doesn't look any better from outside the car. But it doesn't look worse either. Little wins.

Our driver sets the small carry-on I purchased on the sidewalk beside me. I picked up a few necessities for Murphy as well, all of which are packed inside it.

"Can't get any worse." With that, Murphy shuffles toward the building.

"Brian said the door at the back of the building leads to the second floor." I rush after him.

We skirt the structure, and when we find the back entrance, I punch in the code Brian gave me.

The door opens to a very narrow stairway that leads straight up.

"This is the kind of place adults tell kids to stay away from..." Murphy shakes his head and steps onto the first stair. "And my dad moves into it."

"At least there aren't any cobwebs." I don't love spiders. I don't love bugs in general. Especially ladybugs. A shiver races down my spine at the thought of the little red polka-dotted creatures. Gross.

When we get to the top of the stairs, I push the door open and step into a surprisingly large open living room full of...plants? Every window ledge is covered in potted plants. Every other flat surface too.

There are cacti and ferns and spider plants and at least ten other species I can't name. We've stepped into a house plant jungle. And not one of them was in the pictures Brian sent me.

Why the hell would the guys fill the whole place like this?

Murphy sighs. "It's my dad, right?"

"Um." It's all I can come up with. I'm too stunned to form words.

"He's the weird plant guy, isn't he?" It's a question, but there's certainty in Murphy's tone.

I blink. "Maybe?" I can't picture it being Brian or Sully. And yet I've never known Cal to be into plants. His office in New York is plant free, and I'm certain I didn't see any the one and only time I was in his penthouse.

Cal appears in the kitchen doorway, dressed in joggers and a T-shirt, with a mister in his hand, singing softly to himself.

As I assess him, it occurs to me that I've never seen him dressed so casually. It's disconcerting the way my eyes can't help but eat up every inch of him.

The second he spots us, he freezes, his eyes widening, like we've caught him off guard. But an instant later, he breaks into that stupid sexy smile of his.

"Oh, hi," he says, affecting a casual stance, like the room we've just stepped into isn't something straight out of the Jungle Book. "I didn't know you were here already." When neither of us says anything, his expression goes pinched for a second, almost betraying his nerves, but he recovers quickly. "I was just getting ready to give these little babies their special midday showering." His eyes move over the room, softening. "Aren't they perfect?"

"Why?" I ask, looking from one plant to another. And another. And *another*. "Why are there seventeen plants in this room?"

"Because the lighting in my room isn't right." He shrugs.

"No." I scoff. "That's not what I meant. Why do you have so many of them?"

"Jeeze, you sound like Sully." With a shake of his head, he sets the mister on the table. "I thought one would be enough. But then when I went to the store, I realized that if I only picked a single plant, I'd be taking it away from its family. So I got them all. I didn't want anyone to be lonely." Cal surveys his new friends, his shoulders slumping almost imperceptibly. "Turns out taking care of plants isn't as easy as it seems."

"My dad is the weird plant guy," Murphy whispers, "and he's not even good at it."

At this moment it's hard to disagree with that statement. This is already going poorly.

I clear my throat. "How about we get Murphy settled and then can we focus on the plants?"

Cal straightens again, and that smile is back. "Yes, wait until you see your room, it's the best." Still beaming, he rushes towards us.

As he gets close, I'm engulfed in his spicy cologne. I have to fight the urge to lean in and sniff. I'd never admit it but I've always loved how he smells. His scent is just one more annoying attribute on the long list of them that Callahan Murphy possesses.

He snags the small suitcase from me, causing our hands to brush. The brief contact sends warmth rushing up my arm and forces all rational thought from my brain.

"Come on, Lola," he sings, quickly reminding me that I hate him.

"*Lo*," I snap.

"Whatever Lola wants." Cal's laughter echoes off the low ceiling in the tiny hallway as he practically skips toward the door labeled Murphy's room. "I got you the best room."

Murphy says nothing. He just stops a couple of steps inside the door and freezes.

When I follow him in, I see why.

The mattress on the opposite wall is in a blue race car frame. The desk beside it matches.

"When I saw this bed, I knew it would be perfect." In two strides, Cal is on the other side of the room. He drops onto the colorful comforter and bounces up and down. "I got the extra springy mattress. Come try it."

Slowly, Murphy slips his backpack off his shoulders. It lands on the floor with a thunk, and then he's cautiously shuffling to the tiny bed. Carefully he sits next to Cal, making sure to leave a couple of inches of space between them.

Cal bounces again, launching Murphy into the air. He catches the little boy with ease, and while he chuckles, Murphy doesn't even crack a smile.

"Isn't it great?" Cal's tone is full of glee.

A jungle in the living room and a bedroom set up for a preschooler. I fight the urge to shake my head.

The boy doesn't look upset. If anything, he's resigned.

"Sure." His eyes drift over the space, expression flat. "I like blue."

Cal stands up, pride pouring off him. "I knew you'd love it."

"Love" is definitely too strong a word to describe Murphy's reaction. I'd label this situation as more of an epic disaster. I cannot believe I'm leaving this man in charge of a small human.

There's no other choice, so I step back toward the door.

"Since you two are settled." I wave a hand at the too-bright room. "I'll get out of your way."

Cal spins toward me, his smile gone, his usually tan complexion almost white. "What?"

I throw a thumb over my shoulder. "I gotta get back to the office."

Unlike Cal, I have to work today. I'm the one packing up the stuff we'll need here starting Monday. Files, supplies, electronics, and about a thousand other items. Not that Cal or his brother or even Brian have a clue what they need. If it were left to them, they'd show up with their laptops and then be shocked it wasn't enough.

"Okay." Cal side-eyes Murphy, his demeanor going rigid with nerves, but he quickly shakes it off and breaks into a smile. "Okay." He claps. "You can help me with the midday misting," he says to the little guy. "It'll be a jolly good time." With that, he strides out of the room, practically spitting sunshine.

Murphy's focus is fixed on the floor, his hands clasped in his lap where he's still sitting on the too-small mattress. It stays like that for a solid ten seconds before he looks up at me, those blue eyes full of dread. "Is he always like this?"

Fighting the urge to wince, I nod. "I'll stop by and check on you tomorrow. Okay?"

"Great." Murphy pushes off the bed and shuffles out the door.

A bone-deep urge to follow them, to help, thrums through me.

I shake my head. It's always like this. It's hard to let a kid go after

I've spent a few days with them. But my job is done. Cal has to take it from here.

Instead of following the boys into the kitchen like I'd like to, I let myself out, easing down the narrow staircase while Cal explains his spritzing technique.

When we pulled up and I saw the state of the building from the outside, I thought I was prepared for the office. But the second I step in the front door of the office, I'm hit with the realization that I was nowhere close.

On instinct, I cover my mouth and nose with one hand. What is that smell? Ugh. The scent registers somewhere between moldy cheese and poopy diaper. I hold my breath and will myself not to gag as I survey the space. File boxes litter the room, like after the firm's move employees came back and went through them to find what they needed, then left them scattered around the floor and on every flat surface when they were done. The surfaces not hidden beneath boxes are coated in a layer of dead bugs. Shuddering, I rush back out the door letting it slam behind me.

Was the apartment that horrific when the guys arrived? I peer up at the second-floor windows. Maybe I should have given the place a more thorough inspection before leaving Murphy there.

"You've finally arrived," a high-pitched voice calls.

I spin around, finding an elderly woman standing several feet from me on the crumbling sidewalk. She watches me with a childlike wonder, though her bright smile is outshone by the sun as it catches off her gold earrings and what has to be close to a dozen bangle bracelets.

"So vibrant." She walks toward me with more pep in her step than a woman her age seems capable of possessing. "I've been waiting years. *Years.*"

I peer over my shoulder, expecting to find that another person has approached. She can't be talking to me. I have no idea who she is. So there is no way in hell she's waited years for me. I don't even live here.

But I find no one. It's just the two of us.

"Uh—"

"If you loosen your braid the words will flow better dear." She taps her head sending the many bracelets around her wrist jingling as they slide down her arm. The sound is muffled as they get lost in the layers of bright, gauzy clothing she wears.

"I'm sorry." I frown. "You've got the wrong person, but maybe I can help you find whoever it is you're looking for."

She must be confused. At her age, it wouldn't be abnormal for dementia to begin setting in.

"You're exactly the right person, dear. And no, we haven't met, if that's what you're wondering." Her expression is perfectly serene. "You can call me Madame Esmeralda." She claps once. "But you can't find Sebastian. Oh no, that man finds me when he wants." Leaning in close, she arches a brow. "If you do see him, though, tell him enough with the sock-stealing shenanigans. No one in this place will have a single matching pair if he keeps up this joke of his."

I blink. "Wait..." I glance at the building, then back at her. "You live here?"

"Oh yes. Third floor. Terry couldn't get rid of me." With a little bounce, she adds. "Not that he wanted too." She brushes past me, heading for the back. "Do come by soon. We'll free your hair from that braid and loosen you up. Get the words and pheromones flowing."

Confusion swirls inside me. Every word from this woman is utter nonsense. "Pheromones?"

"Sex dear, you could use some." She chuckles, the sound loud and hearty, and scurries away.

I frown again, my stomach sinking. How could she possibly know that?

"Oh," she spins back to face me, a hand splayed over her chest. "Be careful when you lift the lid."

"*What?*"

The word has barely slipped from my lips when she disappears around the building.

I huff in a breath of the not-so-fresh Jersey air, desperate for relief and a little rejuvenation. Instead, all I muster is a mix of annoyance and defeat. Shoulders slumping, I take in my surroundings again. Awful building, putrid smell, weird neighbors. What was Terry thinking when he insisted the guys work here? And how the hell am I going to manage showing up every day even if it's only for ninety days? The cleaning crew better perform a miracle. Just getting rid of the smell will be a feat.

"Ready to go, Ms. Caruso?"

I glance up to find Joe, the firm's driver, has stepped out of the car. With a nod, I start for the black sedan. Halfway there, my phone buzzes, pulling me up short.

I slip it from my bag and check the screen, assuming it's a contact from the cleaning company or maybe Brian.

Instead, I find Sloane's name flashing on the display.

I'd been avoiding her calls for the last few days. I can only imagine what she'll have to say about Murphy, the apartment, and the new office, and I haven't been ready for it. Her head probably exploded when she found out.

It was probably similar to what'll happen to Sully's when she informs him that she's accepted a position working for the man who spent two years trying to steal her from him. God, when he finds out, he's going to lose it.

I hate knowing things. Being the one with everyone's secrets is getting old.

Nose scrunched, I fight the urge to hit decline. Instead, I force myself to slide my finger over the screen and answer the call.

"Hey, Sloane."

"Finally," she huffs. "I know you've been busy with the guardian thing, but jeez, you could have answered a call."

I could have. I just didn't.

"Yeah." I nod at Joe who holds the back door of the town car open for me, and slip inside.

"Did you get him settled?" Sloane asks.

I look up at the grimy building, ignoring thoughts of what the next three hundred and sixty-five days will look like for me if they somehow convince me to stay past the ninety days I've agreed to.

Three hundred and sixty-five. Counting by days makes it seem so much more daunting. I cannot think past ninety days at this point.

I sigh. "I think Cal has it covered."

"Cal?"

A huff of a laugh escapes me. "The boy is his son, so it's up to him to figure it out. And since they're living with Sully and Brian now, I think they will rally." I hope they will rally.

"Cal has a *son*?" she sputters. "And what do you mean they're living with Sully and Brian?" Her voice hits an octave that makes me pull the phone away.

A pit forms in my stomach. "Have you talked to Sully?"

It's been three days. How the hell has he not spoken with his wife yet?

"Lo?" That single syllable is more of a growl.

I cringe. "Talk to your husband tonight when T. J. calls. Please. Because Murphy is an adorable six-year-old boy who is most definitely Cal's son, which makes him your family."

"Not my family. I'm getting a divorce."

That might be true, but the slight crack in her voice every time she says the D word leaves me doubting that it's actually what she wants. The last thing she wants is to speak to Sully. I get that. However, I do not want to be the one to break the news about the trust and its requirements.

"Call your husband."

CHAPTER 7
Cal

"Remember, your babies need extra spritzing in the afternoons so they can stand tall and make you proud."

I adjust my grip on the bottle, ensuring the hold mimics that of the man on the video. Then I point it toward my plant.

When he squeezes, the water comes out in a fine mist. This is a technique that helps keep them damp, not wet. Everyone knows that a plant will die without enough water. But apparently, too much water can kill them too. No plants are dying under my watch, so I'm determined to get this right.

"Why are you standing like that?"

The little voice startles me. I hadn't realized he walked into my bedroom.

I scream and inadvertently squeeze too hard, sending the bottle flying behind me through the air. I whip around just in time to watch, horrified, as it hits my brother, who is standing in the open doorway, square in the chest.

With a glare, Sully picks up the water bottle and disappears with it, leaving me alone with the pint-sized intruder who scared me in the first place. He tilts his head and studies me like I'm an exhibit at the zoo.

"Ah, I was just watering the plants." Side-eyeing the computer screen, I slam it shut. I can feel Peter the plant guy's disapproval. He thinks I'm going to kill this plant. But with one more glance at Murphy, I know that's not an option. "Are you hungry?"

He shakes his head. "Brian's making dinner."

Hands in my pockets, I rock on my feet, willing the nerves skittering through me to settle. This is the first night we're all in the flat, and more importantly, the first time I've spent more than a few minutes with my son.

My son.

It's such a weird word.

I mouth it, rounding out my lips. Son. Sonnnn.

"Are you meditating?"

I blink at the little lad. "Do you like to meditate?"

Frowning at me like I'm an idiot, he turns and walks out of the room.

Yup. He's a Murphy. Just like my father and Sully, he's exasperated by me.

My phone buzzes on top of my dresser, pulling my attention away from his retreating form. I don't even have to move to snag it. There isn't much to my room. If I stretched both arms out and did one of those eighties work out routines like the ladies in the tight trousers with high socks do—the one where they rock from side to side—I'd hit the walls without much effort at all. And I don't even have unreasonably long arms. Sully? That's a different story. Though everything about my brother is unreasonable.

The beige walls of my room have yellowed. The dark wood trim around the window where my plant is perched is scuffed and faded from the sun. The drab interior paired with a single bed with one pillow makes it feel sort of like a prison cell.

Maybe I'm being dramatic.

Maybe not. There isn't even a television in the flat, thanks to the language my father included in the trust that prohibits them.

What the hell did he have against televisions?

It should make for an interesting time for Murphy, I guess. And we can watch movies on my phone. Maybe I'll get him an iPad.

The moment I open my phone and tap on the notification, I gasp and clutch the device to my chest.

Boobs. Huge big boobs fill the entire screen. Whose, I couldn't say. They're as unfamiliar as the number.

Heart hammering, I peer over my shoulder, worried someone else caught sight of the image on the screen. When I confirm that I'm alone, I let out a long breath and hold the phone up again. Then immediately delete both the message and the image. I also block the person.

I didn't read the message, so I don't have a clue who it was from. All I can think about is what would have happened if Murphy had been watching a movie on my phone when the text came in.

Dread swirls in my stomach.

Definitely won't be using my phone for that.

I swear women don't send me boob pictures often.

Okay, not *that* often.

I think it's because I'm British. The accent makes women do stupid things. Even Sully, bad attitude and all, only has to say hello and women bat their lashes at him.

It's pointless on their end. My brother has never looked twice at a woman other than his wife. For as much as Sloane complains about him, she couldn't fault him for giving anyone else attention. Ever. Unfortunately, he just never gave her attention either.

His tunnel vision and obsession with Sloane worked well for me. It meant I got all the love from the women.

I set my phone on the dresser, but I pick it up again instantly, thinking better of it. Grumbling about the rack attack and my fear that it could happen again, I turn it off and stuff it into my drawer, nestling it between two jumpers. There. Murphy can't be attacked by boobs now.

Done caring for the plant in my bedroom, I stroll out to the living room, where Murphy and Sully are sitting at the dining room table

Brian had delivered today. It's dark mahogany with eight chairs. It absolutely doesn't fit the space. Especially because the pool table I ordered was also delivered today. Now they sit side by side, warring for a spot in the open floor plan.

"My pool table came with a top. We should get rid of that monstrosity." I nod at the enormous surface they're perched around as I shuffle to the fridge. Sure, the top is actually a Ping-Pong surface, but it could serve multiple purposes, right?

Sully holds up a bottle of Hanson whiskey, silently offering me a glass. I shake my head and pluck a bottle of water from the shelf in the fridge.

"You can't eat dinner on a pool table." Brian skirts around me with a large platter in hand.

I follow and drop into a chair beside my little guy. Holding back a grimace, I study the meat loaf, then eye Murphy.

Surely the kid thinks it looks as inedible as I do.

I watch as Brian puts a slice on Murphy's plate, secretly waiting for him to tell Brian just that. Murphy cuts a small piece off with his fork and pops it into his mouth without complaint.

Dammit, normally I can count on T. J. to throw a fit about grown-up food. That's when I swoop in to save the day, offering to order a pizza. But it looks like I'll have to eat with the big boys now.

"Is your bedroom okay?" Brian asks Murphy as he sits at the head of the table.

I grin down at my plate. Murphy's bedroom is awesome, regardless of what Brian and my brother said about the race car bed being too little for him. He fits just fine.

Murphy's eyes cut to mine quickly, then veer back to his plate. He stabs another forkful and nods. "Yeah, it's fine."

There's no stopping the smirk that twitches at my lips. That is until I force a bite of meatloaf into my mouth. Ugh. I fight a shudder. I have no idea why Americans like this so much. Tastes like a dry hamburger.

Needing a distraction, I reach out and swipe a Ping-Pong ball off the table behind us. I toss it up in the air twice before bouncing it off the side of Sully's head. I'm hoping for a reaction, but the man hardly gives me the side-eye before he scoops his next bite off his plate. Damn he's in a mood.

A phone rattles loudly in the other room, making us all sit up. It's my brother's. He's got his ringtone set to that loud jangle that screams nineties mobile. I wince every time I hear it.

Sully lifts himself from the table. To anyone else he'd seem unbothered as he moves to his room to get it, but I know better. Rather than his usual slow amble, he walks with purpose, obviously on high alert.

I can almost guarantee his son T. J. is on the other end of the line. This is about the time the two of them talk every night.

When my brother speaks, using the softer tone he reserves only for his son, my assumption is proven correct.

"What do you want to do tomorrow?" I ask Murphy.

He glances at Brian and they share a knowing look before he turns to me. "I guess we need to find the local school so I can register for first grade?"

I nod, stabbing at the meat crumbles on my plate. Why didn't I think of that? "Makes sense. But I thought we might do something fun. Since it's still summer, we probably have time—"

Brian clears his throat. "School starts on Monday."

I reel back. "But it's not even Labor Day?"

Americans celebrate all sorts of frivolous holidays. Some might be absurd but I won't complain about a day off work. I like the Monday ones best because who doesn't enjoy a long weekend?

Brian shrugs. "School starts earlier these days."

"Ah. Then where should he go?" I look at Brian this time. Murphy's smart, but I can't imagine he knows anything about local schools.

Brian shrugs. "Guess you'll have to figure that out tomorrow."

I toss down my napkin with a huff. That's not an answer.

I have access to a better resource, and I'll take full advantage. I stand and march into Sully's room. Before he can react, I snatch the phone from his hand. My nephew is still talking when I bring it to my ear, so I wait patiently for him to finish the stream of consciousness thoughts he's spewing.

Growling, Sully lunges for the phone, but I dance around the room, ducking and spinning out of his reach.

"What are you doing?" he growls.

"Hey Teej," I say when my nephew stops to take a breath. "Can you put your mum on the phone? I need to ask her a question."

"Hi, Uncle Cal," my nephew chirps. "I'll get her."

Without hesitation, he's yelling for his mum. He's probably dying to get off the phone. The kid is rambunctious. He'd rather be goofing off than chatting every night. He's six—just like Murphy; bonus—and doesn't understand why his father suddenly wants to talk to him so much.

It's been hard on Sully, but he made this bed and now he's got to lie in it.

"Hello?" My sister-in-law's tone is laced with confusion when she answers.

"Hi Sloaney, how's my favorite sister?"

Sully scowls at me. I return the expression with a grin. I've always been Sloane's favorite and now that she hates her husband, I've climbed even higher on the list.

"I'm fine," she says. Her tone is a little short, but I swear there's a little affection there too. "What's going on, Cal?"

"I'm not sure if you've heard but I'm a dad now."

She lets out a long sigh. "Lo filled me in. Congrats."

"So, you see..." I drag out the last word. "I need some advice and since you're the responsible one when it comes to your kid—"

"What the?" Sully, who's given up trying to take possession of his phone, pulls at his hair, glaring at me.

I hold up my hand. "Don't interrupt me, I'm asking dad questions."

"I'm a dad," he grinds out.

"I'm asking Sloane." I turn away from my brother and pace to the doorway, which takes one entire step.

"What do you need, Cal?" Sloane says, suddenly sounding exhausted.

My heart clenches. Damn. She used to be the fun one, but in the last few years her attitude has transformed. These days it's reminiscent of my brother's.

"Here's the thing. Brian just informed me that school starts on Monday, and I haven't the first clue where to enroll Murphy. Though it occurred to me only a moment ago that since he and T. J. are the same age, they could go to school together. Wouldn't that be fun? So what's your plan now that we're all moving to Jersey?"

"Bloody hell," Sully hisses.

I turn and am instantly assaulted by his panic-stricken expression.

What the bloody hell is his problem?

"T. J. will be staying right where he is." Her tone is a bit harsh. My question was a legitimate one, I swear. "At the private school he's attended since he was three."

"Okay." I nod once. "Murphy can go there. Can you set that up for me?"

"No."

"Sloane," I whine, "don't be unreasonable."

"Put Sully on the phone." The harshness has officially morphed into anger. Yikes.

Frowning, I hold the phone out to my brother. "I have no idea how you haven't worked this out yet. You're the exact same miserable person."

Face ashen, like he's scared of the device, Sully stares at the phone and takes a step back.

"What?" I mouth.

With a grumble, he shakes his head and snatches the phone from me. "Hi, sweetheart—"

I can't make out what she's saying, but judging by the angry staccato tone that's beating against his ear, she's pissed.

"Yes." He tugs on his hair again. "I was going to tell you about the move but I—No, I know, I just—"

Fucking hell. My brother never told Sloane about our move? Or the stipulation that requires T. J. to also reside with us in New Jersey if we want to keep our interest in the firm?

Yeah, I wouldn't want to be him right now.

Slowly, I back out of the room and close the door with a soft snick. Then I shove my hands into my pockets and head back to the table. Looks like I've done enough damage for tonight. At least I got the name of a school.

CHAPTER 8
Lola

"I'm well aware of how bad this situation is, babe. Trust me. I'm the one who's apartment hunting in Jersey." Words I never thought I'd say. Words I wish I never had to say, honestly.

"Stop being dramatic. Jersey is full of nice places. The view along the river alone is enough to have most people begging to be there." Sloane sighs. "Now that office and the apartment? They're another story. I cannot believe Sully waited a month to tell me about this." Her irritation is palpable, even through the phone.

Honestly, I'm tired of ranting about that damn office, so I change the subject.

"How'd he take the news about you working with Will?"

When she doesn't respond, I'm sure the line has disconnected. I pull the device away from my ear to check, but her name is still on the screen.

God. I want to shake her *and* Sully.

I've witnessed just how hard the last few years have been on Sloane. I get it. Still, it's hard to see the two of them giving up like this.

"Right." I sigh. "Look, I should go. Brian will be here any second."

"Find a place with a good view, a deep tub, and a walk-in closet. Bonus if it costs the Murphy brothers a small fortune."

I giggle. "From your mouth to God's ears."

I've ended the call and am just tucking my phone into my purse when it vibrates, signaling an incoming text.

> Brian: We're having a small issue at the office. Well, a lot of small issues.

I grimace. I shouldn't be surprised.

> Me: What's wrong?

> Brian: You don't want to know. But Cal and Murphy are on their way to you. And I'll be there as soon as I can.

> Me: Great. I'm on babysitting duty.

> Brian: Murphy's easy.

> Me: I was talking about Cal.

Without waiting for a response, I shove the phone into my purse. "Loo-laa."

At the sound of the singsong voice, my hackles rise. I swear the man exists to annoy me.

I take a deep breath, searching for a modicum of patience. There's got to be a little left for him deep in my soul. When I come up empty, I spin, ready to tell Cal to go away. But the outfit stops me short.

He and Murphy are wearing matching navy sweat suits and bright red Nike's. Blinking, I focus on the bold red letters on Cal's chest. *Big guy.* With a scoff, I drag my attention over to Murphy. *Little guy.*

"Big guy." Cal taps his head. "Little guy." He taps Murphy. "See." He beams, his chest puffed out. "Matchy matchy. Father and sonish right. *Son.*"

He gives the little guy a wink.

Before Murphy can respond—not that he looks eager to, Cal says, "Ssssssooooonnn." The word is long and drawn out, his voice low, like he's saying some kind of odd chant. "Ssoonn."

Beside him, Murphy has managed a straight face. This kid has talent, I'll give him that.

"I think he meditates," he explains, his expression still flat.

"No, it's just a fun word," Cal explains. "Try it." He waves a hand at me like I'm going to join his chant. "Sssooonnn."

"Seriously." I fist my hands on my hips. "What is *wrong* with you?"

"Nothing Lola."

The name makes me cringe.

"In fact," he says, his tone much lighter now, "pretty soon you'll realize I'm your favorite person." He steps up beside me and drapes an arm over my shoulders.

I duck, brushing him off. "Don't touch me."

"Oh but Lola you love when I'm close."

Irritation bubbles to life in my chest. "I love when you're close to leaving me."

A tiny laugh escapes Murphy, but he quickly coughs to hide the sound.

"Come on." I sigh. I'm stuck with Cal. Might as well get on with it.

And maybe it'll help to focus on the silver lining here. Cal won't care how much these apartments cost. He probably won't even pay attention. With any luck, he and Murphy will entertain each other while I tour them.

From the outside, the building had promise. But despite the pictures I looked at online that made the lobby appear modest but not too small, there's nothing but a tiny hallway with an elevator bank. That's it. There isn't even enough space for grocery drop-off. That will be annoying.

"You must be Miss Caruso." A bubbly blonde with a high ponytail and deep scoop neck steps out of an open door on the right and scurries over. "I'm Christy, with a C."

It takes effort to keep from rolling my eyes as I shake her hand.

"Call me Lo."

With a polite nod, she turns her attention to the boys behind me. Her smile turns downright radiant as she takes in Cal. His brown hair is perfectly mussed, his blue eyes popping in contrast to the navy hoodie. His very broad chest strains against the cotton fabric in a way that should be ridiculous, but on him, isn't.

The interest in her eyes is annoying. Great. I can already envision how this will play out. She'll only speak to him, and he won't care about the damn apartment. I'll get no questions answered.

I cross my arms, irritation making me prickly. But when I register that Cal, who normally loves a good set of boobs, is looking anywhere but at her, I deflate. What the hell? Christy with a C is his perfect type, yet it's as if he hasn't noticed her.

"Where are the other people?" His forehead creases with what I swear is concern as he finally looks Christy's way. Though quickly that concern becomes annoyance, leaving me absolutely dumbfounded.

"*Other?*" She tilts her head. "Just me today." Her smile becomes a little brittle. Forced. "Most days. It's either me or Dana."

"No." Cal steps back shaking his head. "No, we're leaving." He snatches Murphy's hand and tugs him to the door. "Come on, Lola. We aren't looking here."

Murphy glances over his shoulder, lips turned down, and shrugs.

Christy scoffs. "What?"

Nerves skitter through me. I can't explain Cal's reaction. I'm just as baffled by it.

"I'm sorry. It seems nice. I don't know what the issue is," I blurt as I dart out of the building behind them. "What the hell was that?" I ask the second I'm on the curb next to him.

My choices in Jersey are limited, so pissing off building managers seems like a bad idea.

"Did you sleep with her?"

He rears back like I've hit him. "What?"

Teeth gritted, I cross my arms. "Did you and Christy have a bad date or something?"

"Who?" He blinks in genuine confusion.

I can't help but huff. Seriously? "Christy with a C, the big-breasted blonde we just met."

"No." Glowering, he points down at Murphy. "Little ears."

Murphy tips his head back, his dark hair falling back from his forehead. "I've heard way worse than that."

I sigh. "Cal, come on, can we please go back in and see the apartment?"

He shakes his head almost violently. "That's not the right place for you."

The irritation that bloomed when he arrived grows until I feel as though my chest will burst. "How do you even know that?"

"Because there's no doorman." His tone is neutral, soothing, almost. I hate it. "Like I was just telling Murphy, my father was adamant that Sully and I understand the importance of taking care of the people in our lives. When we can't be there, we make sure they're surrounded by other people who have their best interests in mind." He roughs a hand through his hair. "When you moved into your flat in New York, Dad asked me to tip your doorman."

Confusion threads its way through me, cutting through the annoyance. "What?"

"Tip him to help you." He releases Murphy, and with his hands in his pockets, he rocks back on his heels. It's a familiar move. One I've seen him make a thousand times. "To ensure that he'd always have your groceries sent up to your flat, or help out if your car didn't start or step in if some ass—" He darts a look at his son, his words dying. "If some, uh," he stutters. "Some jerk was bugging you."

For years, Stanley had been my doorman, and he was incredible. He never once forgot my name, and he complimented my outfits just about every morning. He always opened the door for me, and my packages always made it to my apartment without a stop in the mail-room. I just figured he was efficient.

"How often did you tip him?"

"I go by every week." He lifts one shoulder and lets it fall. "We need to find a building with a Stanley. Someone needs to watch out for you when we can't."

His words are matter of fact. Straightforward. But the idea of him worrying about me all these years resonates within me in a strange way.

"Okay?" he asks, brows arched.

I can't do anything but nod. My chest is suddenly full of a myriad of uncomfortable feelings, making it impossible to speak. It's like my heart kind of tripped on itself.

Cal smiles, blissfully unaware that I'm having a weird moment of *like*. Could it be that I almost appreciate Cal at this moment?

He and Murphy take off down the block, but I'm rooted to the spot, staring at their backs.

"Come on, Lola," Cal says over his shoulder, his hand still clutched around Murphy's.

That phrase, that name, is enough to shake me from my stupor. Spine straightened, I stride down the sidewalk to catch up with them. As I get closer, I fight the urge to grind my teeth.

The annoying man I don't like is back. That's much better. This Cal I handle just fine.

Two apartments later, I'm almost smiling at the view of New York across the Hudson.

"This is it," Cal announces behind me. "Let's sign the papers."

I turn, ready to remind him that this is my lease and my choice.

Before I can, he goes on, "The wine rack is perfect for your collection, and you'll need at least one glass of wine after a day with me. Plus, it has a closet with a built-in shoe rack that'll fit thirty pairs of your favorites. I know, I know." He waves a hand. "It's not quite enough, but this is temporary, after all." He turns in a circle, pointing at the bedroom door, then the floor-to-ceiling windows. "Deep tub, great view." He backs into the kitchen, a hand on his heart. "And the six-burner gas stove will be the perfect tool for trying out new recipes. It ticks all your boxes."

My stomach sinks. "How?"

How does he know what my boxes are? This man doesn't pay attention to *anything*. He's never cared about what I have to say as much as he cares about lunch and slushies and shooting hoops with the mini ball and the basket on the back of his office door.

Stepping close, he rests a hand on my shoulder. "Don't look so shocked, Lola, I know what my girl likes."

I peer up at him, my eyes locking with his, and once again my heart stumbles.

His expression goes soft, his irises soothing like calm waters. "This is it, right?"

I swallow the lump in my throat and will the buzz of electricity that radiates from where his hand is still cupping my shoulder to disappear.

Forcing my attention back to the view of the city, I take a breath.

"Tell me it's perfect." He finally removes that hand, but only to bring his fingers to the underside of my chin and tilt my head back.

"If it had a Stella's…" I clear my throat, ridding myself of the emotion welling inside me. "It would be perfect. I'm going to miss the croissants. Ones I can eat are almost impossible to find." And my Stella's must use magic ingredients because theirs are exceptional.

He smiles softly as his hand falls from my chin.

I hate myself for wishing it back. I can't help but wonder if Cal might not be as shallow as I thought. Honestly, that possibility has sent me into a tailspin.

"A girl needs her baked goods," he murmurs as he takes a single step back. "I'll get the paperwork done for you."

I can't look away from him as he hurries across the room to the building manager.

"You like him."

Murphy's comment startles me and I jerk out of my stupor.

"Oh, I—" I swallow.

"You like him." He repeats as he, too, watches his dad, who's now wearing the charming smile he's known for as he speaks to the middle-aged gentleman across the room. "Maybe he's not that bad after all." Murphy's tone is quiet, like he's really talking to himself.

But he's almost mimicking my own thoughts.

Maybe.

CHAPTER 9
Cal

"Are you nervous?" I peer down at Murphy.

Is his backpack too big? It looks a little big for his body. Brian and Sully insisted it was the right size, so I went with it. Now I'm second-guessing myself.

Then again, since he's enrolled in a small private school he won't have to carry it from class to class.

Regardless, I can't help but worry it'll be too heavy or get in his way.

Sloane and T. J. aren't here yet, and I don't want to go in without them. It feels like my own first day of school all over again. Murphy tips his head back and squints up at me. "Should I be worried?"

"No, of course not," I say quickly.

"You sure about that?" His lips flatten out, his questioning tone causing me to shrink back. "Because you look worried."

"Uncle Cal!"

I perk up. My nephew's arrival couldn't come at a better time. With a smile plastered on my face, I turn and stretch out my arms. Like I knew he would, he immediately launches himself at me.

"Hey Teej." I squeeze him tight and nod to Sloane who follows behind him. Her long, dark hair is curled at the ends and she's wearing a pretty gray pale suit that complements her fair complexion, and a pair of white stilettos. Her expression is one of pure amusement, her blue eyes ping-ponging between Murphy and me.

"It's like copy and paste." She stoops over and sticks out her hand. "Hi Murphy, my name is Sloane, I'm your cousin's mom."

He gives her that same arched brow and skeptical look. "Wouldn't that make you my aunt?"

She straightens and shrugs. "Well, yes, though I'm—"

Glowering at her, I clear my throat. We're not going to start the morning out talking about her divorce. It's the first day of school. A special occasion. And honestly, I'm an adult and I'm struggling with the dismantling of our family. I can't imagine T. J. is handling it well. "You can call her Aunt Sloane."

"Or Sloaney, that's what Uncle Cal calls her," T. J. says as I set him on his feet next to his cousin.

"And this is your cousin T. J. Teej, this is Murphy."

"Hi." Murphy's tone is even, confident. Like he's just a bit too cool.

He is, obviously, because he's my son.

T. J. on the other hand is a precocious six-year-old with too much energy.

"I heard we're going to be living together," T. J. chirps.

Sloane glares at me again like I had anything to do with getting the lot of us into this predicament. "That's to be determined."

"Come on, Mom!" he whines with a stomp of his foot. "It's going to be so fun. Uncle Cal will be there." He points at me.

I offer my most debonair smile, but my sister-in-law is less than amused.

"We'll talk about it later." Her lips tug down at the corners, the skin around her eyes pinched tight. "Right now, you boys have to go inside. They're lining up." She ruffles T. J.'s hair, then kisses him on the cheek.

Naturally, he promptly wipes the remnants away, causing me to chuckle.

Her expression is genuine when she smiles at Murphy. "Have a good first day of school. And welcome to the family."

T. J. hikes his backpack higher on his shoulders and says, "c'mon" to Murphy. My guy mimics his movements, and without another glance in my direction, he turns away.

He's taken about two steps when I lunge forward and grasp the handle at the top of his backpack, tugging him back.

"Don't we have to go inside with them?" Nervous energy clutches my throat as I look from him to Sloane. "Talk to their teachers? Make sure they're all set for lunch?"

Sloane's lips twitch like she's trying to hold back a laugh at my expense. "No, Cal, this is where we say goodbye." She places a gentle hand on my forearm. "He'll be okay." With one more sweet smile at Murphy, she says, "Say bye to your dad. I think he's having a hard time."

Murphy tips his head up again and sighs. "I'll be okay, Cal."

My gut clenches. I don't like it. Don't like it even a little bit.

Jaw locked tight, I nod. "I'll be right here at 2:30."

"They get out at 3:15," Sloane gives up any pretense and breaks into a grin.

Chin lowered, I eye her. "I'll be here at 2:30."

Murphy gives me a single nod. "See you then."

Instead of releasing him, I rush for an excuse to keep him here longer. "We need a photo."

"What?" Murphy frowns in confusion.

"A photo." I dig my mobile out of my pocket. "To commemorate your first day of school."

"Come on, Teej," Sloane says, waving a hand. "Stand with your cousin so Uncle Cal can get his picture."

I unlock my phone—surreptitiously checking that there are no inappropriate messages waiting—and aim. I can't hold back my smile when T. J. loops his arm around Murphy's shoulder. Sure, Murphy looks a touch bewildered by the affection, but I'm glad I'll have this memory saved. I've missed so many other things and have no idea if Murphy's mother documented them. Does she have photos of him the day he was born? Or on his first birthday? A video of his first steps?

With a thick swallow, I shake away the thoughts, ignoring the intensifying burn in my chest.

"Can we go now?" T. J. bounces on his toes, his face alight. The kid is never not moving.

Though I don't want to, I nod. If I keep Murphy here any longer, he'll be late.

With one last big wave, T. J. tears off, excitement catapulting him forward. Murphy, on the other hand, moves in a much more subdued manner.

I don't take my eyes off them as they take their spots in line. While they wait to go inside, T. J.'s mouth doesn't stop moving. From here, it looks like he's pointing out the other kids in line, giving Murphy the rundown.

Murphy remains aloof, but when the kids nearby greet him, he gives them polite nods. Then the teacher appears, opening the gate, and the kids file in.

"Have a good day!" I call after them.

Murphy glances my way and gives me what might be considered a half smile. I suppose it could be a grimace but I'm choosing to pretend it was a smile. Sure, I'm a lot to take and he hasn't exactly warmed up to me—and he's definitely not ready to call me dad yet— but I think I'm growing on him.

As the doors close and the noise of the children silences, a knot forms in my gut. How the hell am I supposed to just walk away knowing my child is in there? He doesn't know anyone. His mother just left him with me. Hell, he barely knows me. How—

"Cal?" Sloane prods, her tone soft and gentle. So unlike her lately.

I've known Sloane since she and Sully were in law school almost fifteen years ago. The two of them married right after graduation, and honestly, I barely remember a time when Sloane wasn't part of our family. I hate that she's divorcing Sully.

"Hm?" I reply, but don't look away from the building. If I stay here, maybe I'll spot the top of Murphy's head as he walks through the hall. I could camp out here, look for him between classes. Do kids move from class to class in first grade? For as much as this place costs, they should.

"We can go now. The boys are fine."

I shake my head, squinting at a hint of movement beyond one window. "I'm okay here."

That gentle hand is back, this time with a light squeeze. "You can't stay here."

Finally, I force myself to look at her. "Why?"

She sighs, lips pressed together thoughtfully, as if she's finally understanding that I'm serious. "Because someone will think you're casing the place. Or a pervert."

I scoff, straightening. "For standing outside my son's school?"

"*Cal.*" She takes a deep breath. "Listen, it's sweet that you're worried about him. And it's admirable that you're trying to be a good dad. But you have a job, and so do I, so we need to leave the boys. I promise they'll be fine."

Leave the boys? I'm not sure I can—

My brain screeches to a halt and replays her words. Frowning, I survey her. The pant suit, the makeup, the hair. "What do you mean you have a job?"

Sloane hasn't worked since she got pregnant with T. J.

Before that she worked with us.

But the outfit suggests she's not going home to do housework or headed to the gym or for a coffee date.

"I got a job at Higgins, Smith, and Dodge."

The air whooshes from my lungs. "You're working for the enemy," I hiss, clutching at my chest.

With a sigh, she grabs my arm and pulls me away from the building. "They're not our enemy." She bows her head and shakes it. "I mean they're not *your* enemy."

"No. You had it right the first time. You're a Murphy, Sloane. And you know just as I do that William Higgins and his slimy kid have always been our enemies." Even saying his name leaves a gross taste in my mouth.

She blinks at me, her expression deadpan. "You're being ridiculous."

"And you're being a traitor." I jab a finger at her. "No. I won't stand for this."

Her eyes go wide and her brows practically leap to her hairline. "You won't stand for this?"

I shake my head. "Nope. And there's no way that Sully will either. So enough. You've made your point, now take it back."

She lets out the heaviest of sighs and tugs at the hem of her jacket, straightening it. "Callahan Murphy, I'm only going to say this once, just like I did with your brother, who already knows about the job, by the way, and was smart enough not to throw a tantrum." She tilts her head, giving me a look. "I am my own person. I am not a Murphy. I've agreed to waive my interest in the firm. All I want is my freedom and my child." Her posture sags a little, her bluster dying. "And it wouldn't hurt to have your support too. T. J. loves you, and as annoying as you're being right now, I've always liked you too. I'd hate to think I've lost you as well."

A sharp pain radiates from the center of my chest. I hate this. Hate it so very much. "Of course you haven't lost me." I grasp her arms and pull her into a hug. "You're my sister. Forever. You can't divorce me."

When I release her, she smiles up at me. It's soft and kind, just like she's always been with me. "I wasn't trying to."

"Can I buy you a cup of coffee? I want to hear about this new job." I try not to make a face. It's not true, but I do want to spend time with her, and she's right: if I want to remain friends, then I have to be supportive of her.

By the way she laughs and shakes her head as we stroll toward Lola's favorite coffee shop, I haven't done well hiding my feelings.

We spend the next half hour discussing this new job. She's genuinely excited. Even if I despise the men she's working for, it is nice to see her so energized. The last few years have been hard on her. She's a powerhouse. Always has been. But somewhere along the way, she lost herself. She was hurting, and Sully was too, and no matter how much we all wanted them to figure things out, neither could see past their own pain to make the necessary changes.

Maybe she's right. Maybe this is for the best. Even if it feels like another death.

"You going to eat that?" She points at a small paper bag on the table.

"Oh." I slide it over an inch. "I got this for Lola. It's her favorite." I turn and look at the counter. "Should probably let the barista know I'm ready for her iced coffee too." With any luck, the ice won't be completely melted by the time I get to the office.

Sloane's face lights up. "That's really sweet."

I shrug. It's nothing really. If I have to drop Murphy off in the city every day, I can swing by here and pick up her favorites. Then this will be one less thing she'll miss while we're in Jersey.

"What do you think about taking turns picking the boys up? On my days they can come back to my office so you don't have to drive all the way back into the city until the end of the day."

"Oh." I straighten, cupping my coffee in both hands. "I'll pick them up everyday. You have a job."

She's just starting out. Again. She'll need to be in the office.

"So do you," she says, giving me a teasing grin.

My lips twitch. "Yeah, but nobody will miss me. It's fine."

CHAPTER 10

Lola

"So you're keeping the Philips Estate and the three custody cases, plus your two GALs here in the office."

Brian grimaces. Just as I predicted, he's not happy with this arrangement. The man lives for his cases, so passing several of them to associates in the main office is painful for him. "Considering we have to be open to new cases in Jersey, we can't handle more than that." He sags in his chair.

"We could have kept the Treams Estate and probably the Ferris' custody case too. I was handling those."

Brian cocks a brow. "You're now responsible for all three of us and our caseloads. Not just me."

My muscles lock up at the reminder. Right, I'm working with the Murphy boys as well. Over the weekend I got settled in my new place, all the while actively working to forget the turmoil Cal and his thoughtfulness forced on me. I was fairly successful, and the man has returned to the box in my mind where he belongs. The one reserved for annoyances only.

Especially after his paralegal emailed me, laying out the chaos that is his caseload. The man needs to focus. I might have to start tying him to his desk chair.

"Also." Brian taps his fingers, his attention drifting to a spot just overhead.

Dread threads its way through me. "No." I know this look. Whatever it is, I don't want any part of it.

"I haven't even said anything."

Frowning, I cross my arms. He's going to ask whether I want to hear it or not, so I might as well let him get to it.

He sighs, resting his forearms on his desk. "Somehow we only got one copy of the Narson trial binder, and I need two for court this afternoon."

I grit my teeth and force myself to breathe evenly. "The one with 97 exhibits?"

With a grimace, he pulls the five-inch three ring binder out of a bag he must have hidden on the other side of his desk. "The old copy machine was set up over the weekend, and Sully had a Staples order delivered so we have paper. Think you could whip together a second one for me?"

"Fine." I grab the massive thing off the desk and storm out of his office.

The main space is barely bigger than my office space in New York, yet I share it with the monster of a copier. One wall opens to a large closet for redwell storage, and the carpet is a dingy gold. The walls definitely weren't this drab grayish-yellow color when they were painted decades ago. No, it's the grime and dirt that were permanently absorbed by it.

At least the putrid smell is gone.

My "desk" is a folding table that the guys swear will be replaced "soon," but I'm not holding my breath. The Sheetrock above me creaks like someone is walking around the apartment upstairs, but no one is home. Sully is in his office and Cal has yet to return from taking Murphy to school.

Hesitantly I glance up, suddenly concerned the ceiling might collapse on top of me. Though the paint is cracked, it seems stable, so I let out a sigh and get back to work.

"Lo!" Sully calls. "I'm going to print something I need sent out asap."

"She's working on my binder," Brian yells.

"She can do both," Sully hollers back.

Right, because I'm their fairy godmother I can do all the things. Bibbidi-bobbidi-boo.

The printer groans, then makes the kind of noise that signals that it's going to start spitting out papers. Instead, it thunks and goes quiet. I'm halfway across the room when it lets out a loud beep.

Of course it's jammed. How could the dinosaur not be? I heft the heavy lid, ready to work my magic, starting with the most likely culprit. I pull open the door that should allow me access to the jammed paper, but when I peer in, paper is *not* what I find.

Stomach lurching, I leap back, a full-body shudder working its way through me.

Oh no. God, no. It's full of hundreds, no, maybe thousands of maggots.

"Oh shit." I whisper as I continue backing away from the little white wormy things. "Oh shit." Heart pounding, I shake out my hands. I have to get away from the bugs. Now. When I take another step back, my calf hits a box and I stumble.

I don't stop. I can't. My mind has been overtaken by visions of the creepy-crawlies wriggling along my skin. Half falling, half climbing, I jump onto the box, then clamber onto the card table. My violent movements are a bit too much, sending me sliding off the other edge into a heap on the dingy gold carpet.

"Shit shit shit." I chant.

God knows what I'll find down here but standing up means having to look at the copier again. Neither are great options.

"Lola?"

I leap to my feet, determined to get off what could be bug-infested carpet while turning to keep my gaze from landing on the behemoth of a machine across the room. As I stand, I stumble again, slamming into a hard body.

"Whoa." Cal catches my arm gently. "What's wrong?"

I don't stop moving. Not until I skirt him so he's standing between me and the copier. "The things in the thing. And uck," I stammer, body trembling, arms waving.

Another shudder hits me. Shit. What if I left the lid open? They're probably squirming out and heading for me.

"What?"

"It's infested." I back up again, but he stops me with that gentle hand on my arm.

He ducks his head, catching my gaze, calming me a fraction. With a concerned once-over, he releases me and turns to the copier.

Before he can take a step, I grab his hand. "Don't let them escape. We don't want maggots."

"Maggots?" Cal's lips pull into a line. An expression that might be disbelief. Though there's an equal chance he's fighting a laugh. "Lola maggots don't live in photocopiers."

"Uh, I beg to differ." I point to the dinosaur. "There are thousands in that thing."

Cal yanks out of my grasp and moves to the machine.

No. No, no, no. I should stop him, but I refuse to go near it again.

He lifts the lid, and with a yelp, he jumps back. "Bloody hell."

"I told you."

The door jingles open behind us.

Shit. I whip my head around, praying it's not a client. We can't let them see the maggots.

Who would hire an attorney who has a lifetime supply of decomposers hiding in their office?

Actually...They might come in handy for a criminal attorney.

"Too late, I see." Madame Esmeralda shakes her head, not the least bit surprised or confused by our terror. "I warned you about the lid."

I'm still trying to suck in a lungful of air as I gape at her. What?

"I told you last week about lifting lids."

"Oh." She did.

"You are eerily accurate." Cal, who scurried away from the bugs, though kept himself between them and me, is staring at the snake ring on her pinkie almost like the deep green gems in its eye sockets are hypnotizing him.

Wonder where she got it. Amazon? I should look. Maybe I could use my own to keep him in line.

"Your father said the same thing. Now, where is that brother of yours? I need to sign some papers for my place apparently."

Cal tips his head toward Sully's office and Madame Esmeralda floats across the room. As she passes us, Cal suddenly jerks forward crashing into my card table and sending two stacks of papers onto the floor.

Dammit. I need a better desk.

Before I can comment on it—before I can butter him up and talk him into ordering one for me *right now*—he spins around, backing up so his ass hits the table, and watches, wide-eyed as Madame Esmeralda steps through the door of Sully's office.

"I think she pinched my arse."

I chuckle. "You think?" If I'd been touched like that, I can't imagine I wouldn't know for sure.

He peaks over his shoulder at his own butt and then looks back at me, confusion swimming in his expression. "Maybe?"

The floor above us creaks again, cutting through the silence. I glance up, knowing no one is upstairs.

"Also," Cal says, his tone serious. "I think we have a ghost."

Sighing, I fall into my desk chair.

This is what life has come to, an eccentric ass grabbing seer, a maggot infested copier, and a boss who believes in ghosts.

Damn Terry and his big ideas.

"Oh, you know what?" Cal perks up, his face taking on its typical brightness. "I can fix this." He slides a small paper bag my way, making the table wobble as he does. "One croissant from Stella's and one iced coffee."

Tipping the bag hesitantly, I peek in. Instantly, I'm assaulted by the delicious buttery scent of a croissant and the sharp, addicting aroma of espresso. "You…" I peer up at him. "You got me coffee?"

"Whatever Lola wants, Lola gets." The annoying line is in song form this time.

Normally, his typical response, the damn song lyrics, set my teeth on edge. Today, though, the words are softer. Like maybe he's trying to be nice rather than irritating.

I work hard to fight the smile, but my lips tip up of their own accord. "Thanks."

He rocks back on his heels. "It's only a block from the school."

Warmth blooms in my chest. "How did day one go?"

"Oh." He ducks his head, and I swear his cheeks go pink. "I was so nervous I had to skip breakfast, but I think Murphy did okay. I got him a new backpack." He slides his phone from his pocket, and with one swipe after another, he shows me about seventeen thousand pictures of Murphy from the moment he woke up until he's stepping into the school building, nothing but his blue and silver backpack visible.

"Thanks so much," Madame Esmeralda calls as she steps out of Sully's office.

Not so casually, Cal shuffles back until he's pressed up against the wall like he's keeping his backside safe.

The ceiling creaks again, and I look up.

"Oh, don't mind Sebastian." Madame Esmeralda waves dismissively. "He's very heavy-footed, you'll get used to it." She rushes to the door. "And don't worry, Lo, the only other surprise today will be a ladybug."

Fear grips my chest. "Wait! What? When?" I call out.

It's too late. She's gone. Pulse picking up, I survey the room, though I deliberately avoid looking at the copier.

Sully and Brian both promised the exterminator cleared the place of the beady-eyed red vermin. Though they did miss a thousand maggots in their inspection.

"Do you see any?"

"See what?" Cal asks.

"Ladybugs." I practically shudder at the word.

"Oh no, but they're so cute." He steps away from the wall, face alight as he also scans the room. "I love them."

"They're awful. Those eyes? They're always planning something. Beady little things. They poop on everything. *Everything.* Imagine walking around with lady bug poop on your hands, on your clothes. It will be everywhere just—"

Cal barks out a laugh. "Most people think they're good luck."

"Most people are stupid," I mutter.

"I'll keep you away from the maggots and the ladybugs." He dips his chin, peering at his phone. "Later. When I get back, I'll get you moved into the conference room with me."

I grimace. Share the room with him? No, thank you. "I'll move into the empty office."

"I'll move you into the conference room later." He nods, ignoring me completely. "Right now, I need to go because it's almost Murphy's lunchtime."

"Why?" I frown. "Did you forget to send a lunch?" Poor kid. Day one, and Dad forgot to pack food for him.

"I sent him lunch." Cal scoffs. "Three options just in case."

Tapping my fingers on the card table I study him, confused. "So then…"

"I need to make sure he has someone to sit with."

I suck in a breath. Oh no. "You're going to sit with him?" That's just what every kid wants on their first day at a new school, their dad sitting at the lunch table. Even in first grade, it'll make him a pariah.

"Of course not." He gives me a look of disgust. "If I did that, kids would think he's a weirdo, I'm just going to watch through the window."

I close my eyes and rub at my temples, willing the impending migraine to abate.

In a Cal way, it makes sense.

With a cleansing breath, I zero in on him. "So you're the weirdo, not Murphy."

He frowns, as if he thinks I'm on the wrong side of this conversation. "Just for today. Tomorrow, I'll drop him off, and I won't leave work again until it's time to pick him up. When you have a minute, will you take a look at my schedule and make sure that all my meetings and court appearances happen between ten thirty and two? Thanks."

"What?" He's got to be joking. Court closes from twelve thirty to two p.m. for lunch. He can't expect every judge in our district to be amenable to working with him during those two hours a day only.

He lifts a shoulder, the movement easy. "I have to drop the kids off, so I can't get here before ten thirty, and I have to leave by two p.m., otherwise I'll be late picking them up."

I can appreciate that he's jumping into this parenting thing with both feet, but the man is an attorney. His work schedule cannot revolve around carpool. No, in this line of work, we're all at the mercy of the courts and our firm's clients.

It takes effort to keep my tone neutral. "The judges are not going to agree to this."

"It's for a child."

That argument works in some actual cases, but this is a personal matter, not a legal one. "Yes, but this time *you* are the child. Your child is at school. They're not going to deem it necessary."

"You can do it. I believe in you." His lips turn up in that damn charming smile.

I drop my gaze, focusing on the knot of his tie. There's no way I'll let that expression soften me. "*Can* and *will* are not the same thing." I cross my arms and risk looking up to glare. "I can't work magic with the courts."

Instead of backing down at my annoyance, his blue eyes brighten, and he blasts me with a full-on grin. "Come on, Lola." He rocks onto his heels and dips his chin just a hair. "Be a team player."

"I'm not on your team." It's a reminder to myself as much as him.

He pouts. "But I brought you coffee."

Before I can respond Brian appears, head peeking out of his office door. "Minor issue."

"Besides the maggots in the printer?"

Brian winces. "Well, there's a silver lining here, I guess. I just called the exterminator again. There are several mice nests in the empty office."

I groan. Of course there are. This place is the literal worst.

"That's great news." Cal's voice is way too chipper.

"I hate this place," I mumble, eyes drifting shut.

Brian grunts. "I'm not too crazy about it either, but it's only a year."

I snap my eyes open again and narrow them on my boss. "Ninety days. That's all I promised."

CHAPTER 11

Cal

"Testing. Testing."

The guy next to me is watching, biting back a smile.

"You mind holding this and standing right here?" I ask, holding up one brand-new walkie-talkie.

The man shrugs. "Sure."

I count my steps until I'm about ten feet away, then hold the second walkie-talkie up and press the button. "Can you hear me now?"

He nods.

I walk another ten feet. "How 'bout now?"

When he gives me a thumbs up, I stalk back another ten.

"And now?"

He presses the button on the device in his hand. "Yes."

"My man." I grin. "That's about the distance from here to the school, right?"

Eyes narrowed, he studies me, like he's cataloging my features so he can give them to a sketch artist.

"I'm not a creep, I swear." One hand held out, I dart back to him. "I'm a dad. A new one," I explain.

"Ah." He nods, his expression relaxing. "It's hard to leave them."

"Exactly! I'm Cal." I hold out my hand.

He returns the gesture. "Roger. My daughter is in fourth grade."

"My son is in first."

With a flick of his wrist, he turns the walkie-talkie off. "He'll probably like this. My daughter would never go for it. Ten going on seventeen and all." He chuckles.

"Yeah, I'm really glad my surprise kid was a boy."

His eyes go wide. "Surprise kid?"

Before I can explain, the double doors fly open, and a rush of kids descend the steps.

T. J. is leading the pack, but even once I've scanned the crowd, Murphy is nowhere in sight.

"Uncle Cal!" My nephew launches himself into my arms.

Fortunately I'm used to his enthusiasm, so I catch him easily.

"Are you going to pick me up every day? This is the bestest! I don't like school but if you take me for a slushie, I'll like you!"

Have I mentioned the kid is a con artist as well?

I nod, preoccupied with finding Murphy. Tendrils of panic grip my throat, tightening with every second that passes. "Where's your cousin?"

T. J. shrugs. "Slushie time? I'm thinking a blue one, but if you get a red one and I get a blue one I can have them both."

Ignoring his chatter, I hike him up a little higher and stride for the front of the building.

"Excuse me," I say to the woman standing at the door.

She looks exactly like the strict teachers from my private school in England. Her hair is pulled back in a tight bun, and her clothes have nary a wrinkle. Immediately, I'm transported to that time. Suddenly, I'm a lad searching for my mother in the crowd of parents. My endeavors were always fruitless. My mother never picked us up.

One day, though, she promised she would. My birthday. But she never showed. My driver didn't either; he thought she was coming to get me.

My heart rate ratchets up. I had Sully back then. He and I stood together waiting and eventually walked home. He always had a few quid on him and that day he used them to buy a Lion bar for me. The caramel chocolate wafer was always my favorite as a child. He pretended that had been the plan all along. I knew better, but I went along with it. It helped. But Murphy doesn't have a Sully. He's stuck with me.

Dammit, where is Murphy?

The woman turns my way, her nose in the air, her back completely straight.

My stomach rolls.

"Yes?"

"I'm looking for my son. Murphy Macallister. He's in the same class as my nephew"—I heft T. J., keeping him in my left arm—"but he didn't come out."

Eyes narrowed, she unclips a walkie-talkie from her belt. Instantly, all of my worries fall to the wayside. She can't be that bad if she has one of those.

She presses the button on the side and uses two fingers to cover one of her ears, appearing very official.

I make a note to try it that way next time. Maybe it'll make a difference. "Gerry, I'm looking for a Murphy Macallister. First grade. Could you send him out?"

She pulls it away from her mouth and holds up a finger to keep me from talking. Five seconds later, the device crackles and beeps.

"He's talking to Mrs. Benoit, I'll have him head your way."

She offers me a silent, perfunctory smile. Nothing more.

Alright.

"Who's Mrs. Benoit?" I whisper as I set T. J. on his feet at the bottom of the steps.

"Our teacher."

Hands in my pockets, I pace the tarmac. With each pass, I glance at the door, willing it to open. Is he in trouble? Murphy doesn't seem like the type of kid to get in trouble, then again, I barely know him.

After a literal eternity the door eases open, and Murphy appears wearing the cool expression I've come to expect from him. He doesn't light up in excitement when he sees me, though I swear there's a flicker in his eyes. Like maybe he didn't expect me to be here, and he's not mad that I am.

It hits me then that maybe my son has experienced situations similar to mine. Maybe he's been the kid waiting at the school for a parent who didn't show up. And based on the closed-off expressions, there's a good chance he's been through it more times than I ever have.

He's probably used to people not showing up.

And that breaks my fucking heart.

I take three big steps toward him, not bothering to hide how excited I am to see him. "Mack Attack! How was your first day?"

His brows jump to his forehead. "Mack Attack?"

"Trying out nicknames, what do you think?"

"Everyone else calls me Murph."

I shrug. "But I'm your dad."

He sighs, his little body slumped like his backpack is full of bricks. "Are we going to your office?"

"Actually," I say with a smile, "we're going to get slushies. After, we have to drop T. J. off at Sloaney's office, then we'll head home. That work?"

Murphy lifts those shoulders again like he couldn't care less what we do.

"I told Uncle Cal I wanted a red and he'll get a blue and we can mix them," T. J. grips the railing at the bottom of the staircase and swings himself back and forth. He can't sit still for even a moment.

I back up, waving for them to follow me. "How about we all get red and blue slushies? We can mix them together at the machine."

T. J. says, "Ah, yes, Uncle Cal. Murphy, you're so lucky your dad is the coolest."

Murphy doesn't respond, but I'm certain his lips lift just a little.

"Now boys, we're walking into enemy territory," I explain as we ride up the lift, slushies in hand. I stick out my tongue, assessing myself in the stainless steel wall. My reflection is hazy, making it hard to get a good look, so I spin, my tongue still out. "Is my tongue blue?" The *is* sounds more like *ith*.

Murphy hides his smile behind his extra-large slushie cup. T. J., on the other hand, lets loose a loud laugh.

"No, Uncle Cal! That's why we mixed it with red!"

"Oh." I take another obnoxiously loud slurp. "I thought that was just because it tasted better."

The lift doors open, and an elderly couple stands on the other side, eyes wide. "Scuse us." I hold the door open and motion for the boys to head off the lift.

We step out into a bland reception area where Mozart is playing at a barely audible level. Pretentious fuckers probably don't even know the classic tune, only that it sounds like money.

I've never been inside this office, but I'm not surprised at all by the bland gray and blue hues. It looks like every other law office in Manhattan. Sterile décor, a shot of the Empire State Building at night, and a photo of the New York City skyline included.

If there's anything New Yorkers are obsessed with, it's that.

Best City in the world, I love New York. It's a mantra that many residence seem fond of. Including the lovely Lola, I can imagine. She probably chants the words when she's getting off.

Fuck. I'm a wanker. Why the hell am I even thinking about Lola getting off? Now I'm plagued by images of her in her flat doing just that. Hands trailing between her thighs, a vibrator cranked to its highest setting. If I had to guess, the woman likes it rough.

"Uncle Cal, who is that man talking to my mommy?"

T. J.'s question shakes me from my far too vivid daydream, but it's the scene before me that has my blood running from hot to cold.

Yes, why the hell is Will Higgins talking to *our* Sloaney?

Side by side, they amble down the hall. She's laughing while he yammers on, her arms cradling a file to her chest, her posture easy, her face lit up.

I hate to say it, but I haven't seen her this relaxed in years.

My brother is so fucked.

When she spots us, she goes stiff, guilt flashing in her eyes.

Oh yeah. So fucked.

She recovers quickly, forcing a bright smile—not an easygoing one—and bows her head, focusing on the boys. "Hey," she says, her tone far too chipper. "How was the first day of school?"

Yes, my sister-in-law is feeling guilty about something, and I don't like the looks of it at all.

CHAPTER 12

Cal

Traffic to Jersey is a bitch. The roads are full of people who would rather live in the city but have chosen to do the whole suburban thing, clogging the lanes in their oversized vans and SUVs. Every one of them wears a frown as I speed by them in my Aston Martin DB12 Volante.

Though I'm focused on the road, keeping my passenger safe, my mind is a mess. I keep going back to the way Sloaney was laughing with Will.

Should I tell my brother?

Is there anything *to* tell my brother?

Lola would know what to do. Hell, Lola probably has all the details already, since she and Sloane are best friends.

Hm.

I glance in the rearview mirror at Murphy. "Should we take dinner to Lola? She's all alone in her new flat."

Murphy frowns, his focus remaining fixed on the passing scenery. "Didn't she live alone before moving here?"

"Yes, but she hates Jersey," I explain. She's probably lonely and miserable without us.

Sure, you prat.

Murphy shrugs. "I could go for pizza."

"That's it, lad!"

Wait, does Lola like pizza? Everyone likes pizza, right?

An hour later—traffic really was terrible—we arrive at Lola's flat and I spot Benjamine.

"Benjamine!"

"Cal! Do you need help with that?" He strides for me, arms outstretched to take the stack of pizza boxes I'm balancing. I wasn't sure which Lola would prefer, so I got several options. I ordered a salad as a backup in case she hates them all.

"I've got it." I peer at him over the cardboard. "Can you just buzz me up?"

"Is Ms. Caruso expecting you?" he asks as he lifts the phone.

I grin. Even with me, the bloke's careful. That's exactly what I was going for. Lola deserves that type of loyalty. "Nope, but call her and let her know I come bearing gifts and Murphy."

She can't possibly say no to him.

Me? Possibly. My charm doesn't work on her the way it does with the rest of the world.

He turns away, and as he speaks softly into the phone, Murphy glances up at me, brows raised, like he's saying, *you really think this will work?*

I shrug.

That's the extent of the interaction, but it's got giddiness bubbling up inside me. We just held our first silent conversation.

Head tipped up, I glance at the door so I can hide my grin.

"She said I can buzz you up," Benjamine says.

I break into a cheeky smile and wink at my little sidekick. "Well, look at that."

Murphy shakes his head, but as he ducks, I catch just a glimpse of a smile.

When we get off the lift, Lola is waiting for us in the hall.

She's a proper knockout. The deep coppery hair she typically keeps in a braid is loose, falling around her face in soft waves, her skin which is normally a flawless creamy color, is flushed, and when she spots Murphy, her green eyes glitter.

"How was your first day?"

He responds. I think. The boy's polite enough to make pleasant conversation. But I don't have a clue what he says. I'm too gobsmacked by the woman standing in the doorway. Her oversized sweats are rolled at the waist and sit low on her trim hips, and her tiny tank top clings to her small breasts. The soft swells make it difficult to catch my breath.

It's so odd, this pull I feel. Seeing Lola like this—relaxed and not so uptight—is bloody mesmerizing.

The two of them chatter as she holds open her door for me, but I pause rather than follow Murphy inside because I've just discovered something else about Lola.

"You have freckles," I murmur, my voice gruff.

"Huh?" Those gorgeous emerald eyes of hers narrow on me, and when she realizes how close we are, she shuffles away, though she can't go far, trapped between me and the doorway.

"Freckles." I gesture at them with my chin because I've got five pizza boxes in my arms.

She bows her head, her cheeks going pink. "Oh, yeah, I wasn't expecting company."

Fuck, I need to put these boxes down. But the counter is at least twenty steps away, and I want to stay caught in her orbit. "You're beautiful, Lola. You're always beautiful, but hell, those freckles." I shake my head and huff, annoyed that I can't stop mentioning my newest obsession.

Lola stares at me blankly.

"Sorry, I'll just put this down. I brought pizza. Figured everyone loves pizza." I'm rambling. I can't help it. This close to her, I've turned into an absolute twat.

And she's barely said a word.

Why did I have to bring up her freckles?

Lola clears her throat and gives me a pointed look.

Oh. I'm still standing in the doorway. Wanker. With a sigh, I force myself into the flat.

She closes the door quietly. "I'm—ugh—gluten free."

Eyes wide, I whip around. "Obviously." How could she think I'd forget? "All the pizzas are free of gluten. No gluten in this shisouse!"

Shisouse? What the hell are you prattling on about, you arsehole?

"Shisouse?" Murphy mouths to me.

Cringing, I shake my head. *I know, kid, I know.*

I've lost the plot. With a sigh, I shuffle to the counter and drop the stack of boxes. "Figured it'd be healthier for all of us to give up gluten, right Murphy?"

He stares at me for a beat, expression as deadpan as ever, then nods. "Yeah, that's exactly what we thought."

"Oh," Lola stares at the boxes then she looks back at me, green eyes wide. "That's...oddly sweet. Thank you, Cal."

An immense wave of pride swells through me, my confidence growing. "Of course. Figured we can share. If you want a bite of mine, you can have it. We'll be like those dogs in *Lady and the Tramp*."

Her frown is back.

Might just start calling her frowny face. Imagining how badly that would go, I bite back a laugh.

"That was pasta."

I hum, playing it cool. "I'll get that next time. We could share a meatball."

With a snort, she takes a step back. "I want nothing to do with your meat, Callahan Murphy."

Excitement ping-pongs through me. I think Lola Caruso is flirting with me. With a wolfish grin, I open the first pizza box. "Which do you want, Mackster?"

He shakes his head. "That's a no on the nickname."

Lola laughs. "Good luck with that. I've been begging him to call me Lo for years."

She steps up to grab a slice and as I slide out of her way, I duck so my lips are close to her ear. "Odd, I don't remember you begging, and that's definitely something I wouldn't forget."

Her sharp inhale is impossible to miss. Especially when I'm watching her every reaction. I can't look away.

"*Cal,*" she hisses.

Shrugging, I head to the kitchen table with plates for Murphy and me.

"What do you guys want to drink?" Lola asks.

To my surprise, she holds up a bottle of wine and tilts it back and forth.

It's a bottle of pinot noir and I note the brand she likes for future Cal. I've always known she likes good wine because my father always got that for her whenever he bought her presents, but I never knew which kind. Now that I do, I can take over that task.

"I'll take water," Murphy says. "Please," he adds perfunctorily.

I stand. "Wine sounds good, need help?"

She shakes her head. "I got it."

Bollocks. There are three of us. I refuse to let her carry over all the drinks on her own. By the time she's got the wine bottle open, I've located the correct cabinet and have two empty wineglasses in one hand and a third regular glass filled with water in the other.

When she notices, she shakes her head but she's smiling. "Thank you."

"Did you make friends today?" Lola asks Murphy as she sits across from me.

He shrugs.

"What about your teacher? Was she nice?"

He shrugs again. "She's getting me a different reading assignment."

I straighten and zero in on him. "Why? Do you need help? We can get you help."

I don't know the first thing about his life. Did his mum read to him? What if he can't read?

"Because I read the book we're reading two years ago."

Lola eyes me across the table, brows raised, and smiles. "It's great that she noticed that. So you're comfortable there?"

Wait? My heart stutters. *Is my son a genius?* What am I thinking? Of course he is.

"Is that why you were late today?" I ask before he can respond to Lola.

"Yeah." He nods once, picking up his pizza.

"He was the last one out at the end of the day," I explain to her. "I'd already been thinking about it, but that just cemented the idea. How about—"

"Oh God," Lola hangs her head, like she's certain I'll say something ridiculous.

But this is as brilliant as Murphy. "No, hear me out." I pause for dramatic effect. When I have them waiting with bated breath, I hold my hands up and give them a little shake. "Walkie. Talkies."

Both Lola and Murphy blink back at me.

"Walkie...talkies?" the little man says slowly.

"Yes. I didn't know where you were, and I didn't like it. You're too young for a phone but not for a walkie-talkie."

Lola sighs, wiping her face with a napkin. "No, he's probably too old for one."

I shake my head. "If I'm not too old for a walkie-talkie, he isn't."

Wineglass in hand, she arches a brow. "They'll never let him use it in school."

Huh. Why not?

Murphy shrugs, giving me a pitying look. "Probably not. They're pretty strict."

"But how will I make sure you're okay?"

"*Cal.*" Rather than chiding, Lola's voice is soft. The single syllable is accompanied by the strangest action. Under the table, she gently squeezes my knee. Almost as soon as it happens, though, she pulls back, eyes widening.

I peer at her, wanting her to know just how okay the move was.

That it was more than okay, and I wish she'd do it again. In fact, I wish she'd leave her hand there. *Forever.*

But she refuses to look at me.

Murphy tilts his head. "I'm okay, Cal. I used to ride the bus after school. If you want—"

I shake my head. "I'm picking you up."

He lifts one shoulder, like it's nothing. "I'm just saying if you're ever late or busy—"

Lola straightens. "We'll make sure he's never too busy or late. And if he can't be there, I'll be there. Or Sloane, or Sully, or Brian." Her green eyes are dark, fathomless as she adds, "We've got you, okay?"

Murphy gives us a single nod. I don't blame him. If it were me, I doubt I could muster more. As it is, there's no way I can speak right now.

I'm angry at his mother. She kept him from me. She never contacted me. All this time, she had this totally awesome smart kid and she didn't even take care of him. She allowed him to travel on public transportation in New York fucking City by himself for gods' sake.

But I'm not angry that she dropped him at our door.

I'm not angry that he's here with me now.

And I'm not angry that Lola recognizes how much he needs us.

"Can I call my mom?"

My chest constricts. "What?"

"You have your mother's number?" Lola asks. Thank fuck one of us can speak in full sentences.

Murphy nods.

Tone gentle, she leans forward and asks, "Why didn't you say that before?"

A shrug of a shoulder is all we get.

Lola turns to me, shaking her head.

I'm a second away from catapulting out of my chair and diving into the phone to strangle his mum.

"It takes a long time to get to Bali," he says. "She gets jet lagged. Figured I'd give her a few days to get settled."

My stomach bottoms out. This kid. This fucking perfect amazing kid. My son. With a shake of my head, I pull out my phone. Not because she deserves to talk to him, but because he deserves it all. The whole world.

He takes it and gives me the briefest of smiles. "Thanks, Cal. Can I go in the other room?"

I look to Lola because I don't know what the fuck I'm doing. Do I let him call her alone? Can I say no?

Nodding, she stands. "Sure. You can use my bedroom."

The two of them disappear, and I'm pretty sure my heart goes with them.

I'm angry. So fucking pissed. How could his mum do this? And how in the bloody hell am I going to make it better?

I'm still in my head when Lola comes back and puts a hand on my shoulder. "You okay?"

"No." My voice is gruff, unrecognizable. "He rode goddamn public transport home from school. He knows his mum has jet lag. He knows too fucking much for a six-year-old." I dig the heel of my hand into my eye socket. "He's six, Lola. I've missed everything."

With a squeeze of my hand, she sits beside me, her eyes filled with understanding. "I hate that you've missed so much. But that's changed now. He has you. And Sully and Brian are here."

And you, I want to whisper. *You promised him you are too.* The words almost escape me. The next question clawing its way up my throat. *Are you here for me as well?*

But I choke it back. I'm not a child and she owes me nothing.

"He's smart, Lola." I groan. "He's bloody brilliant."

She smiles. "He is."

My chest deflates. "And I'm not."

She levels me with a glare, those green eyes piercing into my soul. "You went to Harvard."

I slump back in my chair. "But I didn't have to try. I never cared. It all came easy."

Lips pressed together, she assesses me for a long moment. "Sounds like it does for him as well. Maybe you're more alike than you think."

"The difference is that he does care. He wants to learn and I... I don't know how to do this."

She sighs and shifts in her seat. "That admission proves that even if you don't know how, you'll figure it out. You care, Cal and that's half the battle. My parents—" She shakes her head, cutting herself off.

My gut churns. I don't know what she'll say but the defeat in her expression sets me on edge. Normally she's annoyed at me, snarky, strong-willed. At the mere mention of her parents though, she just seems tired.

"They didn't care about school," she explains. "I loved it. I constantly wanted to learn more. They just wanted to focus on the fun."

My throat constricts, making it hard to breathe. She probably thinks that's all I care about too. I'm the fun one. The fun uncle, as T. J. says. I wanted to be the fun dad. What the hell do I know?

She settles her warm hand on mine again. "You're both. You care about the fun stuff, but you care about the hard stuff too. You're doing okay, Cal. I'm—" Her gorgeous green eyes glisten as they settle on me, enveloping me in a sensation that's almost as comforting as a real hug. The kind of hug I wish she'd actually give me. "You'll be fine."

Worried she's on the edge of tears, I clear my throat and shoot for lightening the mood. "Walkie-talkies are fun right?"

She shakes her head, smiling.

I lean forward. "Can you imagine if other things were named like walkie-talkies?"

With a huff, she pulls her hand away. "What?"

"Like that fork." I nod to the unused utensil beside my plate. "It'd be stabby-grabby."

She snorts.

"Your bra."

Her eyes flare with the kind of annoyance I'm familiar with. And maybe even a little humor.

I give her a wolfish grin. "A breastie-nestie."

The laugh that falls past her lips is loud and happy, it rips through the space, filling me with an insane type of joy.

She's still smiling when Murphy appears again.

He sets the phone on the table. "What's going on?"

I clam up, searching his expression for any hint as to how he's feeling.

Lola, thankfully, asks the question I should have. "How was the call?"

Murphy shrugs, unbothered. "She didn't pick up."

The anger that had been bubbling up inside me instantly returns, this time in a full boil. Just as I think I'll explode, Lola squeezes my knee.

"Can we go home?" Murphy asks quietly. "I have homework."

Fuck, I hate this.

I stand, my hands flexing. "I'll clean up."

Lola shakes her head. "I've got it. Thank you for bringing dinner."

I nod. It's all I can manage. Words are too hard right now.

Lola pushes back from the table and heads toward the door, where Murphy is fiddling with his backpack. "Which book did the teacher give you?"

"The first Percy Jackson book. *The Lightning Thief*, I think."

"Oh." She clasps her hands and smiles. "You'll have to tell me what you think of it. I can't decide whether Annabeth is my favorite or Grover. They're both so funny. And the scene with Medusa is definitely the best."

Murphy's eyes light up. "You read it?"

With a nod, she holds out her arms. "Can I have a hug?"

Murphy collapses against her. The sight makes my heart squeeze so tight I'm afraid it'll implode. I clear my throat and survey the kitchen until I've got my emotions under control.

When I finally look back, Murphy is heading into the hallway and Lola is standing by the door, holding it open.

"Thank you," I whisper.

She pats my chest as I slip by her. "Don't have a screamy-dreamy."

I pull up short and frown at her. "Huh?"

"Sweet dreams, Cal." She pops up on her toes and kisses my cheek, surprising the shite out of me.

I don't even bother to fight the smile that tugs at my lips. "*Whatever Lola wants.*"

CHAPTER 13
Lola

The shrill ring of a phone echoes around the room, startling me. When *NJ Judiciary* flashes on the display, I dive for the phone. I've been waiting for Judge Cabello's law clerk to call me back for the last two hours.

"Murphy and Machon."

Two seconds into the call, I cut the kid off.

"You're telling me the judge still hasn't signed the new order?"

Cal, who's sitting across from me—yes, he moved me into the conference room with him, just like he said he would—freezes, focus trained on me. A framed picture of Murphy and T. J. in his hand, hovering a few inches over the table.

I'm trying to ignore him. After last night, it was hard enough. But now that he's so adorably decorating our office with family pictures, feelings are creeping up that I don't want.

The photo just inside the entrance was a nice touch. It's one of the three guys with Terry. But when he hung the picture of his father and me from our Christmas party last year, a lump formed in my throat.

Yeah. I'm definitely ignoring the emotions roiling inside me. I need bane-of-my-existence Cal back. This version of Cal, the one that makes me tingle in all the places I don't want, has to go.

He cocks a brow, and my traitorous stomach flips.

Desperate to fight the magnetic pull, I lower my focus to the table and the pen I'm tapping against a legal pad.

"Well..." The law clerk's mumble is hard to hear over my incessant tapping. "We're working on it."

Irritation is a living, breathing entity inside me. Working on it my ass. For two months, our client—who does not have kids or a child support obligation—has been harassed by probation for the arrears they now think he owes. It wasn't until a few weeks after it began, when he received a letter from probation in the mail, that poor Howard even knew this was going on.

The issue was a result of a mistake out of Judge Cabello's chambers. And for whatever fucking reason, he's taking his sweet time righting the wrong.

"Our client is about to have a lien put on his house because of a child support obligation for a child that *doesn't exist*. You get that right?" There's no tempering my rage.

"Hopefully soon."

I grit my teeth. "I need it *today*."

"I'll talk to the judge." He hangs up before I can insist he do it right now.

Dammit. Now I'm going to have to call probation and hope I can convince them to slow down the process of putting that lien on his house.

A clatter nearly makes me jump from my seat. Cal has set the frame down, but now he's holding a second print of the same photo.

"What are you doing with that one?"

"It's for Sully's office." He gives me a crooked smile, pride seeping from every inch of his handsome face. "I'm livening the place up." His expression suddenly sobers, and he averts his gaze. "Unless you don't want them there."

I scan the pictures he's set out. His dad. His brother. His son...*and me.*

Dammit. That twinge in my chest is back.

Cal has always seemed like a shallow pond, fun and flaky. But I'm beginning to wonder if I've just never given him a chance to be more. With a sigh, I look at him again only to find him watching me, anticipation etched in the lines on his face, like he's waiting for my response. The air grows heavy under his warm gaze. He seems to genuinely care about my response.

"It's perfect there." I clear my throat as my voice cracks.

"Whatever Lola wants..."

The line to that damn song is enough to snap me out of the weird stupor I've tripped and fallen into. "Stop that."

"Lo," Sully hollers from his office. "I'm sending a letter to your printer. It needs to be filed on JEDS to adjourn tomorrow morning."

I stand, my body moving on autopilot toward the new laser inkjet printer. We set it up on the corner table for the time being. Just until we can install a larger maggot-free machine.

The paper is warm as I pluck it from the printer tray. I'll get this done and then attempt to call probation again

"I just printed a consent order," Brian yells. "It needs to be finalized on Tervant, and it *must* be filed today."

I bite back an annoyed groan. Guess I'll call after I do the consent order.

"Don't forget to make sure Judge Avello has Winters ready hold for ten thirty tomorrow," Cal reminds me.

The urge to roll my eyes is strong. But as annoying as his requests are, none of the chambers have given me a hard time with the stupid ready holds. Apparently, Daddy Cal is even more adorable than normal Cal. At least to the secretaries at the courthouse. They all have easily agreed, eager to help him.

I grit my teeth.

"And—" Sully starts.

"Enough," I snap. "I'm one person."

"Aww, Lola." Cal stands and steps toward me, the scent of his cologne filling the air. "You need a wakey-breaky."

I glower up at his stupidly handsome face. "A what?"

He grasps my hand, his body heat instantly soaking into me, and tugs me toward the office door. "Do your own shit, you plonkers. Lola and I are taking a wakey-breaky."

Wakey-breaky? Cal and his damn weird ass words. I'm still trying to decipher this one when Sully appears in the doorway.

"What the hell is..." He crosses his arms, filling the entire space. "Whatever the hell you just said."

"A coffee break."

I fight the urge to smile. I do *not* want that to be cute. But it is... kind of. Just like Cal.

"It's a wakey-breaky, right Lola?" With a wink, he pulls me toward the door.

"Oh no." I yank my hand back, ignoring the way my heart flutters at his touch. "We are not making this a thing."

"Too late. It's a thing," he assures.

I cross my arms so he can't reach for my hand again. "It is not a thing."

He wraps an arm around my shoulder, the warmth of his body presses against mine. Oh no. This is so much worse. I want to hate it, but I don't.

Lips brushing my ear, he whispers, "It's our thing."

It takes everything in me not to shiver. "We do not—"

"Shhhh, Lola. You'll ruin it." Despite his low volume, his words are laced with humor.

And as if they have a mind of their own, my lips lift at the corners.

"Wakey-breaky here we come." He steers me out the door.

Though I'm loath to admit it, the wakey-breaky really does improve my mood. An hour later, I'm almost bummed when Cal slips out of the office without a word. Only then do I realize that although I got all the tasks ticked off the guys' lists, I still don't have my order.

With a grunt, I push out of my chair and head across the hall to Brian's office. "What are we doing about Howard?" The door frame creaks as I lean my shoulder against it.

He glances up, eyeing the molding like it might fall to my feet. When nothing crashes to the ground, he sighs. "This place needs so much work."

"So does the Howard case."

His eyes narrow. "The suit didn't work?"

"What?" I ask.

Before he can explain, the bell over the entrance jingles and in walks a bright orange suit. There's a person in the suit, of course, but it's impossible to focus on him while I'm being blinded by neon orange.

When I finally pick my jaw up off the floor, I ask, "What are you wearing?" Although Cal and I worked in the same building, we didn't work together, and I'd never seen this outfit.

Cal holds out his arms, grinning. "It's my get-it-done suit."

The move causes his lapels to shift, drawing my attention to his chest and the pink polka dot tie around his neck.

Before today, I'd have told you Cal looks good in anything. I'd have been wrong. This suit is not only ridiculous, it's downright painful to look at. "Wearing orange and pink helps you work?"

With a chuckle, he pulls a piece of paper from his shoulder bag and holds it out to me.

Once again, my jaw hits the floor. "My Howard order?" I gasp. "How?"

He rocks back on his heels, tugging on his lapels and smirking. "It's the suit. They can't ignore me when I'm in this baby."

Brian chuckles. "Works every time for the dumbass."

Teeth sinking into my bottom lip, I consider the man in the tacky suit. For once, despite the outfit, Cal doesn't seem like a dumbass.

"*Whatever Lola wants...*"

This time, when the lyrics slip from his mouth, they don't annoy me at all.

CHAPTER 14

Cal

While I've officially settled into my role as a dad and our new living situation in New Jersey, I can't say the same for some of my roommates.

It's been two weeks, yet Brian is more surly than ever.

"What was that man doing in our apartment?" he asks, leering over the conference table, a big ball of negative energy.

Ah. He must have run into the man I hired to handle a little home project.

"When was the last time you had a rumpy-pumpy in the sheets?"

Brian scowls. Lo, on the other hand, snorts. That reaction sends a thrill through me.

"A what?" The edge in his tone warns of the pain he'd like to inflict on me.

I don't heed it at all.

"You know, when was the last time you had your wanker boinked?"

He straightens and runs a hand over his jaw. "For fucks sake."

I grin at Lola, then continue to tease Brian. "A shagging, a banging, get nasty, make whoopie. Any of these familiar?"

His face is red and mottled, like he's ready to explode. Blinking back and forth from me to Lola, he shakes his head. "Why are you smiling at him?"

She presses her lips together, flattening her expression. "I'm not."

Bloody hell. I want to leap across the table and pummel his arse for wiping away that beautiful smile.

"You were." The lines on Brian's forehead deepen.

"You're going to want to stop doing that." With a wave of my hand, I push back and stand.

Brian sighs. "I have a feeling I'll regret asking. Doing what?"

"A frowny upside downy?" I look to Lola for confirmation that the term works.

Her lips tick up again as she tries not to smile, but she gives me a simple nod.

Brian, on the other hand, storms out of the room, blustering and calling for my brother.

I cough out a laugh as I watch him go.

"So who was in the apartment?" Lola's voice is quiet, making it hard to hear as I stand by the door listening to Brian rage in my brother's office.

When I spin around to give her my full attention, I realize that I've made a grave mistake.

Lola is always pretty. I've never been able to ignore her presence, though she's never had trouble ignoring mine. That has always rankled me, so I settled on taunting and teasing her. It makes it harder to pretend I don't exist, and it's easier on me, knowing her annoyance with me is warranted.

Right now she doesn't look the least bit annoyed. There's a small smile on her lips and an excited glint in her pretty emerald eyes. Like she wants to be in on whatever secret I'm about to share. Like she's not only tolerating me but she appreciates my presence. *It's intoxicating.* I could stare at this woman all damn day. I'd do almost anything to get lost in those eyes. To get lost in this feeling she's evoking inside my chest.

"Security company." The words escape me on their own, breaking the spell.

She blinks, as if she, too, was lost in reverie, and tilts her head in confusion.

Leaning against the door, arms crossed, I fight the urge to go to her. It's nice sharing an office with Lola. Though I don't know that she'd agree.

"Why?"

"Wanted cameras for the flat so after school, when Murphy and T. J. are here, they can hang out upstairs, and we won't have to worry about whether they're safe. Madame Esmeralda has a lot of people coming in and out all day."

"Makes sense."

"And if Murphy wakes up at night—"

Lola frowns. "Wait, you had cameras installed *inside* the apartment?"

"Lo!" Sully shouts.

"I miss the intercom," she grumbles, her eyes falling shut, before taking a deep breath, like she's searching for patience. Just as her expression evens out, Sully screams again as if we didn't all hear him and his grumpy arse the first time.

Lola presses her palms against the surface of the table and uses it to push herself out of her chair. As she straightens, a desperate, beleaguered sigh slips past her lips.

"Enough," I bark.

Lola's eyes go wide with surprise and jump to mine.

Shit. "Not you," I say, backpedaling. "Never you."

Jaw ticking, I stomp straight into my brother's office. Sully is alone, squinting at his computer. Looks like Brian got all his bitching out. I turn right back around and knock harshly on Brian's closed door, then swing it open without waiting for him to acknowledge me. "Partner's meeting. Sully's office. Now." My words are staccato and angry. I'm fuming.

As Brian whips his head up, I spin on my heel and head back into my brother's office.

"Did you just bark at me?" Brian almost sounds amused as he appears in the doorway.

I point to the chair in front of Sully's desk. "Sit."

Brian reels back. "Excuse me."

"Sit," I grind out again.

"What the hell is this about?" Sully's annoyed growl rolls up my spine. As always he acts like his time is wort more than all of ours.

Hands in my pockets, I eye them both. "You two are driving Lola insane."

Brian points to his chest. "*We're* driving her insane?"

Sully narrows his eyes. "What's wrong with Lo? Lo!"

I step inside and slam the door, pointing at him. "*That.* Stop doing that."

Sully looks back and forth between Brian and me, brows pinched. "Doing what? Asking her to do her job? We've got work to do, Cal." He grips his armrests and tilts back in his chair. "At least some of us do."

I ignore his jab. I get my work done. Maybe it takes me less time than theirs takes them, but that's not my issue. I've never been good at sitting around, and I won't do it just to make them feel better about themselves and their inability to work as efficiently as I do.

"We're not going to scream at Lola. If you want something done, get off your arse and talk to her."

Brian, the stodgy bastard, actually looks like he might smile.

Sully sighs. "I don't have time to walk back and forth every time I need something. Lola doesn't mind."

"*She does mind,*" I quip. "And we can't lose her."

Just the thought of her going back to New York City like she's always threatening makes it hard to breathe.

Brian relaxes in his chair. "She promised ninety days."

Ninety? But we need her here for three hundred and sixty-five. Bloody hell, this is worse than I thought.

Grinding my teeth together, I shake my head. "Then we need to give her a reason to stay." I pull a walkie-talkie from my pocket and toss it at my brother. *"Here."*

He catches it against his chest and holds it up. "What is this?"

"A walkie-talkie?" Brian answers, though his voice tilts like it's a question.

"Yes. Otherwise known as the Jersey office intercom system," I explain.

Sully's frown deepens. "What?"

"I'll pick up two more. When you need Lola, you simply press the side, say *pardon me, Lo*"—I glare at him—"and once she acknowledges that you aren't interrupting what she's working on, you *ask* her to accomplish the task."

Both men are silent, studying me, for a long moment.

When they finally nod and agree, I turn and stalk out.

As I hit the threshold, Brian calls after me. "Oh, Cal, DCPP called. They'll be by some time in the next forty-eight hours."

At the mention of the Division of Child Protection and Permanency, my blood turns to ice. I swivel around. "Why?"

Brian shrugs. "Court needs to sign off on Murphy's living situation. Ensure it's safe. It's standard."

We may run one of the most preeminent family law firms in the country, yet being on the other side of this—waiting for a judge to decide that my son is safe with me—feels foreign. Wrong.

He's *my* son. If Brandy had told me about him, then I wouldn't have missed all this time with him, and there would be no need for the court to be involved at all. No reason for them to have to *decide* whether I'm fit to take care of him. I've done nothing—absolutely freaking nothing—to warrant the court's concern about whether I have the *right* to take care of my son.

She left him. She should have to explain herself.

Dazed and nervous, I breathe through my nose and stalk out of his office. Just as I step into the hall, I barrel straight into Lola. As our bodies collide, she stumbles back, wobbling on her heels. On instinct, I grasp her arms to steady her.

"Bloody hell, are you okay?" I duck, assessing her.

She blinks up at me, completely silent.

"Do you have a concussion? Should we call a doctor? Sully!"

In an instant, my brother appears. Brian too.

Sully breaks into a smirk, brow arched as he zeroes in on the hands I still have cuffed around Lola's arms. "Thought we didn't yell anymore."

"Wanker," I mutter, eye still roving over Lola's dazed expression. "I ran into Lola. She's not talking. Should we call a doctor?"

"I'm fine." She pulls out of my hold, taking her soft, warm body away. "You just surprised me is all."

"Of course I did. I almost knocked you over."

She shakes her head, like she disagrees, but she doesn't speak, and that mask of indifference she wears so often slips into place.

Brian steps between us and looks her over. "You okay?"

"I'm fine," she huffs.

Relief floods me, though it's instantly replaced with the fear that had consumed me only moments ago. Blood pressure rising, I side-step the group. "I'm going to check on the flat."

"Check on the flat?" Sully asks. "Is this another euphemism for a coffee break?"

"No," I grind out. "If DCPP is sending someone out, I want to make sure it's perfectly clean and organized."

I shake my head. What the hell good will that do? It's up to them to determine whether I'm good enough to be Murphy's dad and everyone knows I'm not.

He deserves better than me. He deserves better than this place.

My heart pounds wildly, the pain in my sternum intensifying. Fuck. Is this what a heart attack feels like? Is this how my dad felt before he died? Probably not. He was probably too focused on the young Ginger to panic like this—

"Cal." Lola steps up close and gently tugs at the hand I'm aggressively rubbing against my chest. "Why don't we take a walk?"

I blink down at her, instantly captivated by her emerald eyes. She's this steady calm in the storm. "They can't take Murphy."

"Cal," Brian starts.

"They won't." Lola shakes her head. "Come on, let's go for a walk. I'll talk you through everything."

"Can you come upstairs and look around the flat? Let me know if there's anything else we need to have done?"

She gives me another one of her soft, easy smiles. The kind she offers to the kids she meets, when she's trying to be the person they need in that moment. It's the smile I've wanted for longer than I'll ever admit. "Yeah, Cal, let's go upstairs."

On autopilot, I follow her up the steps, mesmerized by her swaying hips.

On the second floor, I point to one of the security cameras I just had installed. "See?"

She nods and licks her lips. "Very safe."

Inside, I take in the flat through DCPP's eyes. When I spot the wilting plants in every corner, I wince. "I can't seem to keep them alive. I should probably remove some of them." Head lowered, I take a step toward the closest one.

Lola grasps my arm, stopping me. "The plants are fine. They just need a little more water." She releases me, then pads to the kitchen where she fills a glass with water.

"The man said to spritz them." I point to my spritzer as she carefully pours water into the dirt at the base of one plant.

She lets out a light laugh. "Maybe we try really watering them, see if that makes a difference."

"What if they take him?" The question is a choked whisper. It's all I can manage.

She gives me that soft smile again, and I soak it in. "Would it help if I explained exactly what they're looking for and what happens during these appointments?"

Throat tightening with gratitude, I nod. Legally, I understand how this all works. But emotionally, I feel lost.

"This is all very standard. You're his father but they want to make sure he's comfortable with you and taken care of since you've just met. It's similar to the reunification process but—"

"But we were never unified to begin with." A rush of anger works its way through me. I missed out on so much.

Lola nods. "Yes. You have nothing to worry about though. You're doing everything you're supposed to, dead plants aside."

A chuckle escapes me. This woman has an uncanny ability to make even the most anxious of people feel at ease.

She returns to the kitchen for another glass of water. "They'll come in, chat with you, look at Murphy's room, and do a quick check of the house, than ask about his schedule," she says as she plucks dead leaves from another plant. "They'll watch you interact with Murphy for a bit, and then they'll leave. We'll hear nothing for about two months and then we'll get a letter saying the case is closed. No services recommended."

"That's it?"

She nods, focusing on me. "That's it. Everything will be all hunky-dory."

I break into a smile. "Are you doing my walkie-talkie thing?"

She shakes her head, laughing. "Probably failing, but yes. Did it work?"

"You called me a hunk?"

"No. Saying that something is hunky-dory means it's fine."

Tongue in my cheek, I tilt my head. "Nah, I think you just called me a hunk."

"You're—" She puffs out a breath and shakes her head.

"A hunk, I know. You just told me."

With a snort she strides back for another glass of water.

"Careful, Lola, you keep smiling at me like that, I'll think you like me."

She tucks her chin as she stands at the sink, trying to hide her smile. "I don't."

Twenty-four hours later, Lola's prediction comes true. The meeting with DCPP is uneventful. Now we just wait for that little letter.

At least two months, Lola reminds me.

Sixty days.

And she promised Brian ninety.

I can't let that happen. Lola can't leave. Not when she's finally smiling at me. So I'll use the next sixty days to not only get to know my son, but to convince Lola to stay.

CHAPTER 15

Lola

"Lo."

The walkie-talkie crackles, pulling my attention away from the risk assessment Sully asked me to read over.

Though I'm not sure the Jersey intercom system is any better than yelling—it makes it easier for them to dump more on me—the way Cal defended me to them? Yeah, that was sweet. Which is not typical for Cal.

Maybe that was the old Cal. This new Cal, the one who's taken over since we moved to Jersey, is sweet. And I kind of like it.

"Lo. Ya there?" Brian repeats. "I need you to pull exhibits A through U for Kambrano."

The lightness that had taken over wheezes out of me. Twenty-one exhibits. *No problem.*

I grit my teeth. So far today, I've been tasked with sending out three letters, putting together a notice of motion, and finishing this risk assessment. And it's not even lunchtime.

Apparently they think I possess some magical ability that allows me to do six things at the same time.

I pick up the dumb thing and fumble with it. "No," I say, not totally sure I held the button long enough. "Not available for that." I add for good measure.

For as long as I've been around, the guys have each had their own paralegal, plus two legal assistants and associates to help with the grunt work. Now it's just me. So they are gonna have to learn to step up and do more of the heavy lifting themselves. In fact, I intend to teach them how to use the brand-new copier before the day is over. How is it that they passed the bar, yet they can't even scan a document?

Oh, because they're spoiled asshats.

Brian appears in the doorway. "Why the hell not?"

"She's working on prep for my DV trial tomorrow." Sully pushes past him and drops a stack of papers on my already full desk. "Police reports."

I give him a clipped nod, though I'm pretty sure there's smoke billowing from my ears.

"I'm getting the three letters proofed and up to JEDS plus hard copies sent," I say to Brian. "I have the notice of motion, proposed order and cert. I also did service and fees for the motion you're doing. Before the end of the day, I'll need to follow up on the interrogatories on Jensen. Plus, I'm doing this stuff for Sully." Exhaling, I rub at my temples. "So, no Brian, I don't have time to pull exhibits."

He sighs, his shoulders sinking. "You're *my* paralegal."

"I used to be, yeah. And I could be again if we left this shit hole but for the next"—I squint at the calendar on the wall with the countdown—"sixty-eight days I belong to all of you."

"No one is leaving for a year." With a glare at Brian, Sully jabs a finger at the papers he dropped on my desk. "Flag anything I need to review in red. Yellow if you think it's an exhibit."

As he brushes past Brian, he grits out, "I'm getting my firm and my family back. A year Brian, not a day less."

Brian watches him go, and he doesn't turn back to me until Sully's door slams shut.

"So I'm really pulling my own exhibits?"

Before I can respond, the bell on the front door jingles, announcing Cal's arrival.

Of their own accord, my eyes jump to one of the two computer screens in front of me.

10:22 a.m.

He's later than normal.

"*Lola*," he sings.

Smirking, Brian steps back. A moment later, Cal practically prances into the room. He's in a blue button-down that pulls across his shoulders, showing off just how defined his body is. From here, it looks like he didn't shave this morning, so there is just a hint of shadow dusting his jaw.

Dammit. I swear the man gets hotter every day. It's annoying as hell.

"I come bearing a bag of wakey-breaky and the best nifty-gifty."

Brian snorts. I actually like that one, though. *Nifty-gifty*. I'm dangerously close to giggling before my good senses return and I suppress it.

Have I seriously sunk to laughing at the dumb ass rhymes this gorgeous man spews?

Cal's eyes twinkle like he can read my mind. Shit. I hope not. If he knew how hot I think he is, he'd be insufferable.

"Are you ready for it?" He grins that stupidly handsome grin. "Come on, Lola, get excited."

He strides around the table and pulls me to my feet. Once I'm steadied, he doesn't step away. No, he peers down at me, his blue eyes sparkling.

The heat radiating from him is far too comforting, and his scent is enough to hypnotize me. I'm frozen, unable to move away.

His gaze drops to my mouth, and his lips part.

A bone-deep desire to press my mouth to his crashes over me like a wave.

"Who's in the lobby?" Brian's voice jars me out of the haze, and I quickly step back from the man messing with my head.

I do not like him, I remind myself. Right?

"Is that Amy Reynolds?" Brian's voice is farther away now, but the pitch is higher, filled with horror.

The same kind of sensation swamps me at the name, sobering me completely. Amy Reynolds? The woman was the worst intern in the history of Murphy & Machon.

I rush around the table and out the door of the conference room. Brian stands at the mouth of the hallway, and sure enough, just inside the front door, a brunette dressed in a short skirt and sky-high heels stands.

"Surprise," Cal says from behind me. "I brought reinforcements. I reached out to our favorite intern and she's happy to help."

As she nods, her eyes dart around the lobby area and her smile falls. "You didn't say the office was so gross, Cal."

This might be the first time I've ever agreed with a word from the woman's mouth.

"But, like, we'll get flowers," she says, perking up. "And pink pillows for that sofa. It'll be like amazing." She claps. "Ooo, maybe we can get a coffee bar."

"That would be fun," Cal agrees. He turns to me, his brows lifted. "Isn't it great to have her?"

The irritation that's so common in this man's presence has returned, seeping into my veins. He's got to be kidding me. She's the dumbest human alive.

I take a deep breath, willing myself to stay calm. "Cal, can I talk to you for a minute?"

He slides his hands into his pockets. "Sure, what's up?"

Teeth gritted, I spin on my heel and stride down the hall. "Brian's office."

"Be right back," Cal chirps behind me.

"I know what you're going to say," he says as he steps into the office behind me. "But we're only allowed one *paid* employee. The wording of the trust is ironclad in that respect. This is a workaround."

Brian steps in and shuts the door. "An intern might be a good idea."

I glare at him. The traitor just doesn't want to do his own busy work.

I scoff. "Not Amy." She's far more likely to make my job harder than be of any kind of assistance.

Brian rubs at his chin. "She really was the worst we've ever had."

"Really?" Cal frowns, his brows pulled low.

Head cocked, I cross my arms. "Don't you remember when she emailed the judge the lunch order and sent the protected order to the deli?"

His face gives nothing away.

I fling my hand in the air. "No? So, you don't remember that when I confronted her about it, her response was *that's so weird?*"

"I handled that. The judge was fine." Cal smirks. The expression causes an almost irresistible urge to hit him. "Just took a bottle of wine and night out with me."

I drop my head back and groan. "You can't tell people these things."

"I'm telling you. You're not people." He hits me with a charming smile.

It doesn't work on me. Not in this situation. The idea of him on a date irritates me. And I hate my reaction more than the image the thought conjures.

I pin my boss with a glare. "He's as bad as Amy."

Brian sighs.

"I'm just teasing." Cal's tone is too light for the situation. "I'd never take a judge out on a date. It was her clerk. Anyway," he says, oblivious to how little that distinction helps his case, "trust me, this will be great. Come on, give her a try."

He pulls the door open, and I begrudgingly follow him to the lobby where Amy is staring up at the ceiling, her long beach-waved hair falling almost to her waist.

We all follow her gaze and, as if on cue, there's a thump above us.

"Will it, like, fall?" she asks.

"No," Cal says. "That's just Sebastian. Our ghost."

It takes everything in me not to scoff.

Of course he's bought into Madame Esmeralda's idea of a ghost.

"Cool." Amy smiles, just as easily convinced. "I want to meet him."

"We don't have a fucking ghost," Sully shouts from his office. "Stop saying that or I'll never get Sloane and T. J. to move in."

"Sully," Cal says, "the ghost is the least of your worries when it comes to that."

Sully lumbers down the hall, face red. But before he can continue his rant, Cal plucks a small orange basketball from the lobby desk and tosses it at his brother's head.

Sully catches it and glares.

"Just trying to cheer you up. We need to see the frowny upside downy."

With a huff, Sully disappears again, his door slamming a second later.

"Think the ghost will invade our bodies and give us superpowers?" Amy asks. "That would be so cool."

"See, she's going to be great." Cal smiles at me.

I can't believe this is my life.

CHAPTER 16
Cal

"That's what I'm talking about."

With a grunt, my brother swings at the Ping-Pong ball. He misses, and as it bounces across the floor, he glowers at a gloating Brian.

I grin. This is exactly why I got this table. Everyone's been so bloody tense since we moved to Jersey. We're three single lads living together. Sure, we're also dads—well two of us are—and we're kind of disasters at the dad thing, but we can still make the best of the situation.

"Brian." Lola's angry voice is choppy coming from the walkie-talkie.

Truly this system is bloody brilliant. I brought the men upstairs to blow off steam and to give Lola a little peace. But she can still reach us if she needs to.

Immediately his shoulders straighten and he drops the paddle. "Yes?"

"Judge Gasper called. Instead of sending the letter to the court on Friday, Amy mailed an empty certified envelope, so our objection was not filed in time. If you have any chance of winning Peterson's case, you better get down to the courthouse right now."

With a glare at me—as if this is my fault—he holds down the button on the side of the walkie-talkie and grunts. "How the fuck did she do that?"

"I don't know." Lola's voice is robotic. "When I asked, her response was *that's so weird, right?*"

I grimace. Amy is definitely not Lola's favorite person.

"Need me to get the orange suit?" I offer when Brian sets the walkie-talkie down.

He shakes his head. "This is a three-year custody battle with six experts. Not even a Callahan special can fix it."

Sully points at me. "We should go back to the office."

Agreeing, I follow them down. Then, for the rest of the day, I endure Lola's glowering. Every time she looks at me, she huffs, like I was the one who sent the empty certified envelope.

I'm bloody thrilled when my mobile rings offering me a distraction. "Fisher, my man," I say after seeing his name flashing on the screen, "to what do I owe the pleasure?"

With a scowl directed at me, Lola pushes away from the table and struts out of the conference room. And damn does she look good doing it.

"Calling to confirm that you'll be at Libby's event now that your brother cancelled."

Fisher is a man of few words, so the lack of pleasantries doesn't shock me. We attended Harvard together, and, over the years, we'd see each other here and there. But that ended a few years ago when his brother died and he moved to a little island off the coast of Maine to raise his niece.

We reconnected this summer when I ran into him with his girl-friend, actress Elizabeth Sweet. Now he's living in Boston again.

"What do you mean my brother cancelled?" I scan the empty reception area.

Fisher grunts. "No fucking clue. Just told me he couldn't come. I figured you'd know. Don't you work with the guy?"

I chuckle. "He uses fewer words than you."

Fisher sighs on the other end of the line. "This event means a lot to Libby."

I know it does. It's a fundraiser for a children's charity that assists victims of abuse. This summer, after years of suffering, Libby went public with a bombshell of a secret. Now the entire world knows why this means a lot to her.

"Where and when?" I ask.

"It's this weekend in Boston. We've got a block of rooms reserved. The Langfields, Millers, and Berkshires will be there." For a grumpy bastard, he's a fucking genius throwing those names around. Not only are they the wealthiest families in New England, but they're all clients of our firm in some way. We absolutely shouldn't miss this event.

Though there's absolutely no way Brian will let me go in his place since the Berkshires will be there. At least not alone. They're one of his biggest clients. The moment I mention it, he'll panic that I'll fuck it all up.

But if I brought Lola...

The thought echoes through my mind like a siren's song.

"Text me the info. I'll be there."

"Really?" Fisher's tone is laced with surprise.

"Yes, and tell the lovely Libby that she better save a dance for me."

He lets out a derisive grunt. "Her dance card is full."

Chuckling, I end the call without saying goodbye. He probably hasn't even noticed since he's too busy hoarding his favorite toy.

Lola breezes down the hall, and when she catches sight of Amy, who's staring at her phone while she stands in front of the photocopier, she lets out a judgmental huff.

It hits me then how to get exactly what I want.

It's so easy it's criminal.

She's going to walk right into this one.

Pocketing my phone, I stroll down the hall, an easy confidence pushing me toward my brother's office. "Knock knock."

"Oh, I know this one," Amy calls as she rushes toward me. "Who's there?"

"You've got to be fucking kidding me." Sighing, Lola strolls back this way.

She's like a lioness pacing her land. Setting her boundaries. She may say she hates this place, but she hates the presence of another woman even more.

I grin at Amy. She's beautiful and sweet, but she's got absolutely nothing on Lola. That's no surprise. There isn't another woman in the world who could compare.

Lola is perfect.

Even her annoyed little huffs have my heart racing.

I smooth down the front of my shirt. "Well, Amy, I'm glad you asked." I glance at my brother. "Apparently the *who's there* is a pissed off Fisher Jones and Libby Sweet."

Sully straightens in his seat. "What?"

It's rare that I have the opportunity to scold my brother. He's always right, he's always serious, and he's always been the one doing the right things.

I'm going to enjoy this.

"You bailed on Libby's charity event this weekend." I pinch my chin, like I'm deep in thought. "The charity event the Berkshires are attending."

He rolls back a few inches. "I sent a donation and I've already got a meeting with Henry scheduled for next month."

Henry Berkshire is the patriarch of the family but Sully knows as well as I do that billionaires don't do real business in formal meetings, they do it at events like this. To remain on their radar, we have to be seen. We have to be important. That means being in the places where important people are also being seen.

Like this charity event.

"Why did you cancel?" That's what I can't figure out. It's unlike him to waste an opportunity like this.

He rolls back up to his desk and laces his fingers on the top of it. "It's our anniversary weekend."

I frown. "Your anniversary? Like the day you observe to celebrate a marriage? To the wife you're divorcing?"

"You're getting divorced?" Amy interjects, her voice laced with interest.

I don't even bother fighting a scowl as I turn to her. But she's utterly oblivious.

"No," Sully says this to both of us, his tone clipped.

I roll my eyes. "This again."

"I originally said yes to the event thinking Sloane and I could have a weekend away. I thought—" He snaps his mouth closed and shakes his head.

I'm not surprised he's locked himself down. He's not an emotional guy. It's why he's getting divorced. If only he would get out of his own damn way, stop thinking so hard and show some bloody feelings, maybe he could salvage the relationship.

"She finally agreed to let T. J. stay over this weekend. I won't miss the chance to show her he's safe here."

The floor above creaks loudly, making us all look up.

Amy squeals, clapping and bouncing on her toes. "Can I go say hi to Sebastian?"

In unison, Sully and I say, "no."

Then Sully shakes his head. "I'll send a bigger donation."

I strike at the opportunity he's laid out for me. Pushing forward from where I'm leaning against the wall, I grin. "I'll go."

He shakes his head. "You can't fucking handle this."

Pushing away the hurt that bubbles up at his response, I continue the act. "Why? I'm excellent at schmoozing and giving away our money."

Lola snorts from where she's standing at the photocopier, pretending—badly, I must say—not to listen.

"No," Sully groans. "The Berkshires are our biggest client. Brian can go."

"No, he can't," Lola says, suddenly standing in the doorway. "We were just granted an appearance in front of Judge Gasper. Brian has to fix the empty certified mail debacle." She narrows her focus on Amy who's once again staring up at the ceiling, completely unaware of how Lola would probably like to pummel her with her tiny fists.

"Oh, I love Joey Berkshire," the ditzy intern says.

Huh. Maybe she's listening after all. Joey is the youngest of the three older Berkshire daughters. She just won Dancing with the Stars and has millions of followers on Instagram. On top of all that, she and Libby Sweet are friends. I can't imagine she won't be at this event.

This is my cue to go in for the kill.

Tongue in my cheek, I shrug. "Okay," I say, tone easy, posture relaxed, "Amy can go with me."

If I thought Lola's little angry huffs were adorable, they've got nothing on the fire-breathing dragon she morphs into as she looks from me to Amy to Sully.

She balls her tiny hands into fists, her chest heaving with angry breaths, and my cock jumps.

"Absolutely not."

I've witnessed plenty of angry tirades from this woman. I've pissed her off more times than I can count. But I've never witnessed this tone from her. It's as if the devil himself has possessed her. Or maybe it's Sebastian.

Every single head snaps in her direction.

Even Brian peeks in, hand on the door as if her words forced him back. "What's going on?"

"This one," Lola thumbs at me, "suggested that he go to the Sweet charity event this weekend because this one"—She jabs an angry finger at my brother—"cancelled. He doesn't want to go without Sloane. And these two seem to think that this one"—Her voice pitches higher as she motions toward Amy—"can handle mingling with our biggest clients."

Lola's practically steaming now, her face red, fly-aways escaping her braid. She's completely unraveling.

Because of me.

She's jealous over *me*.

I think.

Just one more tiny push to confirm it.

"What's the problem? Amy would look lovely in a dress"—I give the girl a wink—"and she can help me make conversation."

Lola throws out an arm. "I just caught her chatting with the wall."

"I was talking to the ghost," Amy retorts.

Biting back the laugh that wants so desperately to escape, I say, "No fair, Sebastian hasn't talked to me yet. I even left dinner for him last night."

"These two cannot represent the firm," Lola hisses.

Crossing my arms, I lean back against the wall, my job here done.

Brian, Sully, and Lola talk over one another, arguing it out. In a matter of seconds, I see the lightbulb click on behind Sully's eyes. This is it. It's bloody brilliant and the only real answer to this problem.

"You're right, Lo," he says. "You'll go."

Bingo.

"What?" the fiery little object of my affection growls.

"Yes, you and Cal." My brother turns to me. "I'll watch Murphy. The boys have hit it off. Spending the weekend together will help T. J. settle in. And it'll make Sloane more comfortable. All settled."

They walked right into my plan.

"No." Lola shakes her head, though her voice is resigned.

I push off the wall and take a step closer. "I'll get you a green dress to match your favorite crystal heels."

She whips around, and when she realizes I'm so close, her eyes widen. "How do you even know that I own those?"

"You gushed about them to Sloane the night you bought them, and then you got all frowny upside downy when she asked when you'd have the chance to wear them. Tell me, Lola, have you ever worn them?"

She studies me, her brows knitting together tightly.

With any luck, she's finally getting it. Finally understanding just how long I've been cataloging her every move.

She blows out a breath, eyes falling closed. "Fine. But we're flying straight home after."

I grin. "*Whatever Lola wants...*"

"I can't believe this." With that, she storms out of Sully's office.

Even though she's a little ball of anger, I'm smiling. And I'm pretty sure I won't stop.

CHAPTER 17

Lola

"How is it so perfect?"

It takes every ounce of strength I have not to smile at the emerald green dress Benjamine brought up five minutes ago.

I hang it from my closet door, unable to turn away yet. It's just so pretty.

"He's a Murphy. They all possess some kind of black magic," Sloane grumbles from my phone on the nightstand. It's propped up on the bedside lamp, my best friend's face filling the screen.

Black magic but good taste. I finger the soft material, twisting the dress closer. Light catches on the crystals at the neckline, making them sparkle against the otherwise deep green fabric.

"Did you give him a photo of your crystal Jimmy Choos? No, I bet he did this all on his own," Sloane mutters. "He conjured up the perfect thing without any help. Damn them."

I shuffle over to the phone and give my friend a pointed look. "Instead of pretending you're upset about my dress, why don't you tell me what Sully did?"

She sets her giant coffee mug on the granite counter with a little too much force, and a sigh the size of Alaska makes her shoulders slump. "He talked me into letting T. J. stay in Jersey this weekend. And I'm not even sure how. One minute I was saying no, and then boom, the plans were made."

Ah, yes. It's another Murphy trait. The ability to talk anyone into just about anything while making them believe it's their own idea. This I can relate to. "It could be worse, you could be going to Boston with him."

An almost laugh slips past my friend's lips.

"Hold on," I tease. "Did Sloane Murphy just smile?"

"Oh, stop. I smile."

She used to smile. She used to be the life of the party. For years, she was the sunshine to my black cat. But I haven't seen that side of her in far too long. Somehow, I've become the sunshine half of this friendship, and that's saying something. I've never been called an optimist. I'm not bubbly.

But with all she's going through, I'll give her a break. And I can't deny that it makes me feel better knowing that T. J. will be around to keep Murphy company while Cal is gone.

"T. J. will be fine with Sully. He may have messed shit up, but you can't deny how much he loves him," I remind her as I dig pajamas out of my dresser drawer.

Definitely not black...or red...or—

I give myself a mental slap. Why am I stressing about this? Cal and I aren't even sharing a room. No one but me will see them. I grab a set and then turn back to Sloane. "Plus, you'll have a relaxing weekend to yourself. "

Sloane blinks, her lips tugging down. "That's what you're bringing?"

Ball of material held aloft, I give it a second look. "What's wrong with them?"

"They're satin and lace." Her tone is pure disapproval. "And fancy. Those are the type of pajamas you wear when you know someone else will see them."

"No. Cal and I aren't sharing a room. And he will not see them." I turn to my suitcase, frowning at the green lace bra and matching thong I've already packed. It makes sense to wear pretty underwear beneath the dress. Anyone would do that. It's not like I picked them out for Cal.

Cal would probably like red better anyway.

His eyes would lock in on the red lace, and his breathing would quicken a little. Just like every time we were close. His normally scattered attention would narrow until it was all directed on me. The blue of his irises would darken to almost a navy hue.

My heart rate kicks up at the idea of having Cal's undivided focus. The way his hand would hover over my skin for the span of a breath before he put those warm palms on me and pulled me to him.

"Lo?" The single syllable jars me out of my daydream.

I assess the tan pajamas for a second, then toss them in. "They're the only type I have. You know that."

"Only type." She deadpans. "So you don't own a single T-shirt?"

Nose scrunched, I adjust the stack of clothing in my suitcase. "I don't sleep in T-shirts. They're scratchy and bulky."

"Yes. Our little princess and the pea." Her smile is back.

"Says the woman with five pillows and a sound machine."

The comment distracts her from the pajamas and leads her into a tangent about T. J.'s sound machine and her concerns about the weekend.

Although Sully already got T. J. a sound machine—identical to the one they've used since he was an infant—along with a new set of the same sheets he has at home, I'd rather listen to her rant than talk about Cal, so I don't stop her.

Five minutes later, I'm packed and standing in front of the dress again.

The perfect dress.

How does he know me so well? Has he always paid attention like this? And if so, how have I never noticed? There's no other explanation. It's been months since I mentioned my Jimmy Choos. And yet he remembered.

"Since you've become enchanted with the dress again, I'll let you go. But before I do, let me say this..."

With the dress in hand, I spin back to Sloane.

"Those Murphy men are charming, yes. But it's all talk."

I frown at her. A week ago, those words could have come straight from my mouth. But now, getting to know Cal, I'm beginning to wonder if I've been wrong about him.

"Don't drink too much wine or you'll end up in bed with him. Mark my words."

I scoff, shaking away the second-guessing. "That will literally never happen." It can't. I won't allow it.

"That's what we all say." Sloane takes a fortifying sip from her mug. "Okay, I better pack T. J.'s stuff. Have fun."

"You too." I end the call, then focus on slipping the dress into a garment bag. Once it's zipped up, I dart back to the dresser and yank out a damn T-shirt.

Not that it matters, but whatever.

Cal will be here any minute.

Just as the thought crosses my mind, my phone chimes.

Benjamine: Sending Callahan Murphy up if that's okay.

Me: Yes, thanks

Benjamine is just as helpful as Stanley was. Is it because Cal is tipping him as well? Probably.

The thought sends a wave of mixed emotions through me. Growing up, I never experienced that kind of concerned care from another person. My parents see the world as one big adventure. Worrying isn't in their DNA. When I was twenty-two and told them I was moving to New York, they weren't the least bit apprehensive. There was no fear regarding their young daughter living alone in the city. No, the announcement was met with nothing but excitement.

Their style of parenting meant I was allotted a great deal of freedom. In high school, my friends were all envious. No one understood how difficult it was to not feel cared for like that.

So the idea that Cal has always cared leaves me off-kilter.

"Knockity Knock knock."

My stomach jumps at the sound of his voice.

The whole way to the door, I remind myself that this is a weekend work event and nothing more. There's no reason butterflies should be fluttering in my belly.

I pull the door open and find him with his hands stuffed into his jeans pockets, rocking back on his heels, looking casual and so, so right standing in my door.

"You ready, Lola?" His eyes roam over my wrap dress, his lips tipping up. "Need me to grab your bag?"

All I can do is stare. Why does it feel like he should be here? Like greeting him at the door like this should be a normal thing?

It shouldn't be. This is a work trip. This is not a date. We're not even staying together.

When I don't respond, he sheepishly peers down at his white Oxford and jeans. "What?"

The issue isn't his clothes. It's the boyish charm. Because once again, he's got me feeling off-kilter.

"What do you think about the dress?" He smirks like he's privy to exactly how I reacted.

No way will I give him the satisfaction of knowing just how perfect it is. I need to put him back where he belongs. Back into the box of annoying. "It's fine."

"Fine, huh?" His blue eyes dance. "So the crystals didn't match your shoes perfectly?"

I sigh, giving in. "How did you do it?"

"I called Jimmy Choo."

"Oh, so a stylist picked it out to match." I reach for my suitcase, but before I can get ahold of the handle, he grasps it.

"No, he sent me a photo and I went shopping." He holds the door for me.

My heart thumps against my breastbone. "When did you have time for that?"

"I finished up with Judge Espadrilles early so I stopped on the way to get the boys."

I snort. The ridiculous man gave the judge a nickname based on the kind of shoes she always wears.

"One day you're going to mess up and call her that to her face." I shake my head.

"After all this time, you still doubt me? I'd never mess up like that." His grin makes my lips twitch without my permission.

"Anyway, it gave me enough time to find the dress before the boys got out of school. Then I picked it up on my way home. You know New York has the best shopping. There's nothing that can't be found there."

"New York has the best everything."

He dips his chin. "It does."

"And we're stuck here in Jersey."

"Not tonight, Lola." His eyes flash. "Tonight we're going on the whirly-twirly."

I cough out a laugh. What a name for a plane. I can't help but smile because even if I don't want to be, I'm looking forward to the weekend too.

CHAPTER 18

Cal

"What the hell is this?" Lola gapes at the helicopter I arranged like she's never seen one before.

"A whirly-twirly."

The driver grabs our bags from the trunk, and when I try to follow him, Lola clutches my arm, stopping me.

"What's he doing with our bags?"

I face her full-on, frowning at her wary expression. Is she nervous? This woman dislikes many things but I've never witnessed a legitimate fear of hers. Sure, she's not a fan of maggots, but who is? And she's a bit put off by our office, *and Jersey in general*, but that's understandable. But a helicopter? It's a mode of transportation.

"He's loading them onto the helicopter. That's how we're getting to Boston. The flight's shorter this way. We'll be there in ninety minutes."

Her sharp fingernails dig through my shirt and into my flesh. "You want me to sit in that for *ninety minutes*?" Her words come out just as sharp as her nails.

I gently pry her fingers from my arm, hoping she hasn't already drawn blood, and lace them with mine. Once I'm holding her securely, I can't look away. Her tiny hand—a hand I get such a thrill watching ball into a fist—looks right in mine. The softness of her skin is such a contrast to the hard persona she tries to affect. It's warm too.

"*Cal.*"

I snap my gaze up to hers and tug her forward. "We'll be fine. I'd never let anything happen to you."

She lets out a nervous laugh. "Sure you wouldn't. You've already forced me to move to Jersey and set me up in an office infested with maggots and ghosts and *Amy.*"

I shrug. "My father forced you into that. Not me."

She groans up at the sky. "Terry, do you see what you've left me with!"

A surprised laugh rushes out of me. It's the first time since my father's death that I've felt anything other than sorrow or frustration when I've thought about him. It feels good, honestly, to talk about him in an exasperated way because he sure as hell made a mess of our lives. Though secretly, I'm glad. So I glance up at the sky and holler "Thanks, Dad!" hoping she'll take it as sarcasm, even though the sentiment is an honest one.

Lola pulls her hand from mine and smacks me in the chest, but she's smiling.

I snatch her hand and guide her toward our ride again.

Three strides later, she pulls up short. "Seriously, Cal, I don't think I can get on there."

Turning away from the powerful blades, I stand between her and the whirlybird, blocking the gusts of wind pummeling us. "It'll be fun. An adventure."

Her jaw ticks.

"But if you really don't think you can do it, we can get back in the car and drive."

Lola groans. "It's like four hours on a good day. And it's never a good day to drive through Connecticut."

She's not wrong. The damn highways in that state could make even the most patient man lose his mind.

I shrug. "I'd never complain about having more time with you."

She rolls her eyes but her expression softens. Scrutinizing me like she's trying to figure me out, she takes out her phone. When she taps the screen and checks the time, she deflates. "We'll never make it."

I step in close and gently swipe at the wisps of hair the wind has caused to break free from her braid. For a moment, I keep my hand there, my fingers brushing the sensitive skin behind her ear, and get lost in the emerald eyes I swear will be my undoing. "I'll do whatever you want. I make an exceptional grand entrance."

She presses her lips together like she's trying to keep from feeling this pull that lives between us. But she can't deny this heat. It burns hotter every time I look at her. With every reluctant smile she offers. With every scolding. With every softening glance.

She has to feel this.

I can't *not* feel it.

"Promise it's safe?"

The way she's staring up at me, like she trusts me, sends a powerful thrill through me. "Promise."

Her lashes flutter shut and she sighs. "Fine."

Without giving her a second to change her mind, I haul her forward. As we approach the helicopter, I duck and put a hand on her back, signaling she should do the same. I help her up, then run back to thank our driver and make plans for him to pick us up tomorrow.

Once I've settled beside her, I turn to ensure she's buckled in.

"This isn't at all what I pictured," she admits, her hair adorably windblown.

Attention on her, I hum, "How so?"

She surveys the large compartment. "I always thought helicopters had like jumper seats and I figured we'd have to wear headphones."

I chuckle. "This is Beckett Langfield's. It's a bit fancier than that."

Her eyes widen. "God, you Murphys really do play with the big boys."

"If you say so." I dig my phone out of my pocket and check the security app. Murphy and T. J. still aren't home so all I see are the damn plants that are finally coming back to life.

My heart clenches.

Lola leans across the armrest between us and peers at my screen. "Plants look good."

I nod.

"Why are you staring at the plants, Cal?"

"Do you think it's wrong of me to leave Murphy?" That's the only part of this trip I've struggled with. I'm excited to spend time with Lola, but now I wish I'd brought Murphy too. This was a bad idea.

Maybe she answered. Maybe she didn't. I'm too keyed up and in my head to know.

"We should go back." I dart a look at the door a crew member has just closed, anxiety worming its way up my throat.

"*Cal.*" Lola squeezes my hand, her voice soft.

"I don't want to be another person who leaves him," I rush out. "He's had enough of that.

Understanding dawns on Lola's face. "It's good for him to spend the night with T. J. and Sully. They're his family too."

Like she's pressed on a valve, the anxiety seeps out of me.

This woman always knows just what to say. More importantly, she knows kids, and when it comes to Murphy, I have every confidence that she knows what's best.

"Also." Her tone is stern now, like she really wants me to pay attention to this part, "it's good for him to see you leave. This way he'll learn that when you do, you'll come back."

I sigh and relax a little in my seat. She's right. Because I'll always come back. Murphy is stuck with me for life, and I'll make sure he knows that.

"Tomorrow," she adds. "First thing in the morning."

I grin at her, feeling lighter. "Sometime tomorrow."

"First thing. You promised."

I shrug. "We could have breakfast first. Maybe go to the Revs game. Tomorrow's game is at home."

"*Cal.*" There's that growly little ball of energy again.

The helicopter lifts off then, and Lola hisses, then mutters a "shit," squeezing my hand so tight I think I might lose blood flow.

Chuckling, I pry myself free and grasp it with my other hand, then tug her close and slip my arm around her. The armrest between us makes it a little uncomfortable, but I allow the metal to dig into my hip so that I can hold her and press a kiss to her forehead. "I've got you. You'll be fine."

She doesn't pull back. In fact, I could almost swear she relaxes into my embrace. And I like that a bit too much.

Landing goes about as well as takeoff did. Eyes screwed shut and shaking like a feather, Lola allows me to lead her down the three steps off the helicopter.

Our driver awaits, and as he navigates through Boston, she checks emails and I confirm that Sloane hasn't forgotten to pick up Murphy. She assures me that she's got it all under control, reminding me that she's been raising T. J. all these years without incident. Somewhat mollified, I settle back in my seat and will my body to relax.

The hotel reminds me of Europe. Practically every surface is marble, and the ceilings are covered in incredible artwork. The chandeliers offer little light but plenty of charm.

At the front desk, an attendant greets us with a smile. "Good afternoon, Mr. and Mrs. Murphy, how was your travel here?" He holds out a tray, offering us glasses of champagne.

I take a sip of mine, strangely thrilled by the way he addressed us. *Mrs. Murphy.* I've never really considered having a Mrs. Murphy.

Never thought I'd meet a woman interesting enough to hold my attention for more than a few days.

But Lola? Though it may have only hit me recently, I can't deny she's had it for eight years. Since the day my father called me into his office and introduced me to his new paralegal.

I've always been interested. Now, though, it's become an infatuation. Maybe the Jersey air has done something to my head.

Slowly, I take another sip of my champagne, relishing the crisp flavor. I don't mind feeling this way at all. Maybe we'll just stay in Jersey.

Movement beside me catches my eye, and when I glance at Lola, I nearly choke on my drink.

She scowls at me, then at the man across the counter. "Not Mrs. Murphy. I'm Lola Caruso, Mr. Murphy's colleague."

The man blanches. "I'm so sorry."

"It's fine." I smirk. "I'll take being mistaken for Mr. Lola Caruso any day of the week."

Lola huffs out a breath, the sound sending a ridiculous thrill through me.

"Well, right, okay," the man says.

He's working through an issue. I can see it in the way his eyes keep darting to the package in his hand.

"If you're ready, I'll escort you to your room."

Lola stiffens beside me. "Rooms."

"Room," the man replies.

"*Rooms.*" Lola holds the last sound, *roomzzz.*

"*Room.*" The man holds up the room key. "There is only one."

"No." Lola shakes her head and looks at me, fire in her eyes. "No."

"Yes, unfortunately we're completely sold out."

"This is—"

Before Lola can rant at this poor guy who's just trying to do his job, I grab the key from him. "Perfect. I'll take it from here."

He rounds the desk, smoothing out his vest. "Please, let me show you to your room."

With a shake of my head, I slip him a hundred quid and step back. No need for him to experience the ball of fury she's morphed into. It'll be easier to calm her down without him present.

"Cal," she hisses as I start toward the lift.

I hold out a hand, waiting for her to follow. She doesn't give it to me but her feet clap angrily against the marble floor as she follows along.

"I'm sure there are two beds. It'll be fine," I assure her as I step up to the lift.

She lets out a scoff, arms crossed. "You think Sully requested two beds for his anniversary weekend?"

"Things aren't going well for them." I shrug. "They're going through something, remember?"

"Divorce." She huffs. "Not something. They're getting divorced."

When the stainless steel doors part, she stomps through them.

I follow, check the number on the card the man handed me, and press the button to send us to the fifth floor. "That's to be determined."

"Oh my God, you're just as delusional as he is."

I sigh. Fucking Sully. Things were going so well.

As soon as we step out into the hall, she snatches the key from my hand and storms away.

"Don't worry, I'll catch up," I call after her. She doesn't spare me a glance.

I find the door wide open, and inside, she's standing in the middle of the room, her eyes wide and her chest heaving.

Yup, Sully really went all out for his anniversary.

If looks could kill, I'd be laid out right here in the entry. Lola balls her fists and growls, "This is not going to work."

CHAPTER 19
Lola

"It's a heart." I jab a finger at the ridiculous bed. With a shake of my head, I squeeze my eyes shut. When I open them again, it's still there. I didn't imagine it.

Groaning, I whirl on my apparent roommate. He looks like he swallowed his tongue.

Never in a million years would I have expected this. Sully isn't the least bit romantic.

"There are rose petals and candles and champagne and chocolate strawberries and a bubble bath." I fling my hand at the bubbling jacuzzi tub.

Cal's head tilts. "It's amazing, really."

"This is not amazing." Anger causes my vision to go dark around the edges.

This is weird. Uncomfortable. *Not* amazing.

"Not the room. I'm referring to how high and screechy your tone can get. It takes talent."

A rumble works its way up my chest, as if it's a living, breathing entity.

"Wow, did you just growl?"

I might have. I could do a lot of things at the moment. Because I just walked into a romantic retreat with Callahan Murphy.

I'm freaking out a little, because as much as I don't want to like it, I kind of do.

My eye twitches, so I press two fingers just below my eyebrow to make it stop.

"Okay. It looks as though your head might explode, so I'll give you a minute." Cal steps back, holding both hands up like he's warding off a crazed animal. "Have a tubby wubby. Relax."

Dread washes over me. Yes, dread. Not excitement. Not at all. "Not with you."

"No, no." Shooting me an easy smile, he slips his hands into his pockets. "No tubby wubby for me. I'm going to find a pint and give you a few. A little time apart will be good for our blooming love."

My heart seizes. "Our what?" I shriek.

He lifts a finger to his lips. "Shhh, Lola, you'll ruin it." Without having to look behind him, he backs straight to the door and slips out easily, leaving me alone.

Still rooted to the spot, I scan the space. This time I'm sure I growl. How are Cal and I supposed to stay here?

With jerky movements, I pull my phone out and send a Face-Time request.

"This is your fault," I hiss the second my best friend's face appears on the screen.

"What?" Head tilted, Sloane leans closer to the screen. "Are those candles?"

"And roses. And chocolates and a fucking heart-shaped bed."

"Wow, Cal." She reels back, humor dancing in her eyes.

"No, *wow, Sully*. This is your fault." I stomp a foot. "Your husband did this."

"No way." She scoffs. "Sully doesn't do big gestures."

"Cal"—I hiss— "thought we'd have two beds, Sloane. He believed there would be two squares in this room, not one heart."

She cringes. "I don't know what to say."

I flop back onto the stupid white heart mattress, and like mist from a waterfall, soft, deep red petals float around me and dust my skin.

"It's your anniversary. Sully was trying. And you refused to spend it with him." I sigh. I've tried to stay out of their issues, but I'm irritated about being stuck in this room with Cal. Plus, I feel bad for Sully. He clearly worked hard to make this happen, only to be rejected.

"I'm having dinner with him." She worries her lip.

I jackknife to sitting.

She's willingly seeing him? Wow. Progress.

"Really?"

"Not like that," she says quickly, fidgeting with the ends of her hair. "Really, it's dinner with T. J and Murphy. I want to get T. J. settled and all that."

"Sure." I smirk, only now taking her in.

She curled her hair and put on makeup. There's no way that's for T. J. With any luck, Sully has plans. Not ones that leave me in heart-shaped beds but ones that make his wife smile. She needs it.

They need it.

"It's not—"

"Don't drink too much wine," I say, cutting her off. "You'll end up in bed with him. We both know how those Murphy men are."

Well, if those aren't some famous last words.

CHAPTER 20
Cal

I stayed out of the room as long as I could.

After leaving Lola, I rang my cousin Zara, but she was also getting ready for tonight's fundraiser. Fortunately, her husband Asher was available to join me at the pub. Just as we were finishing off our pints, Cortney Miller and Beckett Langfield appeared, so I stayed for another round. It was only polite seeing as how Beckett had arranged the heli for us.

My second round was nothing more than soda water. The last thing I want is for Lola to accuse me of being drunk.

I snuck in two calls to Murphy. The first to see how school was and the second to tell him where I hid the Ping-Pong balls and to suggest he lob them at Sully's head randomly throughout the night. Don't want my brother to get too comfortable with me gone.

Now it's time to face the music. On the ride up, I dig deep, summoning the courage to face Angry Lola.

With any luck, she'll have had a change of heart. The bed was pretty and the Jacuzzi looked relaxing.

Or maybe that's just wishful thinking. There's a good chance she's been stewing since I left her here, and the moment I step into the room, she'll go off like Mount Etna.

If that's the case, I suppose I'll be sleeping on the floor with one eye open, hoping she doesn't stab me with her Jimmy Choos.

I knock rather than walk in. No use riling the beast unnecessarily.

"Is that you, Callie?"

Callie? Who the fuck is Callie?

"No. It's me, *Cal.* Can I come in?"

"Yup!"

That single syllable is nothing more than a chirp. It's chipper. Filled with happiness. Why does she sound happy? Is it because she's spent the last hour and change plotting my death? That must be it. She's probably going to kill me.

Like an idiot, I open the door anyway. I'm drawn to her. Pulled into her orbit.

Inside the room, I'm hit with her cinnamon vanilla scent. Fuck. She always smells like a damn dessert. A moan escapes me before I can stop it.

The room is a mess, rose petals strewn all over the floor. The bedding is wrinkled, the hot tub is empty, and the bottle of champagne is upside down in the metal ice bucket.

In other words, it's likely my little fireball is drunk.

This should be interesting.

"Callie! Is that you?"

The lightness in her voice as she calls my name—even if it's *not* my name—brings a smile to my lips as I stride to the center of the space.

Lola appears in the doorway of the bathroom, and I'm struck completely stupid.

Lola fucking Caruso. Holy hell. My heart sputters to a stop, and the entire English language vanishes from my vocabulary.

She's beautiful.

Drop dead fucking gorgeous.

That auburn hair of hers flows past her shoulders in loose waves. Though her face is done up, there's still a light smattering of freckles across the bridge of her nose. Like she applied a lighter layer of foundation.

Maybe on purpose?

Could it be because I told her I like them?

My gut twists itself into a knot.

No. It's highly unlikely that she thought about me at all while she got ready.

Regardless, the look she's gone with tonight brings with it a tease of innocence that has my heart thundering in my chest.

And the dress? Don't even get me started on the damn dress. The deep green against her alabaster skin is nothing short of magnificent.

"Why are you staring at me like that?" Her voice is quiet, her head tilted. An empty champagne glass dangles from the fingertips of one hand, her shoes from the other.

Straightening, I will myself to be even half the man she deserves. I won't fuck this up. I won't let my mind short-circuit, and I won't say something stupid, like I do every time I'm in the same room as her. No walkie-talkie jokes from this guy tonight.

"Devastating." The word is gritty, my throat dry.

Her brows lower, confusion swimming in those green irises. "What?"

"You in that dress. You're simply devastating. Every woman we cross tonight will be devastated because she isn't you, and every man will wish he had you on his arm. But me?" I scrub at my face, wishing I could erase every moment of my life before this so she'd be the first thing I ever see. "I'll never recover."

Lola's cherry lips curve into a glorious smile. "Callahan Murphy, are you a secret romantic?"

With two steps toward her, I pluck the Jimmy Choos from her fingers. Then I guide her to the bed and urge her to sit on the edge.

"Not a day in my life, Lola," I say. It's the god's honest truth. "Not a day in my goddamn life. But you, you make me want to be Shakespeare."

I drop to my knees in front of her, lifting her foot, and slide one shoe into place before I secure the crystal strap around her thin ankle.

She shakes her head, her expression still bright. "Smooth, you Murphy men." She bops my nose. "You're dangerous with wine."

With a chuckle, I hold her ankle for another second, pushing my luck and relishing the smoothness of her skin. "Let's maybe have some water, then we can try the wine." I ease her foot to the floor and lift the other.

Lola shakes her head, the movement sending her scent wafting around me.

It takes strength to stay where I am on the floor. I want to settle beside her on the bed and inhale her all night. I dream of wrapping her in my arms and holding her close. Of waking in the morning covered in the smell of her and going to bed to do it all again.

I'm fucking gone. And that's a bloody problem, because tomorrow the spell will be broken. Lola will morph back into a ball of fire, while I'll still be this damn puppy following her around, willing to risk the burn for a chance to touch her.

"Why are you staring at me like that?" she asks.

Her words startle me back to the moment. I'm still holding her ankle, knees on the ground, completely enraptured by her.

"Shh," I murmur as I stand and hold out a hand. "You'll ruin it."

With her hand in mine, she shakes her head. But she's smiling.

CHAPTER 21

Lola

"What?" I don't have to turn in the elevator to know Cal is watching me. I can feel his attention. It's like being wrapped in a warm, soft blanket. It makes my skin buzz with an electric energy. Or maybe that's the alcohol. It's safer to blame it on the champagne, but liquor has never made me feel the way that Cal does.

"I like the freckles." The low timbre of his voice has heat pooling in my belly. "Most of the time I can't see them. But damn are they beautiful. *You're* beautiful."

I would never admit it aloud, but his comment about my freckles the other night floated through my mind as I applied my makeup. Normally, they make me self-conscious, but his reaction emboldened me. That and a bottle of champagne.

"It must be the light."

"No, it's not." He shifts closer, his hand brushing along my cheek.

My breath catches, my heart stuttering as he continues the barely there caress, drifting across my jaw and down my neck.

The stuttering of my heart turns into a pounding beat, the desire I've been fighting, the one that holds me captive more and more with each interaction, washing over me.

"Lola."

My name on his lips sends a shiver racing down my spine.

Slowly, gently, he cups my cheek and leans in.

My heart skips a beat. Is he going to kiss me?

My eyes fall closed, waiting for the moment our lips touch.

When he presses a gentle kiss to my forehead, they fly open again.

"You're beautiful in every light."

The elevator dings, and he steps back. It's ridiculous, the way disappointment seeps through me.

With each sip of champagne, I told myself that no matter how romantic the setup was, no matter how charming Cal was tonight, I'd be immune. But with words like *devastating* and *beautiful* falling from his lips, I'm sinking in his quicksand.

"Come on." He holds his hand out to me and for one second I almost take it. Blessedly, good sense barrels into me before I can. So instead, I steel my spine and strut past the charming man that I refuse to let get under my skin.

To my shock, the man lets out a hearty chuckle. As if my annoyance is his game.

Or, a voice in my head whispers, *he just likes all of your moods.*

I shake that idea off as I approach the doors to the ballroom.

Before I can step inside, he's next to me again, cool and confident and full of light, as always. The ballroom screams Elizabeth Sweet. Clearly, the Hollywood star played a role in the décor. The floral arrangements are enormous, the crystal center pieces elaborate and classy, the place settings so extensive, each is equipped with enough forks for six people.

"Libby went all out," Cal mumbles.

Although I've met Fisher a few times over the years since he's our firm's IT support, I've yet to meet his girlfriend. I'd have to live under a rock to not know who she was though. A child star who became America's Sweetheart for a time. Though recently, she removed the rose-colored glasses her fans have become so accustomed to wearing as she shared about her experience with the dark side of the industry.

"We're not sitting with them, right?" I scan the room, shocked at the number of people here. I've never really attended events like this for the firm. For years, I've been a representative for Brian or Terry in the office and on the phone, but my days have always ended the moment I step out of the office. So, this was new territory for me.

Cal shakes his head. "No. We're seated with the Berkshires, the Langfields, and the Millers."

Brian handles the estates of all three disgustingly wealthy families, so that makes sense. Though most would be intimidated by the thought of spending the evening in their presence, Brian's sister, Dylan, is a Miller these days, and she's one of my favorite people.

Cal rests a hand on my lower back as we move through the room and leans down so I can hear him over the instrumental music floating through the large space. "Don't be nervous, you might not realize this, but I attend these all the time. This will be easy."

His tone is dripping with an unusual confidence, a seriousness I've never heard before. He nods to several people as they pass by, his normal charming grin in place. But his eyes are sharp, focused in a way I've never seen.

Maybe because I've never seen Cal in the courtroom, or the boardroom. I only know the Cal who comes into my office to irritate me. This is the Cal I've heard about but never truly believed existed. This is the magic he possesses. The reason he settles cases so smoothly and brings judges to his side of the fence. One more of the many sides of Callahan Murphy.

With a slight pressure on my lower back, he guides me to the table. Eight people sit at the ten top, leaving our two seats as the only vacant ones. Mr. and Mrs. Berkshire sit on the other side of the centerpiece. Mr. and Mrs. Miller are seated near their son, Cortney, and his wife, Dylan. Liv and Beckett Langfield are here too. This will be a fun group.

"Good Evening," Cal says, his British accent a bit more crisp, just like his movements. "Have you all met my Lola?"

My heart trips over itself at the *my* in that sentence.

Cal, as at ease as can be, shakes hands and kisses cheeks before pulling out the chair beside Dylan and gesturing for me to sit.

"*My*, huh? That's new," Dylan whispers, wiggling in her seat. "I love an office romance. It's my favorite trope. Although I don't know that any fictional story could top Liv and Becks's real-life experience."

Liv is now the head of the Boston Revs baseball team, but she used to run PR for Beckett's company, Langfield Corp. A couple of years ago, they shocked the world and got married in Vegas.

"He didn't mean *my* that way." I tighten my core muscles to keep the butterflies at bay.

"Liv thought that, too." She giggles, gold eyes dancing. "And I can assure you the way Cal is watching you is very, very reminiscent of how Becks spent years watching Liv."

As I shake my head in denial, Cal puts a hand on my thigh and gives it a small squeeze, then he shoots me a wink.

It's ridiculous, really, the way a single wink causes me to melt into a damn puddle.

All night, the pesky feeling lingers. As he orders a club soda for me. When he smiles at me. Throughout dinner, as we engage in lively conversation with the people at our table. In fact, as the night progresses, I become more impressed with him and his ease in this group. So much so that I can't deny that he didn't need my assistance tonight. He could have come with anyone and made the firm look good. He's good at this.

"Cortney." Mr. Miller calls from the other side of his wife. "Did you hear that old man Philips's cancer is back?"

Lips pressed together, Courtney nods. "Taylor told me."

"She's worried about Landon," Mrs. Miller agrees.

Dylan, bless her, leans over, as if she can sense that I'm lost in this conversation, and says, "Taylor is Cortney's sister and she's best friends with Landon Philips, old man Philip's grandson, who also happens to own the New York Metros."

"Terrible situation," Mr. Miller says, though there's a gleam in his eye, "But I can't help wondering if the team will be looking for a buyer soon. I was thinking—"

"Oh no," Beckett jumps in.

With a sigh, Cortney slumps in his seat. He's a giant, so he's still a head taller than anyone sitting around him. "Dad, we've talked about this."

"Absolutely not," Beckett grits out, his green eyes hardening like cut gems. "You are not buying my GM a team of his own."

Beckett owns the Boston Revs, and for the last few years Cortney has worked for him. A situation that, according to Dylan, Beckett orchestrated very specifically. The two have a very weird bromance.

"I just thought that maybe you would like your own team."

Beckett glares at Mr. Miller. "I'll buy the damn team before I let you."

"Don't buy another team." Courtney shakes his head.

Between us, Dylan giggles, her red curls bouncing.

"Easy, boys." Cal runs a hand through his perfectly disheveled hair. "There are plenty of baseball teams for everyone. And no one wants the Metros after this last season."

"Landon Philips does." Cortney chuckles. "And Dad, you and I both know we'll never hear the end of it if you take the team away from her best friend."

Mr. Miller picks up his lowball glass and grumbles, "If only I didn't love the son of a bitch."

"You love him because he's never dated your daughter," Cortney teases.

"Wait..." Beckett jumps in. "Best friends who never dated?"

Cortney bolts forward and narrows his eyes at his best friend. "Don't even."

"I write a great prenup," Cal offers.

Henry Berkshire barks out a laugh. "Always the attorney."

Blue eyes alight, Cal leans forward. "That's why you pay me the big bucks, Berkshire."

"Indeed." Mr. Berkshire holds up his glass in a mock toast.

"How is everyone doing?" Fisher appears behind me, resting a hand on the back of my chair. "Enjoying yourselves?"

Frowning, Cal scans the area around us, then peers up at his friend. "Where's Libby?"

"She's around." Fisher smirks.

It's weird, that expression. I've met him a handful of times, and he's never been anything but serious. Focused. I'd even say he's a grump. He doesn't laugh.

Yet here he is, that mischievous smirk playing on his lips seems to come to him so easily.

With a grunt, Cal eyes the hand Fisher still has on the back of my chair.

"Anyway," Fisher says. He finally moves that hand, but only to hold it out to me. "I thought I'd ask the lovely Lola for a spin around the dance floor."

Every eye lands on me, and suddenly, my cheeks get warm. I shift in my chair, reminding myself that the whole point of being here is to schmooze. I should be as charming as Cal has been. Otherwise, there was no point to him bringing me along.

"I'd love to." I take Fisher's offered hand and allow him to lead me toward the dance floor.

My skin tingles under Cal's gaze as I walk away. At the edge of the dance floor, I finally glance back.

He's... *Is he glaring?* I've never seen such an unhappy expression on the man's face, yet his eyes are narrowed and his jaw is rigid. He stands and takes a step in our direction. For a heartbeat, I think he's coming after me and I don't hate that idea.

But after another step, he turns his back to us and heads toward the bar.

I swallow the disappointment. It's silly really, to be hurt that he isn't chasing me down to claim me, to stop me from dancing with another man. That kind of gesture only happens in fairy tales and romance books. Not real life. Plus, Cal doesn't chase women. They come for him. And I am *not* coming for Cal.

Also, we're mingling. That's why we're here. This isn't some silly fantasy date. It's ridiculous to think that any man would buy the most gorgeous dress for me, then fly me to Boston for a romantic weekend.

"So you and Cal, huh?" Fisher spins and gently rests a hand on my waist.

With a shake of my head, I fall into the standard slow-dance-with-an-acquaintance pose, one hand on his shoulder, the other clutched in his. "He just needed someone to come with him this weekend."

"Hmm." He shakes his head, lips pursed. "I'm not sure his perspective matches yours." He tips his chin, then does a quarter-turn.

Sure enough, Cal, eyes blazing, is heading our way towing Libby by the arm.

His footsteps on the dance floor are loud enough to be heard over the music as he shoves the starlet Fisher's way.

"Yours." Tone sharp, he releases her. Then he clutches my hand and yanks me into his chest. "*Mine.*"

Stunned, I gape up at him. Did he just—did that just—wait, did Callahan Murphy just claim me?

"*Mine?*" I whisper-hiss.

The hard expression from a moment ago evaporates completely, his eyes soft as he brushes his thumb over my lips, once, twice. "Shhh, Lola, you'll ruin it." With a slow smile, he guides my head to his chest and presses a chaste kiss to my crown. It's so quick it feels like butter-flies just danced across my skin.

Normally, those words would rankle me, but absurdly, I don't want to ruin the moment. This man really did come after me. He did want to claim me. And Callahan Murphy chases no one.

Pulling back a fraction, I study his face.

He watches me, his expression open. Like he really sees me. And more than that, he likes what he sees. Like he wants me. Desperately.

I should stay away, but all of a sudden, I can't remember why. Would it really be such a bad thing to have this one night? Maybe we both need it. And I sure as hell want it.

"I'm not ruining anything," I promise. Popping up on the toes of my Jimmy Choos, I press my lips to his.

For one perfect moment, he kisses me back, but a fraction of a second later he pulls away.

My stomach bottoms out as he releases his hold on me. Have I read the entire night wrong? Was I way off base when I noted the desire in his expression?

Before my mind spirals out, he grasps my wrist and drags me off the dance floor.

"Cal, I'm sorry," I stutter, wobbling on my heels. "I just thought—"

"Shhh, you'll ruin it." The words rumble from deep in his chest, far more seriously than the last time he spoke them, as he guides me through the door and into the empty hallway.

Spinning, he presses me against the wall and cages me in with his entire body. When he tucks a curl away from my face and cups my cheek, my breath catches. And when he drops his head, closing the space between us, my knees go weak.

"That kiss didn't count," he whispers, his lips brushing against mine. "This is our first kiss."

Warm and firm he presses his mouth to mine. He doesn't rush. Each move is slow, deliberate. He explores, teasing, tempting me with the suggestion of more. One hand still cupping my jaw, he skates his thumb over my cheek. His other slips behind me, keeping me close.

I arch into him, reveling in the warmth and strength of his body. Begging for more.

After what feels like an eternity, he runs his tongue along the seam of my lips, begging for me to open.

I do just that, letting our tongues mingle and play, until once again he pulls back.

The urge to stomp my foot is strong. I'm ready to give in to it, to whine about the loss of him, when the inferno of desire in his eyes registers.

He isn't letting me go.

Instead, he says, "Let's get out of here."

CHAPTER 22
Cal

The instant the door whooshes shut, Lola pushes me against the metal wall and then her mouth is on me again.

The perfect mouth that's only ever punished me, taunted me, knocked me on my arse time and again, is suddenly breathing life into me. She tastes like champagne and sweet dessert. Each little whimper that escapes her is like a current of electricity coursing through me. It takes everything in me not to grind my erection against her to show her how fucking hard those sounds alone make me.

I'm terrified if I do that, I'll break the spell that's been set.

Thank fuck she drank nothing but soda water through dinner and ate most of her meal. If she hadn't, I'd be worried she was too drunk to consent. I don't want her to regret this. I don't want this kiss to ever end.

When the door to the lift opens, I pull back so I can guide her to our room.

The moment I break the kiss, she grips my shirt and lets out an annoyed little growl. "No."

"No?" I can't help but grin down at her as she holds me close.

She huffs out a breath, her emerald eyes bright beneath the harsh lighting. "I hate how good you feel. Hate how soft your lips are. Hate that I need to know what you can do with them."

Her words cause my cock to harden painfully in my trousers. Licking my lips, I taunt her. "I can do many things."

She pouts. The woman pushes her bottom lip out and bloody pouts. "*Show me.*"

All sense gone, I grasp her by her arse and lift her off her feet. Thank fuck I chose a gown that gives her room to wrap her legs around my hips.

She climbs me as I stride down the hallway to our hotel room, to that heart-shaped bed, and peppers kisses on my neck while I attempt to open the damn door. After three or four tries, the green light finally illuminates, and I throw it open. I charge inside, only pausing to kick the door shut, and head straight for the plush bed.

There will be zero interruptions. Not a thing will stop me from showing this woman what my tongue can do. And my fingers. And my cock.

Head buried in my neck, Lola giggles. "I can't believe Sully got a heart-shaped bed. How are we even going to fit on this?"

With her still in my arms, arse held tight, I spin and fall back, stretching out with her on top of me.

Straddling my hips, she gasps, her eyes going wide. There's no way she can't feel the press of my cock between her hot thighs.

"This seems to work, no?"

She gives me a wicked grin. "So you're saying I'll have to stay on top of you all night?"

"I'm game if you are." I run my hands up and down her back, then trail over the silk of her dress to her thighs.

"I can't believe we're doing this," she muses. "Sloane warned me, you know? I told her it would never happen."

I arch a brow. As much as I want this, I didn't expect to end up here. I just wanted to spend more time with her. Give her a chance to see the real me. Hope that she'd like what she found.

But being allowed to touch her like this? It's more than I could have asked for.

"We don't have to do anything," I promise, squeezing her thighs gently. "We can just snuggle. I'm an excellent snuggler."

She doesn't even acknowledge the offer, she just rolls her hips over my aching cock. With each move, electricity shoots up my spine. Her lashes flutter shut and she lets out a breathy sigh.

Fuck. The sight of her stealing her pleasure unravels me.

"But what if—" She lets out another breathy whimper, this one followed by a moan. With her hands on my abdominals, she slows her pace, as if she's dragging out every little drop of her ecstasy.

I tighten my hold on her hips, eager for her to finish that sentence. Desperate for her to tell me she wants this. To use her words. "What if what?"

Eyes fluttering open, she gives me the laziest of smiles. "What if I want to do more than snuggle? What if I want to forget for a few hours? To just—" She wiggles on top of me.

A telltale tingle starts at the base of my spine. Bloody fucking hell.

Jaw locked, I stare up at the ceiling. Can I do this? Can I allow her to use me tonight? I've certainly used and been used before. I'm just not sure I can separate my emotions so easily where Lola's involved.

"*Cal.*"

The need dripping in her tone is enough to cut through any scrap of patience I've been clinging to. Cuffing her neck, I pull her face to mine. She lets out a surprised squeal, but she doesn't fight me. And when our lips lock, she sinks into the connection.

I nip at her bottom lip, holding her in place with my hand wrapped around her neck. "I don't want to make you forget, Lola. I want you to remember every millisecond that we spend together. I want you to relive it over and over again. I want to completely ruin you."

"So many words, Callahan Murphy." She smiles against my mouth. "You always have so many words."

Easing her back a little, I search for any sign that she isn't on the same page. The smile on her face, the haze of pleasure in her eyes, tells me she's right here with me. "Is that a yes?"

"Devastate me," she murmurs. "Ruin me. Do whatever the hell you want to me. Just make me come."

This time my hips are the ones that undulate beneath hers as I give her exactly what she's asking for. My hands roam over her bare shoulders as she reaches for her zipper, and at the slow sound of it parting, all my blood flow surges between my thighs.

Green silk falls to her hips exposing the most perfect tits.

Greedy, I straighten, sucking one pink nipple into my mouth while I roll the other between my fingers.

"Yes, Cal." The tendons in her neck strain as she writhes above me. "Fuck my panties are soaked. I'm going to ruin your tux."

"Make a mess, Lola," I urge, too blissed out to care about anything but her. "Promise I'll clean your first orgasm from your body with my tongue."

"Shit," she pants as she quickens her pace.

I should close my eyes and think of anything but about how gorgeous she looks, face flushed, teeth sunk into her bottom lip as she thrashes above me, but I couldn't look away if I tried.

And there's no way in hell I'll try. I may be daft when it comes to many things, but I know better than to miss this. I want to memorize every detail of the moment Lola first comes for me. Even if that means I'm close to coming in my knickers.

To help her along, I pinch her nipples and give them a little tug.

"Cal," she hisses, throwing her head back.

The moment she shatters above me, my entire world turns upside down. From this moment on, my one goal in life will be to make her do that again. And again. And again.

I used to live to taunt her. To earn the tiniest bit of her attention by driving her batty. Now I'll live for this.

"Good girl," I murmur.

Without a second's hesitation, I flip her onto her back and push up her dress. I made a promise, and I intend to keep it. Fuck. I need to taste her. Need to clean her up so I can make a mess of her again.

As I ruck the material of her dress up over her hips and the scrap of green lace comes into view, my vision blurs. "Lola Caruso." I paste on the smirk that riles her up so much.

"Yes?" Her tone is nowhere near annoyed for once. No, it's sated, a smile tugging at her lips.

"Did you plan this?" Kneeling between her thighs, I shuck my jacket. The tie is next, followed by the top two buttons of my shirt.

She frowns, though the reaction is delayed, her muscles still languid. "Plan what?"

I trace the wet lace between her thighs with the back of my finger.

Her body shudders, goose bumps scattering over her smooth skin.

"These panties, Lola," I purr. "They're soaked and they match your dress perfectly."

Chin lifted, she gives me a defiant look. "I like to match."

There's my Lola, my feisty, angry little thing. I think I'd die right here if she admitted she thought of me when she dressed this evening. But nothing with Lola has ever been easy. I'd expect nothing less than this sass.

And why would she have done it for me? The woman didn't even want to spend the weekend with me. I'm the one who orchestrated it all. I'm the one who slowly fell for this woman, a little more intrigued with each year that passed, only to find myself hurtling into all-out obsession the moment she interacted so perfectly with my son. Burying myself a little deeper in feelings for her every time she gives me a glimpse of the real woman wearing that tight braid.

"Well, I love them. I need to see them all by themselves though."

I tug her dress over her head and toss it to the floor.

"Cal!" she yelps. "That dress is worth thousands."

I lift a shoulder. "I'll buy you another one."

Her eyes go wide. *"You bought me that one."*

I smirk. "I'd buy a new one every day if it meant I could end the night ripping it off you. Now lie back, I need to see all of you."

She coughs out a surprised laugh. "You really are a charmer." Obediently—a total shocker—she settles back, and when her auburn hair spreads out against the pillow, I can't come up with a damn retort.

"You're exquisite." It's the only thought in my head. I'm too lost in her, too busy greedily memorizing every detail. A dusting of freckles cover her stomach and her hips, like the softest of kisses. I want to roll my tongue over every one.

"I bet you are too. Though I wouldn't know, since you're still fully clothed."

Quickly, I doff my shirt and toss it into a heap with her dress.

But as I reach for my belt, she sits up and grasps my wrists. "Let me."

With her teeth pressed to that plump bottom lip and her warm breath fanning across my stomach, she works my belt off. Rather than going for the button of my trousers next, she presses the most unsuspecting kiss to my abdominals, right beside my belly button.

The sensation is soft and surprising, pulling a laugh from deep within me.

It's sweet. Innocent really. Emerald eyes dancing, she peers up at me. Then she presses one to the other side. "I thought of you when I picked the panties," she admits, voice soft.

Gratification and lust battle for superiority, burning hot, rushing through my blood, erasing every insecurity that's plagued me tonight.

She wanted this. She *wants* this.

"Lie back, gorgeous." I slide my trousers off, though I leave my boxers on. Then I get comfortable between her thighs.

She slips her thumbs beneath the thin straps at her hips. "Aren't you going to take my panties off?"

Clutching her wrists, I guide them away. When her hands are splayed on the mattress on either side of her, I nuzzle between her thighs, inhaling her pleasure, reveling in the knowledge that it's there just for me. "Not yet. I'm going to enjoy you like this."

"But—" She bucks her hips up.

I nip at her soaked panties and hold her in place. "Woman, just let me enjoy you. I've waited years to taste all that sass."

Lola's annoyed whines leave me chuckling, but her scent has me just as desperate for a taste. I pluck the edge of the lace, pulling it away from her body. At the sight of her glistening pink pussy, all my teasing dies.

Bloody fucking hell. The woman is too damn perfect.

My mouth waters and I don't hesitate to press open-mouthed kisses to her sensitives flesh.

Lola takes a fistful of my hair, and gives it a tug. "And all this time I've been trying to figure out how to shut you up." She holds me in place, her tone wicked as she writhes against my tongue. "I just needed to give you something better to do with that mouth of yours."

With a finger hooked around the edge of her panties, I expose her further and lick up the mess she made while she ground against me. Her flavor bursts on my tongue, goddamn exquisite, pulling a low, guttural moan from me. She's a delicacy.

Then I press her thighs down and feast. I lick and suck and tease her until she's thrashing against my mouth and yanking on my hair, showing her no mercy, keeping her right where I want her until she comes on my tongue.

When her breathing stutters and her movements grow jerky, I slide a finger inside her tight cunt. When I curl my finger, she bows off the bed and rides the wave of pleasure. Desperate to experience her orgasm to its fullest, I slip my free hand underneath her and ease her down, pressing kisses to her clit, her thighs, up her belly, between her breasts. Then I capture her lips, licking into her mouth, sucking on her tongue.

"Holy shit," she mutters as her inner walls finally stop pulsing around my finger.

I ease out of her and cradle her body to mine. As our hearts beat rapidly against one another, I tug her onto my chest, holding her there, awash in a peace I've never endured after my own release. Although I'm hard as stone, I'm content. I could lie here with her and that would be enough.

Chin on my chest, Lola looks up at me. "Are you falling asleep?"

I chuckle and hold her a little tighter. "No, darling, but we don't have to do anything else. I told you, cuddling is sufficient."

She runs her nails down my stomach gently, and when she meets the resistance of my boxers, she squeezes my covered cock. "Is this the type of cuddling you mean?"

Teeth clenched, I exhale loudly through my nose. "Only if you want me to come."

She props herself up on one elbow, licking her lips. "I really, really"—she slides those nails down my cock and tugs my balls—"want you to come."

"*Fuck.*"

"Yes, Callahan." She works me through my boxers. "I'd like you to fuck me."

"Condom," I breathe out, throwing an arm over my eyes.

"Where?"

I focus on breathing steadily as I rack my brain. Where the fuck are my trousers? I can't think properly with the way she tugs on my cock. "Floor, wallet, trousers."

With a chuckle, she releases me. Then she's scooting off the bed and sashaying her way to the pile of clothes on the floor.

When she returns with the condom, she tosses it onto my chest and shimmies out of her underwear.

I give myself a few seconds to enjoy the sight of her completely naked. She's exquisite.

And impatient.

Hands on her hips, she stares me down, giving me the annoyed look I so love to elicit from her. "You going to put that on and show me what the big fuss is about, or should I get dressed?"

A thrill zips through me. I shouldn't love being bullied like this, but it's addicting. Without hesitation, I shuck my boxers and toss them across the room.

Her eyes go wide and a hiss escapes from between her teeth. "What?"

"Shit," she breathes, "every part of you is huge."

I give myself a lazy tug, then roll the condom down my length. "We'll go slow." I hold out a hand, beckoning her to me.

With a fortifying breath, she straddles me. "This changes nothing," she warns as she lines herself up.

When she slides down that first inch, I grip her hips, pressing my fingers into her soft flesh. "This changes *everything*."

Fire ignites in those eyes, lust mixed with the fight she wants to have. Before she can start it, I cuff her neck and pull her down against my chest, kissing her quiet. I dip my tongue into her mouth and roll my hips, stretching her a little further, relishing every little moan and whimper as she tightens around me.

Never in my life has sex felt like this. We go slow, our hips tentative, our movements gentle. Our lips never part. Our kisses only grow needier. Messier.

Hands roaming every inch of her, I revel in the feel of her above me, around me, on top of me.

I never want the moment to end. I grit my teeth and clench my abdominals and glutes to stave off my orgasm. But when she pulses around me, her body beckoning mine to follow her into oblivion, my balls tighten, and I come with her.

All the while, I hold her to me, keeping her right where I need her. Right where I want her. From here on out.

CHAPTER 23

Lola

I wake to incessant buzzing.

Two quick vibrations, then two more. With a groan, I lift my head and glare at the phone lighting up on the nightstand.

"No running from me, Lola." Cal tightens his hold around my waist.

Those are the exact words he said as we drifted off last night. He was adamant that I wasn't allowed to disappear on him while he slept.

It hit me as strange then, just like it does now. Sneaking out in the middle of the night seems much more his MO than mine.

When the phone buzzes again, I slip my arm out from under Cal's and snatch it up. As I squint at the too-bright screen, I'm confused. It's not a text notification or a phone call. It takes a good ten seconds to ascertain that it's his Ring app, alerting us to movement in his apartment.

I wince. Shit. If Murphy is up and in need of something and he's not there for him, Cal will freak out. I click the notification and turn the screen his way to unlock the phone with Face ID.

"What are you doing?" he mumbles, his eye cracked against the brightness.

Though I was far from drunk when we went to sleep last night, my head still throbs as I squint at the image on the screen. When I discover the person moving through the apartment isn't Murphy, though, my eyes fly open wide and I gasp.

There, tiptoeing toward the door, is Sloane. Her hair is a mess, and she's wearing the dress she had on when we FaceTimed before her dinner with Sully.

Speaking of Sully, she absolutely just slipped out of his room...

And this is a live video. That means she spent half the night in her soon-to-be ex-husband's bed.

Whoa.

"Lola?" Cal asks, lifting his head.

Breath held, I delete the video and set the phone on the nightstand again.

"I was worried it was Murphy," I rush out. "But it wasn't." I turn toward him and rest my head on my pillow so our faces are only inches apart.

He lets out a soft sigh, his lips ticking up adorably.

I understand now why this heart bed works for special occasions because Jesus we have to be damn near on top of each other to both fit.

"Who was it?"

There's no way I'm telling him that my best friend just slipped out of his brother's room. If I did, he'd only gloat about how right he was when he said the divorce isn't a sure thing.

"Must have been the ghost."

Eyes widening, he reaches past me for the phone.

Unaware if Sloane has escaped, I do the only thing I can think of to stop Cal from seeing the screen: I grab his face and pull his lips to mine.

With a moan, he rolls over me, caging me in with his forearms pressed to the mattress on either side of my head.

As his tongue tangles with mine, I forget about Sloane and Sully and all the issues we left behind in Jersey.

I should stop him. I should tell him we can't keep doing this, but if we only have this one night, I might as well enjoy it. Besides, there's something I never got to do earlier and as nervous as I am, because the man is huge, I am also determined to experience all the sides of Callahan Murphy while I have him. I pull back just slightly and even with just the low din of light spilling in from between the curtains, I can't help but note how he's got this warmth in his eyes as he studies me. "You're so goddamn beautiful," he rasps, his fingers trailing through my hair.

A flush works its way up my chest and to my cheeks. I'm glad he can't see the way he affects me. That I can keep just that little bit a secret from him. Everything Cal has done in the last twelve hours has affected me though.

"What are you thinking?" He tilts his head like he's trying to uncover what I could be working out in my brain.

I'm sure he'll never come up with my real thoughts though. I'm wondering how I'll fit his entire cock in my mouth. And trying to picture what it will feel like. I've never actually done it and I'm slightly nervous to admit that. Will I fight it? I'm not good at submitting but God do I want to submit to Cal for just a few more hours. I want to make him feel as good as he made me feel.

I lick my lips, deciding to just go for what I want. "I'm thinking that I'd like to taste you."

Cal hisses out a "bloody hell, woman," and I smile.

Encouraged by his words, I slide down his body. We're both still naked and as I glide my already damp core against Cal's thick cock, I pause for a moment and enjoy the feel of him as I grind my body against his. "Shit, why does that feel so good," I mutter more to myself.

Cal watches me in this knowing way. A little too cocky for my liking. "If you say because it's you, I'm walking out the door," I warn him.

Cal chuckles and he strokes my cheek again. "No darling, it's because it's us. We've been dancing around this thing for a long fucking time. Don't think so hard, take your pleasure, I love watching you work."

I snort. "Accurate."

He grins, but it's that soft, lazy one that makes me melt. Not a smirk. Not cocky. Just happy, and hell do I like making Cal happy.

I bite on my lip and then continue my descent. Settling between his thighs, I take a deep breath before wrapping my hand around him and stroking up his entire length. He's warm and smooth beneath my fingers and already I feel a tingling between my legs. I miss the pressure of him between my thighs but can't exactly address that yet.

"You needy, darling?"

Of course he didn't miss that. It seems Cal never misses anything when it comes to me. I shake my head and focus on him. "I'm just—" I hesitate to admit the truth and then realize he'll likely notice quickly since, unlike me, Cal isn't inexperienced.

Cal pushes up slightly on his elbows and then with a single finger he lifts my chin so I'm unable to avoid his stare. "You're just what?"

"I've never done this before. Could you maybe talk me through it?"

I expect Cal to beam. To gloat how he's the first. But like everything else about tonight, he does the unexpected. His thumb slides across my chin and then with it he tugs open my lips. "Stick out your tongue."

Forget butterflies or tingles, a fire works its way through my body and I gush between my thighs. Such simple direct words in that damn accent of his combined with the slight shake of his thumb against my bottom lip, and the way his blue eyes dilate. All of it. Every single act has me squirming.

I open my mouth and present him my tongue. Cal sucks in a breath. "You, Lola Caruso, are a gift." With one hand he continues to hold my face, and with the other he reaches for my hand, slides his fingers between mine, and then guides himself into my mouth. "Now suck," he says as his cock settles against my tongue. I suction my lips around him, hollowing out my cheeks, and do exactly as he says.

"Fuck, *again*," he rasps.

It only takes a few seconds for me to adjust to the way I need to breathe through my nose and then he guides our hands up and down the base of his cock in rhythm with my mouth. Oh God, why is it so hot how he's controlling us? How I can barely move without his direction. He bucks up and I gag when his crown hits the back of my throat and a feral growl leaves Cal's mouth. "You're so fucking sexy. Straddle that pussy over my thigh. I want to feel how wet you are right now."

I should be embarrassed. I should stop this insanity. But I don't. Like the wanton thing I've become when I'm with Callahan Murphy, I do as he says, straddling his thick thigh. He lifts up just a bit and the slight pressure does exactly as intended, rubbing right against my clit. I pant around his cock and like a complete hussy, ride his thigh while I suck him off.

"Yes, Lola, just like that baby, you're so fucking wet."

I am. I'm slipping and sliding against him and continuing to work his cock with both my mouth and my hands. More comfortable, I pop off his cock and then lick at his head, loving the way when I run my tongue over the knot beneath his crown he curses and finally his control snaps and he tugs on my hair and starts to really fuck my mouth. God, why is this so hot? I continue riding him and right as I'm about to come he warns me that he is as well. "It's okay if you don't want to swallow," he warns, but I want to. I wanted to taste him and that's what I'll do. I hold onto his hips, keeping myself right there and when he realizes what I intend to do, he comes on a curse, stroking my cheek as I drink up every last drop of him. Then before I've even had a moment to breathe, he's flipping us over and diving headfirst between my thighs. I crumble beneath the pillows and I couldn't tell you how many times he makes me come. Only that I fall asleep with him inside me, and I love every second of it.

CHAPTER 24

Lola

The next morning I'm once again annoyed with Callahan Murphy. Shocking, I know.

"What do you mean we're driving?" That familiar annoyance flares to life in my chest.

Cal leans against the passenger door of the black Jeep. "You hated the helicopter so I rented this for us."

I take a deep breath and clench my fists to keep from strangling him. "Why aren't we flying? It takes four and a half hours to get to the city on a good day."

"Because Sully said Murphy was having a grand time. Insisted we take our time, so we're having an adventure." He grins and damn if it doesn't make my heart skip.

Mentally chastising myself, I school my expression into one of irritation. "No, we're going home."

"Eventually, but first we'll enjoy a day of us."

Taking a step back, I cross my arms. "There is no us."

Cal follows, leaning in close and cupping my cheek. "That's not what you were saying last night." He waggles his brows, blue eyes dancing. "Or this morning. We can't forget about this morning, either time."

My cheeks flame. Dammit. The man is right. I tried to slip out of bed when the first rays of the sun shone in around the curtains, but Cal didn't let me leave the bed until I'd had three more orgasms.

What can I say, I'm weak.

It seems this is Cal's superpower. He is absolutely impossible to resist.

Over the years, more women than I can count have shown up at the office the week after a date with Cal, desperate for a little more of his attention.

None of them ever succeeded, and I refuse to be just another notch in his bedpost.

"*Cal.*" I grasp his wrist and yank his hand away from my face. "We work together. And you don't do more than one night. Just stop." I stomp my foot. Yes, it's mortifying, but I just stomped like a toddler throwing a fit.

Cal doesn't seem to mind my tantrum. In fact, his smirk turns into a grin, like he finds it endearing rather than irritating.

"Cal, I'm serious. When we get back to Jersey, we forget all about last night. This"—I wag a finger between the two of us—"never happened."

He opens his mouth like he's gearing up to argue, but after his eyes search mine and he sees how serious I am, he snaps it shut again and sags a little. "Fine. But until we get back to Jersey, it very much *did* happen, and I'll revel in it."

My shoulders finally relax while the tension eases from me.

He yanks the door open and holds out an arm with a flourish. "So get in, Lola. You can control the music."

With a sigh, I climb in. There is no point in prolonging this.

He jogs around the front of the Jeep and eases into the driver's seat with far too much swagger.

"So, lunch," he says as he pulls away from the curb.

I blink at the clock, then at him. "It's 9:36."

If we headed straight to Jersey now, we'd be there by two. A late lunch—in the comfort of my apartment and by myself—would be perfectly sufficient.

"Not yet." He chirps. "But we need a plan. So Newport or Bristol Bay?"

Rhode Island? That's not even on the way.

I shift in my seat and dig deep for patience. "What do you mean?"

He nods. "You're right. Newport all the way."

He taps the screen on the console, and the robotic voice of the GPS announces that we should arrive at our destination at 11:02 a.m. "Don't worry, Lola." He reaches over and squeezes my thigh. "This will be fun."

As much as I want to hate this time with him, when we pull into the parking lot of the restaurant, I'm smiling.

"Illinois," I shout, pointing at a car already in the lot. "That's nineteen for me. I win."

"You cheat," he accuses with a mock glare. "Twice you put your hand in my lap to distract me."

I lift a shoulder casually. "All is fair in love and war. And the license plate game."

"Hmm." With an arch of a brow, he unbuckles his seat belt. "I'll remember that." He slips out of the car and dashes to my door before I can climb out myself. "Since the restaurant doesn't open until eleven thirty, I thought we could walk the Cliff Walk for a bit."

With a nod, I turn in that direction. "Sure."

"So you've been here before." Cal falls into step beside me and laces his fingers with mine.

My feet falter, and for a moment I stare at our joined hands. His is so much bigger and tanner than mine. The warmth, the steady strength of his grip, is oddly settling.

If he wasn't him, I think I could get used to the entire scenario.

"Until we get back to Jersey," he reminds me. Though he's giving me that cocky smirk, there's a little uncertainty in those blue eyes of his. Like he assumes I'm upset that he's holding my hand. In reality, I'm furious with myself for enjoying it.

"Right," I mutter. "Anyway..." I steady my pace. "My parents loved to come here. Or anywhere. They love to travel. Always looking for an adventure."

He nods. "I can see the fun in that. But sometimes a kid just needs security. Stability."

I nod. "That was not their forte. They're chaos with a hint of creative."

He purses his lips, surveying the tree line ahead. "And yet you turned out so put-together and organized."

I sigh, weighed down by the disappointment that talking about my parents always brings. "Someone had to be."

"But it shouldn't always have to be you. You should be given the opportunity to let loose too." He squeezes my hand. "Don't worry Lola, I'll make sure you remember."

I let out a sardonic laugh. "Is that what today is?"

He pulls me to a stop. "No, today is about us being an us."

"Before we go home."

Though his lips tug down at the corners, he dips his chin in what I take as agreement.

After the Cliff Walk, lunch at the cutest restaurant in Newport, a tour of the Breakers, and an early dinner in Mystic, Connecticut, I can't help but think the day was more about stalling.

The strangest part of the entire experience? Somewhere along the way I stopped wanting to get home.

As we stand on the curb in front of my building, the sun just dipping behind the buildings, there's an ache in my chest that almost feels like sadness.

"Want me to walk you up?" Cal asks after handing my suitcase off to Benjamine.

I take a step back, needing to put a little space between us. "No, you need to return the car and get to Murphy."

He nods, hands in his pockets. "I told him I'd be home to tuck him in."

"And now he gets to see that you'll come back."

"Always." That single word is said with a fierceness this laid-back man doesn't often show. Somehow, he's closed the distance between us without my knowledge. Now, he leans in slowly. Before his lips can make contact with mine, I put a hand on his chest, stopping his movement. Smooth Cal recovers quickly with an easy smile. "Can I call you after I put Murphy to bed?"

I shake my head and glance at the door to my building, desperate to make a run for it. "No. No calling, no kissing. None of that relationship stuff. We're back in Jersey now. The spell has officially been broken."

He smirks like he knows I'm full of shit. "*Whatever Lola wants.*"

As he climbs into the Jeep and drives away, I stand on the sidewalk, rooted to the spot, wondering: What exactly *does* Lola want?

CHAPTER 25
Cal

Whistling, I stride to the back entrance of the building that Lola hates so much. Nothing could put me in a bad mood today. Not after spending a solid thirty-six hours with Lola. Making her laugh, witnessing the way she let loose.

Touching her. Tasting her. Making her moan. Making her *come*.

Teaching her. It was the greatest experience of my life. Even if she's still playing hard to get.

As I push the door open, I'm hit with the sound of Madame Esmeralda's bracelets jangling. I stop just inside and when she comes into view, I smile. "Good evening, Madame E."

"Oh, Callahan," she says as she takes the stairs slowly, "you are just beaming."

I am. Can't even deny it. "It's been a good day."

She smiles knowingly. "I'd say so. You've done better with water. Now it's time to add fins."

I roll her words around in my mind, thinking really hard on the comment.

Nope. It makes zero sense when considering the topic of our conversation. "Beg your pardon."

With a shake of her head, she rounds the landing and heads down the next set of stairs. "You'll figure it out."

"A riddle. I like it." I slip the key into the lock. Instantly, I'm greeted by a room full of energy.

T. J., Murphy, Brian, and Sully are all engaged in a Ping-Pong match, yelling and roasting each other and bouncing around. The older two are the only ones actually making contact with the ball, but the little lads are having a grand ole time, even if they're missing left and right.

The scene is enough to make my chest swell. This is my family. The people I care about more than anything.

Seeing the smile on my brother's face when Murphy finally connects with the ball is the icing on top of a wonderful day. It's been too damn long since I've seen Sully smiling.

"Bollocks!" he shouts as he misses the volley. "You got me!" He points his paddle toward Murphy who is beaming.

"That's a match," Brian says.

As I close the door behind me, they all turn, only now noticing my arrival.

"Ah, look who's finally gracing us with his presence," Brian teases.

"Uncle Cal!" T. J. squeals, tossing his paddle to the table.

"How was Boston? Did you talk to Henry?" My brother's smile is gone, the rare, easygoing demeanor replaced with his usual surliness.

I drop my suitcase to the ground and head straight for Murphy. He might not be running to me for a hug but I'm itching to give him one. Worried it would make him uncomfortable though, I give him a light squeeze on the shoulder. "How was last night?"

He tilts his head back and looks me in the eye. "Good."

That's all I get from the miniature bloke, but it's enough. Confident he's fine, I crouch and open my arms to T. J. who barrels for me. "Yes," I say, looking up at my brother as he lumbers to the kitchen. "I spoke to Henry. And Beckett and Cortney." I release T. J. and stand. "Philips is ill. Have you heard?" I glance at Brian. "We should make sure his estate is up to date. His nephew Landon might be as surprised as we were with the damn clauses in Philips estate."

Brian lets out a heavy sigh, spinning his paddle. "Well, at least he won't have to move to Jersey."

I chuckle.

"Thought maybe you ran into some trouble with a client when you texted to say you'd be back late," my brother says over his shoulder as he pulls open the door to the fridge.

T. J. dashes for his Ping-Pong paddle and goads Murphy into another game.

"No." I wander away from the noise. "Lola isn't a fan of helicopters so we drove back."

Brian looks up from his phone. "It's a four-hour drive. What took you so long?"

There's no fighting my grin. It may have taken us eight hours to get home, but they were the best eight hours of my life.

I can't tell them that, though. Lola would twist my bollocks clean off. So I simply mutter "traffic," then change the conversation. "Madame E gave me a riddle. I need some help."

Murphy sends the ball to T. J.'s side in what should be an easy return, except T. J. has suddenly lost all interest. He bounces up and down, his shaggy hair falling into his eyes. "I love riddles."

"Me too. So what has fins and goes in water?"

Murphy tilts his head, frowning. "Seriously?"

With a shake of his head, Brian slips his phone into his pocket. "*No*. No fish. No fins. No pets."

"Ah, a fish!" I clap once, the sound echoing loudly off the walls.

"I want a fish," T. J. agrees.

Sully nods. "Okay."

Brian growls, arms crossed. "We don't need any more living creatures to take care of."

"Eh." I wave a dismissive hand. "It's a fish, how hard can it be?"

"I agree with Cal," Sully says.

In unison, Brian and I snap our gazes to Sully. He's now focused on his phone though, smiling as he types away using both thumbs.

With a nod at him, I eye Brian and mouth, "Why's he smiling?"

"Why's he agreeing with you?" Brian shakes his head and ducks into his bedroom.

"Should we pick out a fish tonight?" I ask the boys.

"Yeah." T. J. darts around the Ping-Pong table. "Can we go to the arcade place after?"

I peer over at Sully. "Arcade?"

He shakes his head but he's smiling again. "Sloane and I took them to the bar across the street for dinner last night. They have one of those old game machines. They spent a small fortune playing while Sloane and I—" He snaps his mouth shut, his eyes bugging out.

Fucking hell. I don't think I've heard him string that many words together in a decade. And the smiling? I'd forgotten what he looks like when he's not being a broody wanker.

Before I can call him on it, he glowers and grits out, "Food's terrible."

"Please, Dad," T. J. begs, pulling on the leg of his trousers.

Sully's expression is flat when he looks at him. Even so, he'll say yes. It's damn near impossible to say no to his son.

Me? I'm always down for bad food and good games. That's how I've spent about half my time since I moved to America for University. And I've already eaten dinner, so I'll stick with chips or an appetizer. Maybe an ice cream sundae. Oh, that actually sounds really good. Chips—excuse me; fries—with an ice cream sundae.

"Sounds good to me. Let me get changed, and then we can head out."

In my room, I take my wallet and phone from my pockets, pausing to scroll through the pictures I stole of Lola today.

I caught her off guard with the first one. She's squinting at the camera, the Atlantic Ocean rolling behind her from where we stood on the cliff walk. After that, she was a good sport, performing for me when I insisted on snapping photos.

A big, obnoxious smile as she held her hand out at the Breakers, acting as if she owned the mammoth mansion. Oyster in one hand, blowing a kiss my way from across the table. And my absolute favorite: when she snagged the phone from my hand while we wandered across the bridge in Mystic and pressed a kiss to my cheek as she took a selfie.

After all that, the woman still insisted that what we shared wouldn't happen again. She asked for space. So that's what I'll give her. For now. Absence makes the heart grow fonder and all that jazz. Shakespeare would be proud.

Once I've changed, I knock on Murphy's open door and lean on the frame. He's tying his shoes which is a skill T. J. still hasn't mastered. This kid is so beyond his years in many, many ways. I wish I could just be proud, because he's bloody brilliant, but his abilities stem from having to do far too much for himself, and that makes my heart ache painfully.

He straightens, brow furrowing. "You okay?"

I affect a casual expression. "Of course. You just about ready?"

With a nod, he stands. "Is Lola coming?"

The smile that splits my face can't be avoided. I like hearing her name. But more than that, I like that Murphy likes her. That he's asking for her.

"No, she's staying home for the night."

Lips twisted, he breaks into a thoughtful expression. "You know T. J.'s mom?"

I straighten and slip my hands into my pockets. "Auntie Sloaney?"

Murphy nods. He's not quite ready to consider the lot of us family. Aunt, uncle, Dad. The titles may be a step too far for him yet. With any luck, we'll get there in time.

"What about her?"

"She stayed here last night."

"What?" My heart jumps in my chest.

"Yeah." He nods a single time. "She put us to bed and then she had breakfast with us this morning." The blue of his irises deepens as he zeroes in on me. "Why can't Lola do that?"

Tucked the boys in *and* stayed for breakfast? No wonder my brother was smiling.

With a grin, I point at Murphy. "You know, you've got a point. Why can't she?"

CHAPTER 26

Lola

I grimace at the message. Sloane and I have met for brunch on Sunday for years, and after this weekend I'm all in. I need to know what happened with her and Sully.

But in Jersey?

I'd much prefer to make the drive to the city. Meet at one of our usual places, where the staff knows us well enough to greet us with our go-to drinks already prepared. We'll never find that kind of quality or service here.

My phone buzzes again.

My mind goes offline for half a second. The "my" part of that sentence has short-circuited my brain. I shake my head. Before I can think too hard on that, I focus on the other part of his message. Sloane. *Shit.*

Me: How do you know that?

Cal: How do you know that? Where exactly
did she sleep?

Me: I might know something about that. But
what have you heard?

Cal: I know something too. Tell me what you
know and I'll tell you what I know.

Me: I can't do that. You tell me.

Cal: I can't do that.

Me: Oh my God Cal stop being Joey from
Friends and just tell me.

Cal: You stop being Rachel and I'll do just
that.

I snort. I'm oddly proud of him for understanding my *Friends* reference. God, this man is more clever than I've ever given him credit for. Though if I tell him that, it'll only burst his already overinflated ego, so I ignore all of it.

Me: I'm not doing this back and forth. I have
to find a brunch place. Sloane is coming to
Jersey.

Cal: Oh I saw the perfect spot.

Me: What?

Cal: Yeah. Tops Diner. The sign claims it's
the best diner in the world. Do that one.

Me: Really?

Cal: You won't know until you try it.

Me: Why are you texting? It's not a work
day. I'll talk to you tomorrow.

Cal: Whatever Lola wants.

I slide my thumb over the screen, closing out of the Messages app, but before I can navigate to the browser to look up the diner, the device buzzes again.

Sloane: Leaving now. Let me know where to
meet you ASAP.

Dammit. There's no way I can talk her into meeting in the city now, so I look up Tops Diner. Might as well check out the menu.

Instead, my search populates a slew of TikTok's and Instagram reels. After watching two I have to give Cal credit. This place looks awesome.

I quickly call for a reservation, then text Sloane the address. An hour later we're sliding into a booth in a place that gives anywhere in New York a run for its money.

The high ceilings and huge windows make the dining area bright and open. The clean lines and light wood give it a modern feel.

Huh. Who would have thought a place like this existed in the armpit of a state that is New Jersey.

"I'll take a mimosa," I tell the server.

"I'll try the golden patron," Sloane mutters, her tone a little sharper than usual.

"Going for the hard stuff," I tease as the server walks away, eager for the story behind her mood. "Ready to tell me what happened Friday night?"

Sloane shakes her head. "You first."

The giddiness bubbling up inside me goes flat instantly. "Cal and I went to a fundraiser," I say, waving a hand dismissively, "and had to spend the night in your love suite. You know this."

Her lips kick up on one side. "So something happened?"

"It's Cal." I attempt a scoff but the crack in my voice betrays me.

"That's not a no." Sloane puts an elbow on the table and rests her chin in her hand, her long black hair slipping forward over her shoulders. "I want details."

"I don't....no details to tell." I shift on the cushion, unease rolling over me. Cal and I had one night only together. And part of a day, I guess. So I'd rather keep our little lapse in judgment to myself. The last thing I need is to be another Callahan Murphy groupie.

"Sure." Chuckling, she tucks her dark hair behind her ear. "But considering all the nothing that apparently didn't happen—"

I groan.

She cocks her brow, pinning me with a mom look that shuts me up. "It might be time you start looking for a new job. This whole scenario—the four of you working out of Jersey in that shithole—is absurd. Three attorneys sharing one paralegal? That kind of torture should be against the law."

"A new job?" Pain blooms in my chest. Right in the center. It's small, but it flares hot. Yes, I've considered it more than once since the reading of Terry's will. But Brian was right from the start, I'd never leave the firm. Or him. Or Terry's legacy. And now there's a sinking feeling in my stomach at the idea of leaving Cal.

"Yeah, I can talk to Will. We can find you a place."

"Not happening." I shake my head. Even if I did need a new job, there's no way I'd ever work for the enemy.

"But—"

"Not interested." I squint at her. "However, I am interested in the details of your Friday night." I shift the attention back where it should be. On her. "You spent the night at the guys' place."

She swallows audibly. "Uh—"

The waitress appears, setting our drinks in front of us. "Here you go, one mimosa and one golden patron."

I lean forward, not taking my eyes off my best friend. "Saved by the server."

The young woman pulls a notepad from her apron. "Ready to order?"

"You should get the French toast, according to TikTok, it's amazing."

"It's one of our specialties." The server straightens, beaming.

Sloane nods. "Sold."

"And for you."

I order an omelet, ensuring the sides are gluten-free, and when she wanders away, I focus all my attention on Sloane.

"So you spent the night. Where *exactly* did you stay?" I press. "And before you answer, know I saw a video of you leaving Sully's room at 4 a.m."

Her blue eyes widen. "I…I mean nothing happened."

"Sure." I smirk. "And how was the nothing?"

With a roll of her eyes, she leans back against the booth. "About as good as yours, I imagine."

I lift my glass. "To nothing."

Laughing, she picks up her glass and taps it against mine. "To nothing."

We leave it at that. Nothing. When in reality, we both know that mixing wine with the Murphy men never leads to nothing.

CHAPTER 27
Cal

"**G**ood morning," I singsong, carrying Lola's favorite coffee and her breakfast into the office.

I'm not a complete arse, I've got an iced coffee for Amy and one for Brian too. Nothing for Sully, though. My brother would never drink his coffee iced. In his mind, Americans are uncivilized for destroying caffeine in such a way.

Then again, with the way he's been humming and smiling since Friday night, maybe he's come around.

"Morning, Boss." Amy greets me with a bright smile. We had to move her into the conference room as well. It's less than ideal since I'm eager for a few minutes alone with Lola. Though I suppose that isn't in the cards anyway, since Lola is nowhere to be seen.

I set the tray on the table along with the bag. "The iced coffee is yours. Sugar and creamer are in the bag. I wasn't sure how you took it." I ease the second iced drink from the tray and step back. "I'm going to take this to Brian. If Lola comes back let her know her breakfast has arrived."

"You are the best boss ever," Amy coos.

I shoot her a wink, then stroll out of the room. Now that's a way to start a morning. As I make my way to Brian's office, I keep an eye out for my girl but she's nowhere to be found.

Brian is also missing so I leave the iced coffee on a coaster next to his computer. Once I thoughtfully brought him an iced coffee just like this but set it on the desk itself. I never heard the end of it. Every time I set foot in his office in the city, he'd glare at the hint of a ring it left behind on the wood, as if reminding me of my error.

I wander back to the conference room, only to find Amy taking a large bite of Lola's breakfast. Naturally, Lola appears out of thin air at the same moment.

"This is so good," Amy says, mouth full, her voice garbled.

Lola may be shooting daggers, but she's as delectable as ever. Her hair is in its usual braid, and her fitted navy skirt glides over her pretty curves just like my hands did on Friday night.

I fist them at my sides to keep from touching her. "Good morning, Lola." I give her my most winning smile. "I brought you your coffee."

With a heavy sigh, she offers me the weakest of smiles. "Thanks, Cal." She plucks her drink from the tray, glaring at Amy, who's practically moaning over the croissant she's devouring.

I follow Lola to where she sits at the end of the table, as far from our intern as she can get, and settle my hip against the table, essentially blocking Amy from her view. "Did I tell you I got a fish?"

Head dropped back, she groans. "Why would you get a fish?"

I give her one of my extra cheeky grins. "Because it was time for fins."

She doesn't smile back.

"Lola," I singsong as I grasp her chin.

The moment I make contact with her soft, warm skin, the words I planned to say disappear like vapors.

The tiniest of breaths escapes her, and those pretty green eyes of hers stare up at me like she's just as entranced with my touch.

I slowly graze her cheek with my thumb, and her lashes flutter shut.

I'm reminded of the way I held her chin as she asked me to teach her how to suck my cock. Fuck, my trousers tighten at the mere thought. At the reminder of the sounds she made as she rolled against me, chasing her own orgasm as she gagged around my dick.

Caught in her orbit, I dip my head, breathing her in. I can practically taste her sweet lips.

"The croissant was good," Amy says, startling us out of the stupor we've fallen into, and Lola jerks back, "but next time can you get me the chocolate one?" Amy's whiny voice has Lola pulling back from my grasp and her rolling chair hitting the wall. "This one tastes like it's missing something."

The look Lola gives me is scalding. It says *we're at work and I told you not to touch me at work. Or ever again. But* really *don't touch me at work.*

"That's because it's gluten-free," she growls out.

My lips twitch. Fuck, what I'd do to kiss her right now. It's clear my girl is hangry, a situation that must be rectified.

"Why would you order it like that, Cal? The gluten is the best part," Amy muses.

Lola grits her teeth and launches to her feet. "Because it was for me."

As she stomps out of the room, I try not to laugh. Hangry and horny. A terrible combination.

I'll have to rectify both.

I follow her out of the office like the smitten man I am. "Lola."

With a file held tight to her chest she spins, her expression carefully blank. "I've got to work, Cal. I don't have time for games."

Bollocks, she really is in a mood.

I take a step forward, hand out, certain that I can calm her with a touch.

She arches a brow, shutting me down without a word.

So I shove my hands into the pockets of my trousers, rocking back on my heels, and try a different route. "What's your favorite restaurant?"

"Why?"

Chin dipped, I take a risk and lean in a little closer. "Humor me."

With a shake of her head, she huffs. "Rare on 22nd Street."

I hum. Excellent choice. But... "Pick something in Jersey."

Her shoulders sink. "I don't know. Jersey sucks."

"Okay, forget that. Tell me what you order at Rare on 22nd."

My fingers itch to tug at her braid, to ease the ties from it. I want to comb through her soft locks, watch as they fall against her shoulders. To inhale the cinnamon sugary scent I'm addicted to. The combination is so perfect for her. Sweetness and spice. All things sassy and not so nice.

"Filet mignon medium-rare, asparagus, and the freshly baked bread."

"Bread?" That was the last thing I was expecting.

"It's gluten-free." She closes her eyes, and her expression goes dreamy, as if she's remembering the taste of it. "And it's delicious."

"Okay." I skirt around her, giving in to the temptation, finally tugging on the end of her braid, and breathe in her scent.

"Where are you going?" she calls after me as I head toward Brian's office again.

I don't look back as I say, "I've got research to do."

I like leaving her wanting more. I'm always the one staring after her. Chasing her.

It's only fair she wonder where I'm off to.

Brian hasn't returned, so I settle in his chair and power on his computer.

When the lock screen blinks at me, I tilt my head. *Hmm.* What might his password be?

He's a lonely sod, with no life outside of work.

His sister's name, maybe?

I type *Dylan* into the password section and hit return. An error message appears on the screen.

I love New York? Nope, if that's anyone's password, it's Lola's.

His niece? I try *Willow*. Nope. If it's not her, it's unlikely his nephew, but I try *Liam* anyway. Negative.

I sit back in his chair, the leather creaking beneath me. There's got to be something, someone, in this world that matters enough to become his password.

Eyes closed and fingers steepled, I will the answer to come to me. And like a light flicking on, I get it.

Jessica. BINGO! The ex-girlfriend. The one who got away.

Oh, Brian, you're so utterly predictable.

Now that I've gained access to the computer, I put my genius to work, searching for a restaurant in Jersey that has excellent steak *and* gluten-free bread.

Half an hour later I return to the conference room where Lola is typing away on her laptop.

She doesn't even acknowledge me so I amble around the table and lean over her shoulder. "Whatchya doing?" I murmur, my lips a hairsbreadth from her ear.

She lets out a heavy sigh. "Working."

I press a kiss to her cheek and pull back before she can wallop me. "Go to dinner with me tonight."

She turns, glaring. "No." She enunciates the word.

She's turned me down, not a surprise, but I'm too focused on the way her lips move to be disheartened.

"Please?" I offer her a dazzling smile.

"Cal, we talked about this. *This*"—she points between the two of us, rolling a few inches away—"can't happen."

I stare into her eyes, long and hard, silently begging her to give in. When she doesn't, I pull back and pivot to plan B. "Fine. Can you do me a favor?"

Brows lowered, she shakes her head. "I have to work."

"This is work. I need you to set up an appointment for me."

With a sigh, she picks up a legal pad and pen, ready to jot down my request. "Fine."

"Fair warning, the person I need to meet with is really difficult and won't want to come. But I need you to make this happen."

She rolls her eyes. "Someone doesn't want to hang out with you? No way."

"Shhh, Lola, you'll ruin it," I warn as I straighten my suit jacket.

With her pen pinched between her fingers, she rubs at her temples. "I'm getting a headache. *You're* ruining it."

I chuckle. "Okay, okay. This is what I need: Call Berns Steakhouse and make a reservation for two at eight thirty tonight."

She documents my request in the same manner she takes dictation. "Eight thirty reservation for two at Berns Steakhouse." Face lifted to mine, her eyes widen. "Is that right?"

I nod. "Yup. Thank you."

With a charming grin, I turn on my heel and stride away, letting her wonderful little jealous mind do all the work for me.

CHAPTER 28
Lola

I glare at Cal's retreating form until he disappears, willing him to trip and fall on his face.

But the man doesn't even miss a step. Like he didn't notice how pissed I am. Like he didn't think it would drive me out of my mind wondering who the hell he is taking to dinner.

I say no one time and that's it? He doesn't even bat an eye as he moves on?

Hands fisted so tight my nails dig into my palms, I storm out of the conference room and go straight to Brian's office.

"Who's Cal taking to dinner tonight?" I demand as I cross the threshold.

"Is that what the ass was doing on my computer? Making dinner reservations?" Brian grumbles without looking up from the screen. "Every time he's in here, he adjusts the setting on my mouse and never puts it back."

Using Brian's computer is disorienting, since it's set up for a lefty. Even I've been known to change his mouse setting so it's easier to use with my right hand.

"It takes two seconds to put it back, that's not the point."

The point is that Cal apparently already has a backup date lined up. Like I am suddenly just one of many.

Sighing, he rests his forearms on his desk and finally meets my eye. He knows me well enough to know when I'm on a roll. "What *is* the point?"

I cross my arms and glare. "Who is Cal taking to dinner?"

"How the hell would I know?" He tosses his hands in the air and leans back, making the leather chair crack. "He goes out with a different girl every night. He can't even recall the woman who birthed his child."

The wind leaves my sails and my stomach crashes through the floor. He's right. None of this is new information.

How the hell did I let *Cal* get me so twisted up in knots?

He goes and acts like a sweet human to his son for a few weeks and I simply forget who he was before Murphy showed up, but it's not like Cal had a personality transplant. Eventually, he was going to go back to his old ways. Dammit.

As anger and irritation and hurt battle for the top spot inside me, I zero in on the sweat that's formed on the mostly full drink on Brian's desk. One bead of moisture breaks free and rolls down the plastic, picking up speed until it collides with the coaster beneath it. It was inevitable. Destined. Just like Cal will inevitably go out with another woman. Many nameless, faceless women.

This is exactly why *that night* was supposed to be just *a night*.

Cal was always going to move on. And I refuse to let myself get hurt.

"Lo." The single word is a low rumble as Brian pushes to his feet and splays his hands on the top of his ultra-organized desk, his knuckles going white. "*Why* are Cal's dinner plans upsetting *you?*"

Eyes narrowed, he glances over my head like he's searching out Cal. Expecting him to pop in any second.

I choke back my emotions. This is work. I am a professional.

And Brian is a stickler for rules. The firm has always had a no-fraternization policy, so he wouldn't be thrilled if he discovered that Cal and I hooked up.

On top of that, he's always been protective of me. When I started working for him, I was only twenty-two, and from day one, he made sure the staff knew that anyone who messed with me, messed with him.

It dawns on me now that the sentiment still stands, and Cal is included in the *anyone*.

I shake my head. "It's nothing. He told me to make a reservation and mentioned that the person he's meeting with is difficult as hell to deal with. So I was hoping for some insight before I dive into that fight."

Brian runs his tongue over his teeth, amber eyes hardening.

Shit.

"He called it a business meeting," I toss out, evening out my tone.

Finally, his muscles relax and he drops back into his chair. "Oh, that kind of dinner." He smooths the front of his shirt. "Probably Jerry Atshire. He's a blowhard. In his mind, it's absurd for the wife in the Wooden case to be imputed to a full-time income. Even though the assets are 50/50, he thinks the debt should be all Cal's guys' problem."

That eases the unwanted jealousy that's bubbled up inside me. "That sounds like Jerry. Though if he were representing the husband, he'd be singing a different tune."

"I despise attorneys like that." Brian shakes his head.

"Me too." My blood pressure levels out as I take a step back. "But you know me, I'm great at wrangling that guy."

Brian's eyes are on his computer again, but he gives me a hint of a smile. "Just one of the reasons we love you."

"Right." With one more backward step, I'm in the hallway. Then I'm striding to the conference room.

Amy is tapping away at her computer, but Cal is kicked back in a chair, his feet up on the large table, tossing his bright orange basketball up over and over. He doesn't even glance my way when I slip past him.

"I don't understand legal research," Amy whines. "Shouldn't like...the judges know what they say and the rules they make?"

Although both were silent as I walked in, this seems to be a continuation of a conversation.

"Like why do we have to tell them about it?" She frowns at Cal, twirling a lock of her dark hair absently.

I lose all hope for mankind every time I remember that this woman is in law school. Good god.

But Cal, ever patient with her nonsense, shrugs, his focus still fixed on the ball he tosses up again. "There are thousands of judges in this country. They can't be aware of every word every one of them has ever said. So we remind them."

"It's too bad they can't just have a Snapchat or something to remind each other. It would save us time."

"Maybe one day. But until then"—He drops his feet to the floor and straightens, finger tapping the notepad next to her—"legal research."

"The. Worst," she grumbles at her computer screen.

I take the seat farthest from her. Just in case her idiocy is contagious.

I've just pulled up the phone number for the restaurant when the walkie-talkie crackles. "I need someone to assemble the Crown Motion," Sully says, his words choppy. "Amy, can you come in here?"

"Gross. I hate assembling things. It's such a pain to keep the papers in order when there are so many of them. I swear it's impossible to keep track of what's Exhibit A and what's D." She pushes to her feet. "Cal, you should hire someone to do the assembling."

I rub my temples, silently reminding myself that stabbing people is wrong. Plus, if I murder her, then I'll be the one stuck assembling the motion.

Not that I won't be going through it once she's assembled it today.

She wasn't wrong about how difficult it is for her to arrange each document in the correct order.

Once she's left the room, Cal beams at me. "Look how much better she's getting." He tosses the little ball and catches it easily. "She didn't even insist that you do it."

I have no words. So I turn away from him and dial Berns Steakhouse. Even as I make the reservation, I'm in disbelief. I can't seriously be making arrangements for the man I slept with just a few days ago to go out with someone else.

When the person on the other end of the line asks whether Cal would like a table in a corner with lower lighting or one in full light with a view of the restaurant, I turn and relay the question woodenly, a lump in my throat.

"Huh." He taps his fingers on the table, looking perfectly at ease while I feel anything but. "What would you pick?"

Anger floods through me like a violent wave. Is he joking? This motherfucker is asking for my advice about the date he's planning for someone who isn't me?

"Full light," I grit through my teeth.

His stupidly plump lips tug down as he takes in my answer. "Huh, wouldn't have thought that."

"Looks like we're both being shocked by the unexpected today," I snap back.

In response, he breaks into a grin I want to smack off his face. The man needs to learn to read a room.

I relay the request to the hostess and give her Cal's name. When the perky woman ends the call, I slam my cell to the table with a grunt.

"Careful, Lola," the bane of my existence chirps. "If you break that, then how will the two of us talk?"

If only smashing my phone meant I wouldn't have to speak to him. "That would be tragic," I grouse.

"It really would." With one more of those obnoxiously devastating smiles aimed my way, he turns back to his computer.

I pull up the Case Information Statement for the Winters file and have just begun adjusting the expenses per the client's updates when my computer pings, notifying me of a new email.

Like Pavlov's dog, I'm conditioned to click on the icon immediately.

To: Lola Caruso
From: Callahan Murphy
Subject: Business meeting

I've scheduled a business meeting for 8:30 p.m. at Bern Steakhouse. Your presence is mandatory.

Cal

My heart skips as I take in the words. All that for dinner with me?

Ignoring the butterflies threatening to take flight in my belly, I glare across the table. "What is *wrong* with you?"

CHAPTER 29
Cal

At eight fifteen, I slip into one of the two chairs at the table in the corner of Bern Steakhouse. I'm early for our date—as every man should be—and armed with an oversized bouquet that I've laid on Lola's seat.

"Would you say this is a well-lit dimness?"

The server frowns up at the light hanging over the table. "Um, sure."

I nod. Though I don't know that dimness is the right word for this lighting, I do think it's the perfect balance of light to dark.

Lola's pretty face will be easy to see, yet the lighting won't be harsh enough to cause a headache. The candle on the center of the table adds a nice touch too.

It's mine. A new acquisition, picked up specifically for tonight. It's battery operated so it's not a violation of code or anything. The waitress did seem a bit thrown when I asked that she remove the centerpiece to make room for it, though. It was a simple daisy. As if that would be enough to impress my Lola.

According to the images I found of Rare on 22nd, their tables are equipped with baskets of gluten-free bread and candles. *And whatever Lola wants...*

"You're sure this bread is gluten-free?"

"Absolutely," the young woman says. Her tone is a little short, though she's still wearing a smile. She's in her early twenties, meaning she's got enough life experience to know that food allergies are serious, though she's young enough that there's a chance she doesn't care. That she's only here to earn money for a night out with friends.

Hm. Can I trust this twenty-something to be adequately concerned about Lola's gluten allergy?

No. I really can't.

"You take a bite then." I lift the basket, shooting her the most serious expression I can muster.

Frowning, she takes half a step back. "But I don't have a gluten allergy."

"Even better," I counter.

"Leave the poor girl alone," a familiar voice says.

A voice far too deep to be Lola's.

Brian steps out from behind the young woman, his auburn hair almost brown in the restaurant's lighting. My brother's right behind him. Both are still dressed in the suits they were wearing at work.

My heart lurches, and I clutch the edge of the table. "Who's with Murphy?" I picked him up like I always do, but left work at five so I could prepare for this date. They promised they'd take care of him.

We had a plan. They're mucking up my plan.

And where the hell is my kid?

They eye one another silently, then turn matching frowns on me. "With Lola, like you planned."

"No." My heart hammers in my chest. "I made no such plan."

"Then why would she tell us we had a business meeting with you tonight?" Brian clears his throat. "She said, verbatim, 'I'm watching Murphy. Don't be late.'"

He gives me a nonplussed look. One that means he thinks I'm being ridiculous.

Only *he's* the ridiculous one. I am not ridiculous.

"Why would she say that when I specifically invited *her* on this dinner date?"

Brian's eyes widen. Sully's do too, a second later.

Bollocks. Shit, shit, shit. I backpedal. "I-I mean dinner meeting," I stammer. "A work meeting. Lots of work to be done." I nod succinctly to emphasize my point. "Forget it." I push back from my chair and drop my napkin on the table. "You two enjoy dinner. I'm going home."

"*Wait.*" Brian snags my arm and with more strength than I knew he possessed, he whips me around, eyes narrowed, and grip tight. "You better not fuck this up. She's our paralegal. We need her here. She's not one of your usual girls."

With a scowl, I break free of his hold and smooth the front of my Oxford. "Of course she's not. She's Lola."

Brian sighs, rubbing a hand over his jaw, and takes a step back.

That's better. She may have been his paralegal and they may be friends, but if anyone is going to claim her, it's me.

I'll fight him for that right. Regardless of nearly two decades of friendship and a partnership on the line, I wouldn't hesitate. Lola is the prize here.

"You and Lola?" Sully asks in disbelief.

I poke at his chest. "You can't talk. I know secrets too."

Jaw ticking, Brian glares at Sully. "You too?"

"Don't even start." My brother pulls the chair back, making it screech along the floor. He's dangerously close to taking out Lola's bouquet with his big arse when he spots them and freezes. With a sigh, he snatches them up and shoves them into my chest. "She's my wife." He drops into the chair with a huff. "I told you I'm going to get her back."

Groaning, Brian sits in the seat I just vacated. "You Murphy men are going to cost us the firm, you know that?"

I pay him no mind. I'm too busy studying my brother.

I get it now. I get why he's so sure he'll get his wife back. A woman like Sloane—like Lola—is worth everything. There's no giving up when there's a possibility with her on the line. No inconvenience, no difficulty, is too great. Sure, these women will put us through our paces. They won't show up for dates. They'll tell us they don't want to give us a real shot. But that's all bluster. They're just scared. Scared we'll do what we've done in the past. Underwhelm them. Disappoint them. Screw it all up.

So it's time to prove them wrong. We'll show Brian that there's more to life than work. If we lose the firm? Fuck, that would be terrible. But losing Lola? That's just not an option.

CHAPTER 30

Lola

One step outside Murphy's room, the smell hits me. It's mouthwatering. Savory and a little yeasty.

My stomach grumbles, reminding me I haven't eaten tonight. Neither the chicken nuggets nor the mac and cheese I made for Murphy was gluten-free. When I searched the kitchen for something I could eat, I came up empty, so my dinner will have to wait until I get home.

The main area of the apartment is darker than it should be, as if the lights were turned off while I was reading to Murphy. I refuse to believe in Sebastian, ghosts are not real, however weird shit does happen around here. When I left the office yesterday, there was a stack of files on the table near where I've set up my work station, but when I came in this morning, they had been moved to the floor. They weren't knocked over, either. The Redwelds were laid out in a checkerboard pattern on the dingy carpet.

Cal's sure it was Sebastian.

I blame Amy.

But Amy isn't here tonight, so I can't accuse her of turning the lights off.

I'll be really concerned if I discover a ghost in the kitchen, making a meal.

Halfway down the hall, I can see what looks like candlelight dancing off the leaves of the ferns I replaced yesterday. When people have séances to call ghosts they set candles, but do ghosts do it when they are coming to meet people?

I hope not.

Heart in my throat, I step into the main living area. If I find a floating specter, I'll dart back into Murphy's room.

Shit. Can ghosts pass through walls? I don't know. But I can't leave Murphy, so I can't bolt from here the way my feet want me to.

Instead of an apparition, I find the man who has taken up entirely too much space in my head.

"*Lola.*" Cal smiles that ridiculously charming smile, practically singing my name like he always does. Beside him, the Ping-Pong table is set with two plates, a breadbasket, water and wine glasses, a vase of flowers, and two battery-operated candles. "You attempted to skip our meeting."

"No, I skipped your nonsense. Surely your business partners were capable of handling whatever you needed." I feign annoyance, but in reality, the scent of freshly baked bread makes it impossible to be anything but hungry.

"If you'll remember, I told you the meeting was mandatory." He pulls out my chair. "So I brought all the nonsense and the gluten-free bread to you."

Without my permission, my feet bring me closer to the table. Dammit, he's annoying, but I'm hungry.

"I can hear your tummy doing the grumbly-rumbly from across the room." His eyes sparkle in the dim lighting. "Come on Lola, you know you want dinner."

I eye the steak. I really do. "Fine." I huff, though the sound that escapes me is more of a moan.

And if the way Cal presses his lips together like he's fighting a laugh is any indication, he noticed.

"How's the lighting?" he asks as he guides me into my chair. "Is it too dim? I know you prefer full light. The overhead lighting at Berns really is exceptional. It cast the perfect shadows." He slips into his own chair and shakes out his napkin. "Next time we'll have to do this there."

"Next time?" I ball my hands into fists, cursing the way my stupid heart skips at the possibility. Hating that the effort he put into tonight has me melting a fraction.

He grasps my hand, his warmth seeping into me in a much too comforting way. "Yes, Lola." His eyes lose the playful glint and he gives my hand a squeeze. "There will be many, *many* next times."

I tamp down on the flutter that passes through me and pull my hand away. This is getting out of hand. We work together. It can't be more. "You have that much business to discuss?"

Not at all deterred, he smiles. "I do. Brian says you're the best at getting Atshire to sod off."

I chuckle. "That's not the way to approach him. I promise."

Brow cocked, he pushes the basket of bread closer to me. "Eat. Then explain the best way to get him to stop posturing."

Mouth watering, I break off a hunk of the still-warm bread and pop it into my mouth. The outside is perfectly crusty, while the center is soft and warm.

My eyes drift shut while I chew. "Mmm, it's as good as 22."

"You wanted bread, and whatever Lola wants."

That statement has irritated me for years. Like nails on a chalkboard, it's clawed at my brain, making me want to scream.

Now, though, sitting here with Cal, it hits me differently. The words leave his tongue in a way that is almost...*sweet*. Endearing maybe. An emotion settles inside me, one that has nothing to do with annoyance.

After a second bite of bread, I sip my water and clear my throat. "Like any bully, Atshire does better if you call him on his bullshit."

Cal leans close, his expression earnest and eager, like he's hanging onto my every word.

As I explain how Brian and I have handled Atshire in the past, I give in and cut into my steak. The knife slices through the perfectly medium-rare filet as if moving through warm butter. And the first bite? I swear it melts in my mouth.

I've just popped a third bite into my mouth when I'm hit with a thought.

"Wait. You've gone against Atshire more than Brian has, I'm sure." I set my fork down and hit him with a stern look. "Why are you wasting my time? You don't need my help. You're known as the silver-tongued golden boy who can charm any attorney into settling."

Cal sets down his own fork and focuses all his attention on me. "Needing and wanting are two completely different things, Lola."

He inches his hand closer. Though he doesn't take mine, he brushes his pinkie over my own. It's the slightest touch, yet it's enough to send electricity coursing through me.

"I *want* your opinion. On everything."

My traitorous body leans toward him, caught in his magnetic field.

"I crave your thoughts and your words. Could I do this without you? Sure." He cups my cheek. "But I desperately don't want to."

My breath catches, my pulse racing.

He's so close. It would be easy to just lean in. Press my lips to his. Give in to the fire growing hotter inside me. The one I can't douse no matter how hard I try.

But we work together. Hell, we share an office. And he's Cal.

Finally snapping out of his spell, I shift back and breathe in deeply.

Disappointment flashes in those deep blue eyes, but it's gone just as quickly. He clears his throat and forces a smile.

"So finish your story." Fork in hand again, he takes a bite of his own steak. "And then we can watch *The Proposal*."

That's my go-to movie, when I need a pick-me-up or when I just want to chill. The assistant who hates his boss, but falls for her anyway.

Watching a movie with him is dangerous territory. Watching *that* movie with him? God, it's such a bad idea.

"Come on," he says when I hesitate, his tone challenging. "You can't say no to Andrew and Margaret."

He's right, I can't. So that's how I end up sitting a little too close to him on the sofa, laughing at the scene where Margaret runs around the yard with a white fluff ball offering it to a bird in exchange for her phone.

I do not remember falling asleep or being moved, but I wake up before six in Cal's bed.

Alone.

At first, I don't know where I am, but when I see the electric blue fish floating sideways at the top of the small tank on the dresser, it all comes back to me.

Shit. He killed the fish. At least I was expecting it. With the number of plants I've replaced in the last few weeks, I had a feeling this would happen. So I stopped by the pet store and purchased a few Bubbles just in case. Unfortunately, they're all at my apartment.

I sit up and scan the room. With a sigh, I realize I have no choice but to take the entire tank with me. Cal will be crushed if he comes in and discovers that Bubbles has died. And if that happens, he'll spiral. He'll doubt his ability to take care of Murphy, despite what a great dad he is.

And that won't do because Murphy needs him.

I slip out of bed, only then noticing the sweatpants I don't remember putting on. The way-too-big sweatpants that slip down my hips. I roll them a few times, biting back the smile that hits me at the thought of wearing something of Cal's. I'm not supposed to like these things, but I can't seem to help it.

As I unplug the light and filter from the small tank, I consider my options. In the end, the best choice is to borrow Cal's car. Lugging this tank the half mile to my apartment is out of the question.

Since it's early, I make it out of the apartment without running into a soul. I'm not so lucky coming back in.

I've just unbuckled the tank from the passenger seat when the back door opens and Madame E sashays out.

Her entire face glows as she smiles at me. "I see ten more of these in your future."

Shoulder slumping, I huff a breath. "I only got five."

"In that case, you'll need to make a few more trips to PetSmart," she says as she passes me.

"Hey, Madame E," I call.

With her driver's door open, she pauses and turns.

"Stop telling Cal to take on more responsibility. One kid is enough."

She shakes her head. "I only see what I see."

I huff. "Stop seeing things."

Madame E may think that Cal can handle more living things, but I'm not sure I can.

Without another word, she climbs into a bright green Mini Cooper and pulls out of the small lot.

Anxious to get the tank set back up without incident, I hurry inside and up the stairs. Before I even reach the top steps, I hear the guys' voices. Dammit. It's almost seven. Of course they're all up.

I've already committed to this though so I push the door open and feign nonchalance.

At the creak of the hinges, three sets of blue eyes and one golden pair turn my way.

"Morning." I chirp, my own traitorous eyes straying to Cal.

His lips kick up on one side, as if he's pleasantly surprised that I returned.

I give him a small smile, though when Brian glares at my bare feet and the enormous sweatpants I'm wearing, the expression falls.

Dammit. He's going to have so much to say about this.

I refuse to look like I've done anything wrong. All I did was *sleep*. This time at least.

"I thought Bubbles needed a walk," I offer stupidly.

"Oh." Cal blinks. "I didn't realize fish needed exercise like that."

He shuffles across the room and takes the tank. "Look at that." Smiling, he peers at me over the tank. "Seems it did him some good. He looks brighter."

I bite back a wince as he turns and takes Bubbles to his room.

"Coffee?" Sully holds up the pot, looking far less annoyed by my presence than Brian.

In fact, he is almost smiling.

Could this out-of-character easiness have anything to do with Sloane? I'll have to hound her for details later.

He fills a mug and slides it down the counter without another word.

Soaking in the warmth radiating from the ceramic, I sit at the table and take slow sips.

"So, it died." Murphy tilts my way, his voice a whisper.

"Shh." Although he's been helping me change out the plants, we agreed this was our secret.

He shrugs. "If you want to hide a couple of extra fish in my room, we can do that."

"Probably your best bet," Brian grumbles. "While Cal might believe that fish need to be walked, everyone else will think you're a loon if you mention that again."

Murphy giggles, the sound making my heart swell. This kid never used to laugh, but day by day, he's coming out of his shell.

"I like having girls over for breakfast," he announces.

"Me too," Cal agrees as he reappears.

Brian frowns. "Girls?"

"Yeah." Murphy nods at me. "Like Aunt Sloaney and Lo. Do you have a girl, Uncle Brian?"

Uncle Brian. This kid really is settling in.

Cal perks up, a bright smile overtaking him as he surveys his son.

Sully scoffs. "Not since Jess."

"We won't be having any more girls over for breakfast." Brian's tone is cutting, his words final.

I sigh, defeat threading through me. Even if there was a chance that Cal and I could be something, there's too much at stake. The company, the relationship between these three guys, my job.

As much as I hate to admit it, it's not worth the risk of jumping into a situation that won't last.

CHAPTER 31

Cal

"*Lola*," I sing her name like I always do, dragging out the syllables, eager to put a smile on her pretty face.

The woman is doing anything but smiling lately, and that irks me.

"Join me for lunch?"

She lets out a little puff of a breath, a huff if you will, without looking up from her computer screen.

While most men might take it as their cue to stop trying, it only spurs me on.

My phone dings, notifying me of a new email. She's once again forwarded the email she's been using as a response to my advances over the last two weeks.

Because yes, it's been two weeks since our date/non-date—she says it was not a date, I disagree—and she still won't give me the time of day.

Since I'm a glutton for punishment, I navigate to my inbox and click on her message.

FWD: Reminder of Professional Conduct
Murphy & Machon has a zero tolerance fraternization policy. This

includes dating, sleepovers, and **breakfast**. If you are found to have violated this policy, you will be fired, effective immediately.
Sincerely
Brian Machon, Managing Partner of Murphy & Machon

First of all, who the hell made the wanker a managing partner? I suppose I should make a habit of paying attention during our meetings. The policy is ridiculous. Sure, it's technically been in place for years, but it's never been enforced. How could it be when Sully and Sloane once worked together. I can't imagine my brother having a hand in the resurgence of the issue. Not after his little sleepover with Sloaney.

Not one to be deterred, I bat my lashes at my reluctant lady. "What's your favorite fruit?"

Lola jams her fingers into the computer keys, and my phone chimes again. Yet another copy of the damn email.

It's infuriatingly adorable how hard she's working to resist me. But Brian's rules are rubbish. He's only harping on them because he's a miserable sod who never got over his college girlfriend.

The man needs to fall in love. Try as I might, it's been nearly impossible to find a woman open to loving such a curmudgeon. Especially when he refuses to do even the barest of minimums to put himself out there. He won't even talk to Beckett Langfield, the self-appointed love whisperer. Especially after he discovered that the zoom meeting I scheduled for the two of them was a romance consultation rather than an estate-planning session.

Beckett will live forever—his words, not mine—he's not planning for death.

Anyway.

"*Lola—*" I sing once more.

She holds up a hand. "Enough. I am your employee, Mr. Murphy."

I bark out a humorless laugh.

That's another new development. She's begun calling all of us—including Brian—by our last names.

And boy is Brian pissed. Lola may be following his rules but she's now erected a steel wall where he's concerned.

He said no fraternization and she ran with it. For years, the two of them have started their day with coffee and a chitchat in his office. Now? All he gets is a *Good morning Mr. Machon, is there anything you need from me?* When he tries to engage her with conversation, she reminds him of the zero fraternization policy—though a little more politely than she does me—and excuses herself.

"You are also the object of my desires, Ms. Caruso."

Eyes closed, she blows out a breath. Like she's silently wishing I'd stop being so wonderful. Like she wants to forget the night we shared. The incredible day that followed. As if she believes that if she closes herself off to what is clearly right in front of her—a man begging for even an ounce of her affection—she can turn off her feelings.

But I know better. She wants this. She's just as gone as I am. And Brian and his stupid policies will not stop me from making her mine.

My daft fool of a partner is just making it categorically more difficult.

"Cal, stop. Please. I've already ordered myself apology Tulips, gluten-free cookies and cupcakes, chocolate-covered strawberries, and a gift card to a ridiculously expensive spa. No matter how many gifts you shower me with, we can't do this. For you, this is fun and games, but I'll lose my job if I give in."

My chest pinches at the annoyance in her tone. She has every right to be irritated, I'm just as miffed. I just wish she'd direct her anger at the right person. Brian is the problem, not me. The man will pay for making her feel this way.

But right now, I can't promise her she won't lose her job—though Brian wouldn't dare let her go. And I'll get nowhere if I continue to push.

"I'm sorry." I stand and push my chair in. "I'll do better."

Her green eyes widen in shock.

"Need anything from me before I get out of your hair?"

I'd do anything to take away the weight on her shoulders.

She gnaws on her lip, like she actually does have a request, and God, I can't help the bolt of excitement that zips through me.

Does she want a parting kiss? A back massage perhaps? Maybe a secret orga—

"Could you find out what's taking the exterminator so long? Once my space is cleared, the two of us won't be stuck in here like this." She waves a hand, as if the conference room is a prison cell. "That should make things easier."

Right. Because, despite how desperate I am for more of her, she'd prefer to see less of me. The last bit of hope I've been clinging to shrivels even as I force an even expression and smile. "Of course. I'll get right on that."

I suppose I should actually call the exterminator now. I've been putting it off for the last six weeks, but if that's really what Lola wants...

Fuck, not even my little song could make me smile right now.

"Why did you bring us here if you weren't gonna get a slushie?" Across the booth, T. J. slurps his red and blue drink through an enormous straw.

Murphy's slushie is only blue, and unlike his cousin, he takes his time sipping the frozen high-fructose corn syrup goodness.

With a groan, T. J. slaps a hand to his head and squeezes his eyes shut. "Brain freeze! Ow, why does that always happen?"

Murphy chuckles. I try to do the same, but it's pointless.

I'm depressed. Not even a dose of red dye slushie will lift my spirits. I want to date Lola. I want to spend time with Lola.

But all she wants is for me to disappear.

"You didn't answer the question." T. J. dives in again, taking another long pull of his drink.

I sigh. I'm not a good liar. Even if I was, I don't have the energy to come up with an easy excuse for this emotion pushing against my chest. "Lola doesn't want to sit with me anymore."

There. It's a simple explanation. Age appropriate too.

T. J. nods, a dribble of purple liquid running down his chin. "Bryce said he didn't want to sit with me at lunch and my dad said—"

He yammers on, but his words don't register. Not when I notice how gaunt Murphy's face has gone. Bollocks. I'm a jerk for bringing up my issue with Lola in front of him. The two of them are close. He's intimated how he'd like her to spend more time with us—sleepovers and all. And I encouraged it. I gladly let him push her.The boy's lost too much already. His own mother doesn't return his calls. The last thing he needs is to worry that another person he cares about will disappear on him.

When T. J. runs out of steam, I hold up a hand. "It's not like that. She's got work to do, and I talk too much." I look Murphy in the eye and add, "She'll be right down the hall from me. She's not going anywhere."

T. J. gives me a big smile. "Of course she's not. She's Lola. She's been around my whole life."

Murphy takes a long sip of his drink, not meeting my eyes.

As if he's no more comforted by that fact than I am.

It seems we've both fallen pretty hard for Lola Caruso.

T. J. insists on popping in to see his dad when we return, and then we stop by the conference room, where I smile at Lola. I do my best to appear completely at ease, hoping to sell how okay we all are to Murphy.

T. J. bounces off the bloody walls within minutes, making it impossible to herd him upstairs. While I'm trying to peel him off the ceiling—or so it feels—Amy stops me to ask a question regarding a motion she filed that the court rejected.

By the time I've explained that she filed it in the wrong court, my brother is screaming for me to get the kids under control. As if that hasn't been my goal all along.

Unfortunately, at that point, I realize T. J. is missing and Murphy is watching me with a wide-eyed expression. Basically, everything is going wrong and I'm failing at this whole parenting thing. I ruffle his hair, still off-kilter by the way he's clammed up again. "Do you know where T. J. is?"

He gives his head a shake, his dark hair flopping in his eyes. It's about time to get the boy a proper haircut. "I'll find him," he says. "Lola needs your help."

My heart leaps. "She does?" I lean back, peering into the conference room.

Amy's there, but no Lola.

"Yup." He points to the storage cupboard. "She's in there. Mumbling about what she'll do if a ladybug jumps out and surprises her. She needs paper for the copy machine but can't reach the box."

"Oh." I smooth my tie and straighten my cuffs. "Okay, you find T. J. and I'll help Lola. Then we'll head upstairs and I'll get the two of you set up to do your homework. Deal?"

Murphy nods solemnly. "Deal."

I march toward the supply cupboard, a pep returning to my step because Lola actually *asked for my help*. She hasn't done that in... I don't know how long. Come to think of it, asking me to call the exterminator aside, I don't believe she's ever counted on me for anything.

With a flourish, I pull the door open. When light spills into the space, she sags in relief. "Oh, thank God—"

Before she can finish her sentence the door slams shut behind me and we're blanketed in darkness.

CHAPTER 32
Lola

I dart around Cal, grasping for the doorknob, but it's too late. Now we're both trapped. I jiggle it anyway, as if it's not exactly what I was doing, without success, before Cal appeared.

"Shit." I sigh. I've been knocking on the walls for a solid five minutes to no avail. The closet is on the wall near the street entrance, not near the offices, so I can only imagine that even if the guys could hear me, they've assumed my pounding is noise from outside.

"Does the door lock from the outside?" Cal rubs his jaw. Even in the dim light of the old bulb dangling from the ceiling, the light scruff there is visible. He's typically clean-shaven, but for the last few days, it's as if he hasn't felt like it. Or maybe he's been too tired. With every day that passes, his brightness dulls a little more.

He's not the only one. Each morning, when I have to push Cal away, I get a little more cranky. And as we drift farther apart, the ache in my chest grows. It is next to impossible to work in such close proximity and not want to touch him. To make him smile. To laugh when he says, *whatever Lola wants.*

"I don't know, Cal," I huff. It's easier to snap at him than give in to my longing. "But I've been stuck in here for at least five minutes."

With one wall covered with cabinets and a counter and the other lined with shelves, the space is hardly big enough for the two of us. We're only three steps apart, and God, is it tempting to close the distance between us.

I garner every ounce of self-control I can muster, like I have every day for the last two weeks, and stay where I am.

"Why didn't you have Murphy open the door for you rather than coming to get me?" He scans the shelves above my head. They're all empty because I'm too short to reach them. "What did you need help getting to?"

"I have no idea what you're talking about." I cross my arms and shuffle back. "Murphy and T. J. were playing tag, making all kinds of noise. I caught T. J. and sent him upstairs because they were driving Sully insane. It took longer to find Murphy. When I did, he told me you asked if I'd pull out a few reams of copier paper. When I came in to get it, the door locked behind me."

Face falling, Cal turns to face the door and scrubs a hand over his brow. "My kid's involved."

I sigh and let my arms fall to my sides. "They were just playing. Being kids. Murphy wasn't being bad or anything." On instinct, I put a hand on his back, noting the tension in his muscles.

"No, Lola." He spins around, out of my hold, and crosses his arms in a closed off gesture that looks so foreign on this always jovial man. "My kid is involved. He locked us in here. O*n purpose.*"

My hand remains in midair, my heart aching. He's never pulled away from me like that. "What?" I mumble.

"He locked us in here so we'd be stuck together. He knows I'm upset that you don't want—" He ducks his head and gives it a shake. "That you don't want what I want. What Murphy's hoping for."

"I-uh." The ache in my chest morphs into a more acute pain. Because dammit, I want it too, but I can't say that. There is too much at stake. So I look away and swallow back the words.

"*Lola.*" He grasps my hand, cradling it in both of his. His warmth rushes across my skin settling me. "I can't let my kid get involved in this. He *can't* get hurt." With a sigh, he releases me and leans against the counter behind him, his focus fixed just past my shoulder. "So as much as I'd love to spend the rest of my life chasing you, if you don't really want to be with me, then it's time we call this."

And my heart has officially cracked in two. Everything is spinning out of control and I grasp at the only thing I do know for sure. "I don't *not* want to be with you."

He sucks in a breath, bringing his focus to my face, his expression a mixture of hope and doubt.

I spin and hop up onto the counter next to him so our shoulders touch. "But there is a lot at stake, Cal."

He turns, studying me, but he doesn't interrupt.

"We work together. And Sully and Brian are depending on us." I bow my head, avoiding his gaze. "And you've never been in a relationship that lasted a week, let alone months."

"Because I've never wanted one until now." His voice is a whisper, the words laced with a sadness I never could have imagined happy-go-lucky Cal experiencing. There's defeat there too. It's enough to cause those pieces of my heart to crumble. I want him to laugh, to smile. I want to be the one who cheers him up. Not the person who hurts him.

The thought of working alongside him for the next year while no longer having the ability to make him happy is devastating. It hurts more than the idea of losing the law firm. Of finding a job somewhere else. Of no longer being on the receiving end of the harmless grumbling that Brian and Sully do every day.

"Cal, I..." I'm not sure how to explain it. How to say the words.

"It's okay." Shoulders slumped, he forces his lips into the world's most pathetic imitation of a smile. "Whatever Lola wants." He shifts away.

"No. *Wait.*" I snag the front of his button-down and pull him toward me.

His eyes flash, but he quickly regains his composure. "Be very careful with your next move." His whisper floats against my lips.

The warmth of him, of the knowledge of what I really want, washes through me and my lips tip up in a smile. "Shhh, you'll ruin it." Then I press my lips to his, hoping, at least for now, that this says everything I can't quite put into words.

CHAPTER 33
Cal

Before her mouth has made contact with mine, my lips curl into a smile. This damn woman just used my own joke against me.

Not that she could do anything to ruin this moment. Nothing could dampen the pure joy surging through me. Not the uncertainty of the future. Not being locked in a closet that smells a bit like mold.

Because Lola just kissed me. Lola is *still* kissing me. I pull her to my chest and hug her tight. This is nothing like the lust-induced snogging the night of the charity ball. It's far superior to the morning after.

This is like coming home. It's comfort. Like for the first time in my life, a person I can rely on completely exists. A woman made just for me.

She nips at my lips and wraps her legs around my hips, pulling me close. Between one kiss and the next, that comfortable feeling slips into lust. Desire hurtles through me like a freight train.

Fingers threaded through her hair, I tug, forcing her to look at me.

She pants, her warm breath skating over me.

"Is this real?" I ask her. I need to know before I get ahead of myself. Because with Lola it's nearly impossible not to get ahead of myself. I'd blow my entire life up for this woman. Gladly. But not if it'll hurt my son. Before we're too far gone, I need to know she's sure.

"It's real, Cal. I like you." Her green eyes search mine, uncertainty and need mingling there. "*A lot.*"

Chuffed, I peck her lips again and again. "Oh yeah? Like how much?"

With a snort, she shakes her head. "Enough. Don't let it get to your head."

"Lola." I cup her cheeks. "I'm halfway in love with you. I promise I can handle it if you *like* me."

Her mouth drops open, and a gasp escapes her as if the woman is shocked by my confession. She shouldn't be. Has she not been paying attention these last several weeks? And was she not listening when I told her my son is falling for her? If I wasn't feeling the feelings I currently am, the smart thing would be to back away.

She may not have made a grand confession of love, but if she feels even a smidgen of what I'm feeling, if she's really willing to give us a shot, then there's hope I can give Murphy everything he deserves.

With two fingers beneath her chin, I gently push her mouth shut. "I probably shouldn't have been so forward, but I want you to understand where I'm at. And what I'm hoping for."

With an audible swallow, she nods once. "Okay."

Something akin to hope floats between us. "Okay?"

The most beautiful smile creeps across her face. "Okay." Then her lips are on mine again.

Yeah, not a damn thing could ruin this. Elated, I lift her in my arms and spin her. It's a challenge, keeping her from smacking into the shelving in this bloody cupboard, but I'm filled to the brim with love and I've got to let it out somehow. We're laughing and kissing and teasing when a shaft of light appears in the cupboard and widens, followed by the booming of Brian's peevish voice through the tiny space. "What the hell are you doing?"

Scratch that, being scolded by this tosser definitely puts a damper on the moment.

I set Lola on the ground, though I don't release her and I don't look away. "Okay?" I ask again.

Because now that we're in the literal light of day—under Brian's very angry gaze—I need to know she's good with what I'm about to do.

Lola doesn't hesitate. "Yes."

It takes all the restraint I have not to pull her into my arms and do another celebratory spin. As a consolation, I thread my fingers with hers and turn to Brian, grinning like a simpleton. "Lola and I are together."

Jaw ticking, he lets out a long breath through his nose. "I don't have time for this right now. Henderson didn't show up at the airport with his son. Now Judge Sanders is demanding both sides meet in chambers to figure out why the man can't, as her clerk says, 'ever listen to a damn thing he's ordered to do.'"

Lola takes a step back, frowning. "Why didn't Craig bring Larson?"

Brian huffs an annoyed sigh. "He says if he did, then his ex wouldn't bring him back. She's been itching to move the kid to Michigan and Craig is convinced she'll disappear with him."

I frown. "She could do that?"

Outside of law school, I have little experience with custody issues. That's Brian's department. I'm the money guy.

But I'm listening now. I'm ready to research from sunrise until sunset. Because it's only now occurred to me that a mother could just disappear with her son. That Murphy's mom could come back and take him from me.

"That's why the judge wants everyone in chambers. She wants to hear what her attorney has to say to that."

"Okay," I say, stealthily lacing my fingers with Lola's again, "but why do you need me? This doesn't feel like an orange suit situation."

Brian growls, his hands balled into fists. "Obviously, not. Though if you want a shot at wooing the judge, I suggest you wipe the lipstick off your face."

Smirking, I run my thumb along my lip. I'm certainly not wiping away the evidence of Lola's kiss. "Why aren't you dealing with this?"

"Because I've got to pick Craig up and get him and Larson to the airport and on a fucking plane."

Makes sense, I suppose, now that I'm thinking about it. Again, this is out of my wheelhouse.

"So I have to go to court?"

"We don't have associates to send, Cal, so yes, you have to go to court. Plus..." His focus drops to where I'm clutching Lola's hand.

"Plus, it's your Judge Espadrilles." Lola's simple statement has my smirk falling. "And she likes you."

That stupid nickname and all my jokes slam into me like a punch to the gut.

Heart in my throat, I turn to face Lola head-on. "You know I was kidding when I said I take the judges out right?"

"I don't care what you do," Brian grumbles. "I need you to make sure Henderson doesn't get locked up tonight. While you're at it, ensure we have an order in place that requires the ex return the kid by end of week. Think you can handle that?"

Rankled, I straighten my jacket. "Of course I can."

"Good." He steps back and holds the door open for us.

Before Lola can scurry out of the cupboard, I tug her to my side. "But I won't handle it until you apologize to Lola for being such a giant arse these past two weeks."

"Cal," she hisses, trying unsuccessfully to pull away.

Brian scoffs. "This is absurd. I simply reiterated company policy. Which you've both violated, by the way."

Lola goes rigid beside me.

"Company policy which was written by a major arse."

"At least speak English when you're being an ass," Brian mutters.

"I am speaking English you big"—I scramble for words—"sod of a man."

He coughs out a laugh. "Is that an insult?"

"Oh my God, you two," the beautiful woman still locked to my side huffs and once again tries to push me away.

I shake my head and pull her closer. "No. He owes you an apology and a promise."

"Oh, now I've got to make a promise too?" Brian grouses.

"Yes. Lola is the best paralegal we've ever had."

Brian nods, mouth pressed in a straight line. "I agree."

"And she's not at risk of losing her job." He sucks in a breath, but before he can respond, I hold up a hand and go on. "No matter who she dates."

With his hands on his hips, he shoots me a glare. "Obviously, but—"

"No buts. Do you want me to handle this hearing?"

He rolls his neck and stares up at the ceiling. For a moment, he remains like that. Eventually, though, he lets out a heavy sigh. "Yes, Cal, I want you to handle this hearing."

"Then tell her."

Lola's face has gone pale, and she looks like she wants to sink into the floor.

Brian cocks his head to the side, ready to give her shit, I'm sure. But as he takes her in, he straightens, his expression sobering.

Good, he should feel like shite for making her feel anything but good about herself.

"Your job is safe, Lola." His words are measured, genuine. "No matter what. I'll fire him before I'd ever fire you."

"Much better." I turn to Lola. "Isn't it, darling?"

Though she shakes her head, she breaks into a light laugh. "You're insane, you know that?"

"I do." Cuffing her neck, I pull her in and kiss her softly. For a moment, I soak in just being able to share the same breath. "We're not done with the conversation from before." I press one last kiss against her lips, then pull her out of the cupboard. As I stroll past my brother's office, I tap out a little rhythm on the doorframe. "Sully, you're on babysitting duty until I get home."

It's after eight before I cross the state line into New Jersey. The judge wasn't available until after four, and after an hour in chambers, I spent another hour on the phone with Brian and our client, assuring him that all would be well and that his son would be returned at the end of the week. It took another two hours in traffic to get this far.

If I wasn't so hopped up on thoughts of Lola, I'd be concerned I might fall asleep at the wheel.

This side of family law is rough. I'll take working on the money side any day. If I lose, then my client is pissed. But how the hell does Brian cope with the possibility of getting it wrong when there's a kid at stake?

And what happens when both parents' arguments are legitimate? Not many people set out to be bad parents. But sometimes the *how* is what gets in the way of it all.

How do we raise this child? How can we best support the child? How can that parent possibly love this child more than I can? I'm the one who should be making decisions because I know my child best.

It's utterly exhausting. Today's events absolutely reaffirmed my choice to work on cases that don't involve children.

How the hell do Lola and Brian do it? There's no bloody way I could fight this kind of battle day in and day out.

I suppose Brian's surly attitude makes a little more sense now. If this is the kind of rubbish he's always working on, it's no wonder he's in a perpetual bad mood. It's also easy to understand why the bloke has no faith that I'm in this with Lola for the long haul.

I'll just have to prove to him that Lola and I won't be like those other couples.

Lola. I want to see her as badly as I want to see Murphy after such an atrocious evening. I tap the button on my steering wheel and dictate a text to Sully, asking him whether Murphy's still up. I hate missing his bedtime and we definitely need to talk about the whole locking us in the closet thing, but if he is asleep, then I'll use this opportunity to stop by Lola's. Because we also have to talk.

> Me: Just getting back to Jersey. Is Murphy awake?

> Sully: Lo just put him down

My heart leaps as her name echoes around the car in that robotic voice. Lola's at our place? I come to a stop and pick up my phone, this time reading the text.

> Me: At our flat?

> Sully: ??? Where else would Murphy be sleeping? Yes, at our place. Lo brought groceries, made dinner, did homework with Murphy, and is in his room reading to him now.

> Sully: I'm not sure what's going on with the two of you but if you listen to one thing I tell you in this life, this better be it: Don't fuck this up.

I cough out a laugh, at an absolute fucking loss. Never has anyone gone out of their way like she has for me. She stepped in and cared for my kid when I couldn't be there. She fed him and ensured his school work was done and read him a book before bed.

She's still there.

I grip the steering wheel, tempted to step on the gas so I can get home faster but the red light taunts me.

Me: Don't let her leave.

Sully: Doesn't look like she's going anywhere. Murphy's asleep, and she and Brian just sat down in the kitchen to talk.

Fuck. I glance left, then right, and when it's clear my car is the only one in the vicinity, I gun it through the red light.

There's only one person who could ruin this for me, and for once, it's not me.

Brian better not fuck this up.

CHAPTER 34
Lola

"**B**uluga Gold, huh?" I sidle up to the counter across from Brian as he pours vodka over ice.

After two extra chapters of *The Lightning Thief* I finally convinced Murphy to close his eyes. And when his breathing evened out, I snuck out of his room.

Cal still isn't home, so that leaves me alone with the one person I don't think I'm up for talking to tonight. I understand rules and the reasons behind the policy. I even understand Brian's desire to look out for the firm, and probably me too. But he's overstepped, and it's time for him to back off. We are more than past that point.

"I didn't think I'd convince you to sit and have a drink with me if I offered you the cheap stuff." He fills a second glass, his pour a little lighter this time, then adds a splash of club soda and a lime.

When he slides it across the counter, I look from him to it and back again. Does he really think I'll just pick it up and tap my glass to his, forgetting all about the way he threatened my job? Is this really the best he's got?

I sure as hell hope not.

Arms crossed, I take a step back, waiting for a real apology.

"Gonna waste it?" He grunts.

"Maybe." I lock eyes with him, lips pressed together.

He holds my gaze for the space of several heartbeats before he bows his head and watches the clear liquid in his glass slosh as he swirls it.

I inhale a cleansing breath, determined not to back down. I want to be here. Not in this kitchen with Brian, but in this apartment where Murphy sleeps soundly, where Cal will return to when he's finished tonight. I'll give Brian a chance. But if he doesn't pull himself together and own up to his mistakes, then I'll wait in Cal's room alone.

The ice clanks against the glass as Brian lifts it to his lips. After a long sip, he sets the drink on the counter. "It's a company policy—

With a huff, I turn away. The pretense is ridiculous. This man knows me. He's a friend. A person I've always thought I could count on.

Before I can stomp away, he sighs and says, "Lo, wait."

Despite how sick I am of the way he's dragging this out, I give him a minute while he scrubs a hand down his face, collecting his thoughts.

"We need you." His shoulders droop. "The firm needs you. I need you."

I step up to the counter again, hands splayed on the Formica. "I'm not going anywhere."

He zeroes in on me, challenge in his eyes, though the words come out low, halting, like he hates them even as he says them. "And when things go bad with Cal, when he moves on to the next woman, you're telling me that you won't be hurt? That you won't want to leave?"

I choke back a retort. Snapping back will only make me sound like every other dumb girl in history.

So with a slow sip of vodka, I collect my thoughts. It burns down my throat, and when the sensation dissipates, what's left behind is the same feeling that's lingered all day. Certainty. The highball glass clinks against the counter as I slam it down.

Frustration floods through my veins. How could this man I've trusted so completely try to cloud my mind with doubts like this?

"What Cal and I have *is* different. He's different. And you should pay attention to that."

He lets out a humorless laugh.

"Seriously. He's not going to hurt me." The sureness of the statement settles through me as I voice the sentiment.

Forearms on the counter, he hangs his head, like he's weighed down by the conversation. Rather than fight back like I expect, he shakes his head. "That's good because I'd hate to break his pretty face."

I snort.

"We redheads have to stick together, you know." He smirks, a hint of light returning to those golden eyes.

I shake my head, softening a little. "Dylan and I are redheads. You got the annoyingly perfect chestnuty auburn color I always wished for."

"Nah." He chuckles and lifts his glass. "You burn too brightly for that." He downs another mouthful of liquor. "Plus, Cal likes redheads."

At the sound of a throat clearing behind us, I whip around.

Cal stands across the room, his hair sticking up all over like he's run his hands through it. His tie is loose and the top button of his shirt is undone. The less than perfect presentation looks damn good on him.

"Cal likes *this* redhead." Pointing at me, he drops his briefcase on the Ping-Pong table and stalks across the room.

Warmth blooms in my chest. His presence used to annoy me, set me off, but now it's like my favorite hoodie. A comfort I long to come home to and snuggle up with.

"*Just* this redhead." He bands a strong arm around my waist and pulls me in until my back is flush with his chest and his lips are pressed to the crown of my head. "*Always* this one." The words dance across my scalp, and I shiver.

"How long have you been here?" The contentment his presence brings is stamped out by fear. Because Brian's comments were not complimentary. I can only imagine how upsetting they'd be.

But the unease is wiped away as he tightens his arm around me.

"Long enough, Lola. Long enough."

"Well." Brain clears his throat and sets his now-empty glass of vodka on the counter, still hunched over. "I guess I'll leave you two be."

"In the general sense or for now?" Cal's voice lacks its normal lightness.

"Both." He pushes off the counter, his eyes a little bloodshot. "Lo, I'm sorry I was a dick." He gives me a quick smile, though when his gaze slides to Cal, his lips turn down. "And dumbass you better be as devoted as she believes you are. If you hurt her, I will break your very straight nose and then I'll be forced to let her leave before her ninety days are up."

Rather than bristle, Cal laughs. "Won't be an issue."

"I'm good here," I say. "Promise."

Brian shakes his head. "Who are you and what have you done with my paralegal? Are you seriously choosing to stay in Jersey for *Cal*?"

"I wouldn't go that far," I mutter. "But at least I can see the skyline from my window."

Behind me, Cal's chest puffs out. "Because I picked a good flat."

I pat the arms still banded around me. "Yeah, babe, you picked a good one."

He gasps, squeezing me a little too tight. "Did you hear that? *Babe*. I've got a nickname. It means she's getting attached." He practically vibrates behind me. "I like it."

This man is ridiculous. I have a feeling I'll be rolling my eyes at him even more than in the past.

With a huff of a laugh, Brian shakes his head. "And with that, I'm out." He sets his empty glass in the sink and pads toward his room.

As soon as his door clicks shut, Cal spins me around and cages me in with my back pressed to the island. "Before I get too excited about all of this, what exactly does it mean that I walked in and found you here?"

His blue eyes dance down like he knows the answer to the question, but he's going to make me say the words out loud.

"It means," I say, walking my fingers up the front of his white button-down. "We're giving this a try." I stop at the knot of his tie and loosen it. "You're going to see if you can be in a relationship. You might hate it."

He scoffs, his expression one of offense. "I will not."

I purse my lips to hide my grin. "You have to use your words. Talk to me."

He breaks into a blinding smile, as if my statement isn't the least bit off-putting. "Oh my God are we doing the *thing*?"

"What thing?" Is he complaining? Already?

"The thing." With a waggle of his brows, he pushes off the counter. He mutters to himself about *the thing* as he rifles through the drawers in the kitchen. He opens one after another and eventually sighs in resignation, apparently not finding what he wants. "The thing with the Post-it."

"Post-it?" I frown. All this excitement over a Post-it? I still haven't caught up to *the thing*, and now he's moved on to sticky notes?

"Yes, we need a Post-it? You always have them." He stalks over to me and cups my face.

True. At my desk. But I don't carry a stack in my purse or anything.

"Cal." I grasp his wrists. "I don't know what you're talking about."

He drops a kiss to my nose, murmuring about freckles, then pulls back again. "You know the show with the doctors." He squints, wearing a look of concentration he usually reserves for poring over a case file. "Fuck." He shakes his head, a whisp of his dark hair falling over his brow. "You know the one. Sloaney made us watch ten seasons when she was pregnant with T. J. and on bed rest."

His face is fixed in a look of expectation, like he's sure I'll under-stand, but I still don't have any idea what the fuck he's talking about.

"The show with the docs," he says, desperation lacing every word. "That dreamy guy."

I bark out a laugh. "McDreamy? Like Grey's Anatomy?" I've seen episodes here and there, but I have no idea what the television drama has to do with Post-its.

"Yes!" He beams. "The Post-it."

I still don't get it, but he's on a roll, so I don't bother asking him to explain.

He grasps my hand and kisses my knuckles in the most endearing way. "We need a Post-it for the rules and promises."

I hate disappointing him when he's this excited but I can't help it. "Cal, I don't have Post-its with me."

"But." He smirks. "You've probably got loads at your desk down-stairs. Come on." He tugs me down the stairs and into the dark office.

He doesn't let go until we're in the conference room and he's snatching up a stack of Post-its.

"What color?" He fans out the individual stacks. "Choose wisely, because this will be framed on my desk until I retire."

My nerve endings light up in a way I've never experienced. This man's excitement is contagious. I suppose I just haven't allowed myself to give in to it until now. "How about the light blue?"

"Perfect." He peels the top one off and snags a dark blue pen from the table. "So." He glances up at me, pen poised above the small square of paper, eyes sparkling. "These will be our forever promises. Our vows to each other."

I move closer, looping my arm through his.

"We will always talk," I whisper, heart suddenly lodged in my throat.

Without hesitation, he writes the words.

"We always stay, no running," he adds.

"We put each other first, before work."

He nods, jotting down the sentiment. "Lola gets coffee and breakfast every day delivered by Cal." He stabs the note with the pen, punctuating the promise with a flourish.

I snort at the ridiculousness of that vow. "As long as Amy doesn't eat it."

"Of course. I'll hide it from now on." He winks, making my heart trip over itself.

"That it?" I peer at the neat words he's printed. As silly as I thought this idea was, seeing our promises written out like that brings with it a feeling of security I never could have imagined having with Cal.

He tugs me onto his lap, his warmth enveloping me.

"One more." He presses his lips to my temple. "You kiss me." The words dance across my skin, sending goose bumps skittering down my spine. "Everywhere, all the time."

Despite the giddiness that's overtaken me, good sense rises to the surface. "Cal, we can't kiss at work."

He ignores my argument, scribbling the rule onto the page. "We're at work. Does that mean you won't kiss me right now?"

I huff a breath and sag against him. "Different."

"So"—He leans closer, his eyes locked on my mouth—"will you kiss me now?"

My breath catches. In this moment, I think I'd do just about anything to feel his lips against mine.

I shift so our mouths are inches apart, our noses brushing. "Well, it is a rule."

He glides his tongue along my bottom lip, and I don't even try to fight the moan that slips out.

"Lola. Kiss me." With that order, he closes the distance.

Our lips meet, and instantly, I burst into flames. Like the first time, our kiss is so much more than desire. It's pure need. Neither of us can get close enough. He lifts me onto the conference table and settles between my thighs, pressing his already hard cock against me. In unison we both groan as I rock slowly against him.

"Fuck." Cal's growl is low and feral as his large hands snake under my dress and he lifts it over my waist. Every brush of the tips of his fingers are like an electric spark. It has been too long. Too many weeks since I felt his hard body pressing against me. The need to feel him pressing *in* to me becomes more desperate. A pounding desire building deep in my core.

"Cal," I whimper against his mouth.

He pulls back enough to yank the black dress over my head and his breath catches. "Bloody hell woman, you slay me." His hand cups my breast through my lace bra. I arch into his touch, and he runs his thumb against my nipple.

With his eyes locked on me, and his fingers working their black magic, my nipples pebble beneath his touch.

"I can't imagine how I waited so long to touch you, because now looking at you—" His eyes drop lower focusing on my black thong and he wets his lips. The move makes my pussy clench. "I can't imagine not touching you, tasting you, every day of forever."

"Then touch me," I beg.

"Whatever Lola wants." The words are gruff this time. Like he can't make it to the next octave to sing them. Like I've stolen all his oxygen.

I love it.

He leans forward, brushing his lips against mine before slowly working down my neck. The scruff of his five o'clock shadow brushes deliciously across my skin. Every nip and suck of his lips spurs me on. Lighting my body up. He kisses a straight line down between my breasts, continuing to where my body is begging for him. His thumbs slip under the elastic of my thong and in one motion it's down my legs.

When he shifts, I know what he wants. Leaning back just slightly, resting my palms on the table, I spread my legs. Opening myself to him.

His desperate blue eyes lock on the juncture between my legs. He's enamored. "Look at you glisten for me." Reaching up he barely brushes his thumb over my pussy and I moan.

"Don't tease me."

He chuckles darkly and the sound echoes somewhere in the ethers of my soul. "Demanding woman."

Desperate, I tug his tie, pulling him toward me. "Yes, I am. So make me come, Cal, make me come so hard I scream."

Teasingly, Cal dips his head between my thighs, so close I can feel his ragged breath against my pulsing clit. I need more. "*Cal.*" I'm whining and I don't even care. I *need* this. I thrust my hips closer, trying hard to get him to give me what I crave.

Cal's blue eyes are molten when he raises them to look at me as he slides his tongue flat against me, giving me one painfully slow, long lick.

"Yes," I cry as I fall back against the table.

"So fucking good," he mumbles against me before diving in. His fingers dig into my hips as he pulls me closer and I grind against him as he laps and sucks, driving me closer and closer to the edge.

"Please," I beg moments before Cal slips a finger inside of me, curling it at just the right angle. The man knows how to play my body in a way that has my orgasm ripping through me. "Yes, yes," I chant as my body explodes in pleasure.

My walls clamp down, searching for what I really need. His cock, deep inside me.

Tugging his hair, I try to get him to stop, so I can feel him. Cal growls, "Every drop. I will get every drop of your pleasure, Lola." He continues to lick me over and over and although I just came, my pussy quivers as pressure starts to build all over again.

I'm crazed. "Cal, I want your cock. I need it."

CHAPTER 35
Cal

"**C**al, I want your cock. I *need* it."

This must be what heaven feels like. Those words falling from her lips. Those emerald eyes which I find myself searching for in every room. My comfort. My everything.

Fuck, I don't know when or how it happened but this woman went from being the treat of my every day to the air I breathe. The delight I sought out to break from the mundane to the source of my joy.

One last lap of my tongue against her soaked pussy and then I'm rising to give her what she craves. Spread across the conference table, from the neck up she still looks like the stern Lola I love to tease. Hair in a braid—*still*—and makeup covered freckles.

I shake my head. God, she's my obsession like this, but I want *my* Lola.

I search for a tissue and when I spot the box she keeps beside her computer, I grab it and hand it to her. "I need you bare, every inch of you."

Lola frowns in confusion.

"Your freckles, beautiful. I want all your constellations. Every perfection."

Those pretty cheeks pinken as her lips lift, and though she tries, she can't hide her smile. "I really have no idea how you hid it so well for so long."

"Hid what?" I ask as I watch her swipe the days makeup away. The dusting of freckles appears lighting up my heart like little fireflies on a summer night.

"You're a hopeless romantic, Callahan Murphy."

I reach for the tie in her hair and tug, then lift her to bring her to the very edge of the table, stroking my hands through her hair until it's falling in sweet waves over her shoulder. I press a kiss first to her forehead, then my lips dust across her cheeks, trying to capture every freckle, to taste her sweetness. It feels surreal being able to kiss her so openly. To have her like this. In my office. On our workspace. With that beautiful smile lifting her lips, like I'm also the source of her joy.

"Yes," I admit. I'm hopelessly gone for this woman. "Don't break me, Lola, I'll never recover."

That smile of hers goes soft. "I don't think you get it, Cal."

"Hm?" I hum as I continue stroking my hands through her silky strands.

"You've burrowed yourself right here." She taps her fingers against her heart and I swear my breath goes shallow as I wait for her next words. "I look for you in every room. I wait for the moment you walk into this office every day, wondering what you'll say to make me smile, smiling at just the thought of you."

"Fuck, baby, you're making my heart sing right now."

She snorts and I tug her closer, holding her heart to my own. "Need you to take your clothes off," she rasps as she tries to reach for the buttons of my shirt. "Need to feel your warmth."

I could never say no to this woman so despite wanting to just hold her close and hear her tell me all the ways she's come to crave me, I allow her to show me instead. First, though, I undo the clasp on her bra, enjoying the way she sighs as her breasts drop free. Then I kiss her while she works to undo the buttons on my shirt.

We laugh as she struggles and then like a caveman I grasp the middle and rip it off.

"Oh my God that was hot," she mutters shaking her head, teeth digging into her bottom lip. I kick off my shoes and one goes flying toward Amy's computer. Lola laughs as I make a face, hoping I didn't just break it. If anything, though, it makes Lola more feral. She reaches for my belt and tugs down my trousers and boxers in one move.

Finally naked, standing before her, I sigh, knowing in only a few seconds I'll be buried deep inside her. Her eyes widen and she licks her lips as she stares at my hard cock which is straining toward her. Lazily, I stroke myself.

"I forgot how big you are."

"We know you take me beautifully, baby. You were made for this cock."

She licks her lips like she's remembering my taste and if I don't get inside her soon, I'll blow just from watching the hunger in her gaze.

I take a step closer and then a disastrous thought hits me. "Fuck, condom."

Before I can go in search for one—where I have no fucking idea—Lola reaches for my arm, tugging me close. "I want you this way. Bare."

My eyes swing to hers and my heart works double time as do my lungs. I'm drunk with a need for this woman but she has to be sure. "Once we do this, there's no going back."

Lola smiles at me as she reaches for my cock and guides me between her thighs, pausing as my crown notches against her bare pussy. "This changes everything," she whispers as she pushes closer, swallowing each inch of me.

A groan rips from deep within my chest as I sink inside her and she wraps her arms tight around me, taking me to the hilt. "Fuck, Lola, you're magnificent."

She whimpers as she tries to roll her hips against me. From this angle she can't get what she wants so I drop my hands to her waist and pull her just so, then I slowly pull out before thrusting deep inside her.

"It's never like this," I say with a whisper, my lungs not strong enough to fully speak. She's stolen my breath right along with my heart. "Your pussy was made to grip me. Made to make me throb."

She rocks her hips against me and I groan. Our Post-it promises are beside me and I stare down at them, thinking we should add this to the list. Fucking her on every surface I can find. Bare. Filling her. I'm in a frenzy then, just thinking of all the places I want to take her. Of all the ways I can have her. "You know how many times I wanted to fuck you on this table. How many times I've dreamed of having you here, and on my desk, and on..." I'm lifting her before I can even finish my sentence, knowing where I need to have her right this very fucking minute.

Lola laughs. "Where are we going?"

I ignore her question, keeping a steady grip on her as I walk us through the office, completely naked. With each step, I push deeper inside her heat and she clamps down around me, forcing me to close my eyes and pause so I don't come on the spot. "Fuck, Lola, do that again," I mumble, even as I start to walk again.

She squeezes her pussy and pleasure ricochets through me, drawing my balls tight. I speed up knowing I'm about to blow and I need her in position when I do.

"You have a perfect ass, and I can't wait to spank it while you're spread across Brian's desk. Punish you for being his for so many years when you always should have been mine."

"Cal!" Lola screeches as I enter Brian's office and round the table, sitting my bare arse down on his leather chair. The seat bends back under both our weight and her eyes widen. "We're going to break it."

I motion toward his desk. "Hands on the wood. And hold on tight, I'm not going easy on you."

"Brian is going to freak."

I chuckle. "The wanker deserves this after what he's put us through."

She bites her lip but I see the moment she realizes I'm right. The moment we become the team and he's on the outside of that. I love this moment. Maybe that makes me an arse but for so long I've had to watch from the outside, knowing I was the right one for her. For some reason, I truly need this. I need to know that I come first.

Well, she'll definitely come first. All over his goddamn desk. "I'm going to make you squirt," I promise and those words seem to prompt quicker movements as she settles her beautiful body across his desk, giving me a perfect display of her small round arse. I lean back in the chair, appreciating the view for a second. My dick throbs between my legs, but I won't rush this. No, I push forward in the chair, and it rolls with my movement, until I'm right behind her. I place one hand on her back, keeping her in place, and then press my lips to one of her cheeks. "Tell me, Lola, how bad do you want me to spank you right now?"

She growls in annoyance and my cock pulses in excitement. "I'm not begging you to spank me."

I pause and wait, knowing she wants this. My put together, prim and proper girl, with her hair down and her arse up. It only takes a moment for her to wiggle her arse and I chuckle. "Cal," she whines.

The smack comes down on her bare arse and the sound of it echoes through the quiet office, the sound of her whimpers the only thing more beautiful. "Shit," she breathes out.

I kiss the spot I spanked and then before she can prepare, rain down on her other cheek. She spasms beneath my touch, her hips bucking like she's empty and ready for me. "Am I making you drip yet? Are you begging for my cum all over your boss's desk?"

Lola humps the desk like a needy little thing and I smile. "You are such a dirty girl."

"Please Cal, please." I don't even think she knows what she's begging for now. Her tiny fists are gripping the edges of his desk, her hips are rolling as she waits, her hair's a mess and she looks over her shoulder at me, pleading for me to spank her again.

I give her two more and with each smack of my hand she becomes needier, but it's not until I see the evidence of her leaking all over his desk that I finally give in. I slide her cheeks apart and lick up the mess between her thighs. Then I pull her right to the very edge and spear her with my tongue, fucking her slowly with it, in and out as she grinds against my face. "Holy shit," she mumbles incoherent words and I love what a beautiful disaster she's become for me. "I think I'm going to come," she warns.

"Not without me." Flipping her over, I stand and line myself up, thrusting inside her without warning. Lola whines around me as I fill her over and over again, my fingers circling her clit until she explodes around me. Her hands flail wildly with each thrust, knocking down Brian's neat files, his stapler, a jar of pens and number two pencils. With each thrust I make more of a mess, of her, of his desk, of this office, until finally I can't take it anymore and I bury my head in her neck, inhaling that sugar-sweet scent as I come in hot spurts inside her.

"Bloody hell," I mumble as I come back to earth. I kiss over each inch of her skin I can find, until I reach her mouth and stare into those beautiful eyes of hers.

She smiles as she runs her fingers through my hair. "He's going to kill you."

I grin down at the woman who's completely ruined me. "Worth it."

CHAPTER 36
Cal

"**I** don't understand why you get to be Gomez," Sully grumbles, repositioning the bald cap on his head again.

"Because"—I grin at our reflection in the row of doors ahead—"I have a better head of hair. You make a much better Uncle Fester."

"Bullshit," he grits out.

"Shhh, language." Lola smirks as I hold the door open so that my Morticia Addams can enter the Halloween party at Murphy's school.

My son is dressed as my son, because of course he is. T. J. wanted to be Cousin It. Because of course he did.

"Why couldn't I have been the Frankenstein guy?" Sully tugs at his thick, boxy black costume.

"Just be happy T. J. didn't assign you the role of grandmama," Lola teases.

T. J. tosses his head back and cackles. "Aw, man. I should have." He points across the room. "There's Mom!" Without hesitation, he rushes toward Sloane, who has her hair in braids like Wednesday Addams.

"Even she got to pick the character she wanted." Sully sags beside me.

"Cheer up, mate." I elbow him. "Aren't you trying to win over your wife?"

"Not sure it's possible in this." He plucks at the rough fabric of his robe, and with another beleaguered sigh, he follows after T. J.

It's been two weeks since Lola and I officially started dating—and two weeks since we defiled Brian's office—and I intend to celebrate tonight *after* the Halloween party.

Not in Brian's office though because the way he looked at both of us for the entirety of last week, like he was trying to figure out *how* we made such a mess, has me wanting to keep Lola all to myself.

Lola comes over for dinner most nights and insists on cooking quite often, which we're all bloody grateful for. Her healthy, gluten-free meals are loads better than anything Brian makes. After we read a little more of Murphy's book to him each night, and he drifts off, I drive her home and spend a little time alone with her. It takes bloody discipline to tear myself away from her night after night, but I never want Murphy to wake up and find that I'm gone.

Not that he has ever woken up calling for me. Regardless, I'm not taking any chances.

When a kid calls his name, Murphy lights up. "Can I go say hi? That's Jase."

"Of course. Yes. Right. Go."

My heart clenches at the sight of my boy chatting with a friend. And when a whole group of children in costumes surround him, talking a mile a minute, making him laugh and smile, my eyes get hot.

I blink back the sting of tears. He's got friends. And people.

Lola slips her hand into mine and squeezes. "You look tired."

She pushes back my hair—temporarily sprayed a deep black for my role as Gomez Addams—then runs her fingers down my cheeks.

I sink into her touch. "Just emotional is all."

It's the truth, though, she's right, I'm knackered. Murph and I have to be out the door by six thirty to make it to school on time, and my need for time with Lola alone means I'm not getting to bed until after midnight.

I can't tell her that, though. If I do, she'll insist I stay home rather than spending my nights with her. I'm unwilling to even entertain that thought. I like having her around. I wish she were around all the time.

My fish looked almost as done in as me this morning. He wasn't even swimming, just hanging out upside down like moving his fins was too much work. I worried something was wrong, but my fears were assuaged when I checked on him after work and he was bright and chipper. He must have snagged a nap this afternoon. A few hours of sleep and he looked like a new fish. His color is even brighter. I could have sworn he was more blue, but today, his scales have taken on a teal hue.

Who knew I'd be so good at taking care of plants and fish? It's a good thing, since Murphy's case still hasn't been closed. I need all the evidence I can muster to prove I can care for him.

"You're a good dad, Cal." Lola watches me, those green eyes full of honesty. It's the sweetest compliment I've ever received.

"If the two of you are done mauling one another with your eyes," Sloane approaches, thumbing over her shoulder, "the party is in there."

My sister-in-law looks far more weary than I do. She also looks pissed, though that's to be expected when dealing with Sully. The glare she directs at him does throw me for a loop, though. I thought they were turning a corner.

I suppose it was wishful thinking on my part.

The door on the other side of the lobby is closed, though every time it's pulled open, loud music thrums and lights flash.

"Ah yes, I do think Mrs. Addams and I would like to get our dance on." I hold out my hand to Lola, and when she slides her fingers into mine, I fall into character and press a kiss to her knuckles, then work my way up her arm.

"Oh my God," Sloane laments. "You two are—"

"Adorable," I offer.

She shakes her head.

"Amazing." Lola breaks into the brightest of smiles.

Sloane rolls her eyes.

Sully grunts, fiddling with the cap on his head again. "Annoying."

Sloane points at him. "Finally, something we can agree on." With a shake of her head, she sighs. "Sorry, I'm being a bitch."

"Yes, you really are," Lola agrees.

Sloane shakes out her hands and bounces on her toes. "Okay, I'm done. Let's go find sugar, maybe that will help." She slips her arm through my doll's and guides her toward the party.

Sully and I follow, because we're nothing if not smitten with our girls.

In the UK, Halloween isn't quite so over-the-top. The school's PTO has pulled out all the stops. It's unsurprising, if not cliché, that the PTO would put on such a lavish affair.

In one corner, I spot a film screen, complete with at least two dozen bean bags for the viewers.

"What's the film they're playing over there?"

"Oh, Hocus Pocus," Lola says. "I loved that one."

Sloane nods. "Great movie."

"What's it about?" I slip my hands in the pockets of my trousers and watch the scene playing out. The characters are at a party that looks a lot like this one, the lot of them dancing. I happen to like the music they're playing better than what we've got on in here.

Lola shrugs. "There are three witches, and it all starts a hundred years or so ago, when they're hanged for killing a child."

Sully lets out a garbled curse. "That's not appropriate for children."

"It's a Disney movie." Sloane waves a dismissive hand.

Hmm. Then these women must be butchering the storyline. "Go on."

"But they cast a spell. If a virgin lights their magic candle, they'll come back to life."

"A what?" I suck in a breath, clutching my chest, and scan the crowd for Murphy. Thank fuck he's across the room running in circles with his friends instead of listening to this shite or watching this abomination of a film.

"Don't be such a prude." Lola sticks her tongue out at me.

"You said it's a Disney film." Sully's normally surly demeanor is only intensified by the dark circles painted around his eyes.

Sloane sighs. "It is."

"What happens after the witches are killed?" I ask. Surely the witches' curse is reversed by a magical prince who blows rainbows out of his arse or some other nonsense.

"In present-day Salem, a virgin lights their candle. The witches return, but the only way they can stay alive is to suck out the souls of children."

I stumble back, appalled, though Lola doesn't notice.

"Right now," she goes on, smiling at the film screen, "the witches are singing to put a spell on all the parents at the party. Once they've put them all to sleep, they'll go fly and try to take the lives of all their children."

"That's abhorrent." I straighten and scan the people around us. "Excuse me, who here is in charge of this film?"

Lola clutches the lapels of my pinstripe suit jacket and tugs me closer. "What are you doing?"

"The film must be turned off. These kids will have nightmares."

Head tilted and lips twitching, Lola points at the children who are all smiling, as if they themselves are entranced by the singing evil witches. One of them is even clapping along. "Do they look like they'll have nightmares?"

I straighten the knot of my tie, frowning down at her. "*I'm* going to have nightmares."

Lola nuzzles into my side. "I'll keep you safe from the evil witches, I promise."

"Cal!" Murphy barrels for me, his tone urgent.

Panic-stricken, I drop to my knees and inspect him, looking for injury. "What's wrong?"

With the biggest grin I think he's ever worn, he shakes his head. "They're doing a father-son relay race, will you do it with me?"

My heart stutters to a stop, then takes off at a run, pounding loud enough to drown out the tune of *Monster Mash.*

"You want me to do it with you?" I point to my chest, then look over my shoulder to be sure he isn't speaking to someone else.

Murphy nods, his expression sobering. "Unless you don't want to."

"Oh, I so totally want to." I yank him to my chest and press my lips to the top of his head.

The little bugger leans into me, I swear, and I tip back. Before I can land on my arse, I catch myself, my smile so wide my cheeks ache. Because my boy just asked me to do a father-son relay race with him. He may not call me dad, but this might be the best moment of my life.

"I can't believe we didn't win," Murphy grumbles as we walk out of the party.

"I can't believe my hair color came out in the bucket." I wipe my face with a paper towel to keep the dye from further staining my skin.

When I wiped at my face after I dunked my head in the bucket of water and my hand came away covered in black streaks, I nearly screamed.

Lola laughed so hard she might have peed herself and declared me Zombie Gomez.

Sully pulls off his bald cap and shakes out his hair. "Perks of being Uncle Fester, I guess." He holds out a fist to T. J., who bumps it.

Yes, the sod and his spawn beat us. Even Sloaney was screaming wildly for them in the end. Though when the award was handed out, and T. J. tried to bring her up to accept the schlocky little trophy, she waved him off, and as they stepped off the stage after, she slipped out.

"I'm just glad we got to play." I ruffle Murphy's hair.

Head tilted back, he gives me one of his half smiles. "I've never been to a family event at school before."

On my other side, Lola hums. "Me neither."

Grinning, I loop an arm around Lola's waist and squeeze Murphy's. "You know," I say as I guide them to the car, "Madame E said the weirdest thing to me as we were leaving tonight."

Sully glowers at me. He still doesn't believe in her magic. It's a pity, really. Bet she could give him help winning Sloaney back.

"What did she say?" Lola asks cautiously.

"She said she saw two ears and purring in my future."

"Bloody hell," Sully grumbles. "You are not getting a cat."

Laughing, I snap my fingers. "Oh, that's what she meant. I thought maybe you wouldn't show up dressed as Mrs. Addams, Lola Caruso."

She rolls her eyes but snuggles in closer. "I told you I would."

Murphy blinks up at me. "Are you for real?"

Chin tucked, I arch a brow at him. "What?"

"You really didn't know she meant cat?"

I shrug.

"I like kittens," Lola says softly.

Murphy nods. "Kittens are cool."

Hmm, they both like kittens.

My brother curses under his breath. "You're not getting a cat."

I smile. He's right. I'm not getting *a* cat. I'm getting the *best* cat ever.

CHAPTER 37
Lola

"I hung up on him."

Brian blinks. Twice. "I'm sorry, you what?"

I don't know why he's surprised. This asshole isn't the first client I've hung up on during my time at the firm.

"Lo?"

Shoulders pulled back, I force my jaw to relax. I wasted an hour on the phone attempting to sort out which of our client's answers to the lifestyle interrogatories were the truth and which were full-out lies. I'm over it.

"I warned him. Told him that if he lied again, I'd hang up."

With both hands thrown up, Brian rocks back in his chair. "All our clients lie to us, Lo. It's practically a rule. Lie to your fucking attorney. And then expect them to magically fix all your fuck ups."

I frown at him. I suppose it's true in some sense. In our line of work, we see people at their absolute worst. In most other types of law, in a courtroom with an attorney, people are on their best behavior. But when it comes to divorce? The worst parts of them shine. Especially in custody battles like Brian takes on. Every misstep they've taken, every mistake, every poor choice, ends up on the pages of the filings. I don't envy the invasion of privacy they're put through when I sift through years of personal messages and ask questions that in any other situation would be none of my business, so I tend to brush off flippant comments they make about their exes and what they'd do to them if they could get away with it. But I can't do my job without information. *Honest information.*

"The guy lied about going to college. *Why?*"

A harsh chuckle slips past his lips. "Charlie does play fast and loose with the truth. "

I give him a deadpan look. "Charlie is a compulsive liar."

"But he's so nice about it. It's hard to hate him," he says. "The guy just smiles and shrugs and says, '*well, that's not exactly the truth.*'" Brian's impression is terrifyingly good.

"You may like him, but I don't," I mutter.

The guy is a piece of work. And his custody issues are of his own making. He and his wife convinced a doctor to diagnose him with schizophrenia so the state would pay for childcare for their youngest son. It worked out well, but only until the wife filed for divorce and used Charlie's *mental instability* as grounds for seeking full custody.

"I made it clear that he can call back when he's ready to give me some honest answers to the hundred and eighty discovery questions we need to turn over to opposing counsel by next week."

"I should probably ask for an extension." He leans forward and wiggles his mouse, waking his computer.

"I was thinking a substitution of attorney."

Smirking, he shakes his head. "I'd say Cal's drama was rubbing off on you but you two have always been neck and neck when it comes to the battle for the title of most dramatic."

I stick my tongue out at him.

"*Lola.*" The two syllables, sung so sweetly, that used to grate on my last nerve, now have the tension easing from my shoulders. "I have a surprise."

"Oh, fuck me." Brian slaps a hand to his face.

I peer over my shoulder, and my heart lurches. I whip around and take a step back. "Holy shit Cal is that a tiger?"

The feline looks nothing like a tiger, really. It's fluffy and dark gray, and its almost white mane makes it look like a lion. But the bright yellow eyes scream tiger.

"What is that?" Brian pushes to his feet, sending his chair rolling back.

"It's Fuzzy Wuzzy." He runs a hand down the beast's back. "Our new Maine coon."

"It-it's huge," I stutter. Lump in my throat, I can't look away from the cat's piercing yellow eyes. They hover near Cal's waist even though all four of its enormous paws are planted firmly on the ugly gold carpet.

The feline tips its head, focusing those yellow eyes on my boss, its tongue flicking out, whiskers twitching.

"Is it safe?" Voice cracking, Brian takes another step back.

"He's amazing. And I talked the guy down to five grand. That's a steal for one of these gentle giants of the cat world," Cal gushes. "Don't you love him, Lola?"

I open my mouth but words don't come out.

"You always wanted a cat."

"Kitten," I correct numbly. Dammit. My budget might have room for replacement plants and cheap fish, but there's no way I can afford to replace this thing.

Brian makes a strangled sound. "Damn it, you did not spend five k on that awful beast."

Cal covers the massive creature's ears, thankfully not letting go of its—*his*—leash. "Shh. You'll hurt his feelings. You know as well as I do that you can't put a price on happiness."

Brian rubs his eyes roughly with the heels of his hands, looking disheveled when he pulls them away. "Happiness?"

I rub at my sternum. "I'm not sure this feeling in my chest is one of happiness."

Cal breaks into one of his devastating smiles. "Shhh, Lola, you'll ruin it." He releases the cat's ears and tugs on the leash. "Come on Fuzzy Wuzzy, I'll show you your new place."

For a solid minute, Brian and I stare silently at the empty doorway. When the floor creaks above us, I snap into action and stomp into Sully's office.

"Did you know?" I snap.

Sully looks up from his phone, frowning. "Know?"

I fight the urge to slap a hand over my face. Did this man seriously not notice when his brother paraded a zoo animal through the office? Sloane has always complained about how oblivious he is, but there's no way he missed the massive cat.

"Yes." I cross my arms and huff out a breath. "Did Cal tell you what he was doing?"

"Bloody hell." Sully slumps in his chair. "What grand plan has the wanker come up with now?"

I scowl, suddenly hit with the urge to defend my guy against the insult. It dies quickly, though, when I remember the price of his new pet.

"Your brother bought a five-thousand-dollar cat," Brian explains from the doorway.

"A cat that's the size of a small horse," I add.

Sully's brows knit together in confusion. "Okay." He draws out the word.

"Not okay," I snap. "I can't afford to spend thousands of dollars on replacing a cat." I pace in front of his desk. "I have no idea how to bury a body. Yeah, I can flush the small ones, and I've tossed a few small flora corpses into the dumpster. But a human-size cat?" I stop and whirl on Sully. "How do I make that disappear without a trace?"

"There is a lot to unpack in that statement, Lo." He rolls his lips and looks over my head at Brian.

"She's talking about dead fish and house plants. Not people," Brian clarifies. "She's been covering up all the animal and...what'd you call it?" He arches a brow at me. "Flora? Deaths Cal is responsible for."

My heart sinks. "He can't know."

Sighing, Sully runs his hand over his face. "I'm gonna regret asking this, but, *why?*"

"I have no idea." Brian props a shoulder against the doorframe.

"Idiots." Eyes closed, I pinch the bridge of my nose. "Cal thinks that taking care of plants and animals will help him learn how to be what Murphy needs. He's using them to convince himself that he can be a good dad. So they can't die. Because he is a good—*no* he's a *great* —dad." I ball my hands into fists. "The three of us will make sure he knows that. So this cat will not die."

I jab a finger at Brian. "You will walk it every day." I spin back to Sully. "You will feed it. And you'll both take care of the litter box."

"Fuck." Brian shakes his head. "The litter box has got to be the size of a sandbox."

"Probably. The thing is massive."

Sully scoffs. "It can't be that big." He stands and rounds his desk. "Where is it?"

Brian tips his chin to the ceiling and Sully pushes past us, headed for the stairs at the back of the office. Silently we tramp up the steps, one after another.

At the top, Sully pushes the door open and immediately stumbles back. "Fuck me."

I skirt around him just in time to see Fuzzy Wuzzy pounce on Cal, who's sprawled out on the floor. The cat's massive paws span the width of his chest, his claws long enough to shred the Oxford beneath them with one swipe.

"Where is Cal?" Brian steps into the room behind me.

"Under the monster." Sully's face is still a mask of shock, but his voice is subdued, as if he's worried he'll anger the beast if he's too loud.

"Good one, Fuzzy. You got me." Cal lifts his head and grins at us. "See how good Fuzzy Wuzzy is at this game. I knew he'd be the best cat ever."

The huge cat stalks away, then quickly pounces again.

Cal grunts on impact. Maybe the cat really is playing, but that doesn't stop my heart from lurching at the sight.

Sully turns to Brian. "What the fuck did he do?"

I pull my eyes off my boyfriend and his new pet and back toward the stairs. "I can't take any more of this fun game. Remember your jobs." With that, I spin on my heel and dart back to the office. I've dealt with enough chaos already this week.

CHAPTER 38
Lola

The sound of the front door shutting is followed by a familiar jingle.

"Fuzzy Wuzzy's back." Amy announces like we aren't all painfully familiar with the tingle of the bell on his collar. "It was sooo smart of you to give his collar a sound so he doesn't scare anyone."

"Yeah." I nod, lips pressed together to keep from laughing. Or crying. I'm not sure which. "Brian says people stop staring as soon as they hear the bells."

"Right." Amy nods, completely missing the snark in my tone.

"Damnit. This way." Brian hisses down the hall. "No, not my office."

Fuzzy drags Brian past the conference room door.

"Dammit."

"Stop saying that." Cal jumps out of his chair and chases the two down the hallway. "Fuzzy is getting confused about his name."

I don't even try to hold back my laughter. The cat has been here a week, and he does seem to be answering better to Dammit than to Fuzzy.

The shabby puke-green sofa in Brian's office—the one he wanted to have hauled away—has become Fuzzy's favorite lounger. As much as my boss hates it, the cat is attached to him.

"He wouldn't follow me in here." Cal reappears, shoulders slumped. "Still likes Uncle Brian best."

"You have Murphy, and Sully has T. J.," Amy says. "I think he knows that. And he can probably sense how lonely Brian is."

I close my eyes and focus on breathing steadily. I just can't with her.

"Cal," I say. "Fuzzy plays with you all the time."

"That is true. And"—hands on his hips, he turns in a full circle—"we don't have a sofa in here." He eases into his chair. "Maybe we should change that." Under the table, he glides his foot up my calf. "Sofas are more comfortable than tables, wouldn't you agree?"

He waggles his brow.

Eyes wide, I make a show of frowning and glancing at Amy. We are at work. I've drawn lines, but Cal is determined to obliterate them all.

"Ames, go see what Sully needs," he suggests.

"Why? Are you two going to have sex again?" She pushes to her feet and sighs. "If so, just don't do it in Brian's office. He's still complaining about that."

Cal chuckles and my face heats.

As soon as we're alone, I lunge forward in my chair. "I can't believe you told him."

Cal grins. "He asked, I couldn't lie."

"Yes," I grit out, "you could."

"Okay, Lola," he says, his tone placating. "Next time I will lie for you."

"No next time," I grumble at my computer screen.

At a featherlight brush along my neck, I startle, covering my mouth to stifle a shriek. The sneaky bastard is suddenly right behind me, hovering close.

He drags his lips along my neck, and despite my best effort not to react, goose bumps pepper my skin.

"Oh, there will be many, many more next times." His low whisper makes my stomach dip.

"We are working, Mr. Murphy," I remind him, my tone far too breathy for my liking.

"Ooo, I love it when you get all formal." He nips at my collar.

"Really. I have a lot to do today. *Too much.*" Though I fervently fight the desire coiling in my core, a whimper slips from my lips.

"Give me fifteen minutes, then we'll both put our noses to the grindstone for the rest of the day," he promises.

A thrill flows through me, but before I can give in, the front door opens and slams shut again.

"Hellooo!"

My body goes rigid at the sound of the far too familiar voice.

I yank back from Cal. "What is my mother doing here?"

He frowns at me, his expression one of genuine confusion.

"Anyone here?" My father calls.

Panic pulls my heart right into my throat. "Both of them?"

Maybe I'm overreacting. My parents aren't awful people. Not at all. It's just that they don't share the respect I have for responsibility and planning ahead.

They just go where the wind takes them, oblivious to the havoc they cause when they disrupt schedules and organized lives.

"You okay?" Cal assesses me, his brow knitted in concern.

"Fine." Resigned, I stand, smooth my skirt, and head to the front entrance.

"Lola!" My mom, who's talking to Amy, rushes to me. She throws her arms around me, her long blonde hair covering my face as she rocks from side to side with the exuberance she possesses at all times and for every occasion.

"Hi, Mom," I mutter when she finally releases me.

"Buttercup." My dad's hug is next. Rather than rock, he lifts me off the ground and arches back, causing his leather jacket to crinkle oddly between us. "How is my girl?"

"Ready to be put down," I tell him.

He laughs in response, easing me to my feet.

They are a pair. My mother is dressed in ripped jeans, with some type of lacy shirt thing under her denim jacket. My father is decked out in head-to-toe leather. And they wear matching bulky black boots. It's a relatively new look. When I was a kid, they were more hippie than biker. Though they went through a goth stage during my teen years. In my experience, it's the kid who typically goes through that kind of phase. Not in my house. In my house, I was the stability.

Two years ago, they discovered a passion for motorcycles. And when they find a passion, they go all in. At least until a new passion comes along.

"What are you doing here?" The moment the question is out, I wince. It sounded more like an accusation than I meant for it to.

"We're meeting some friends nearby. Then we're headed up the coast to see the leaves." My father shrugs, as if he couldn't care less about the leaves; he's just happy to ride.

"Leaf peeping," my mother corrects. "We're going leaf peeping in Vermont."

I dip my chin. That kind of thing is right up their alley. But... "So you're here because..." I let the sentence trail off.

"When we realized we'd ride past your new office, we thought we'd come by for the day."

My stomach sinks. "The day?"

"Of course," my mother chirps. "We want to see our daughter."

"But I'm working." And they didn't call. Or text. Or send a carrier pigeon so I could plan ahead.

"Oh pish." My mother waves a hand. "Surely you can take the rest of the day off."

This has always been the problem. Careers and commitments mean little to them. And they've never understood my drive or dedication to my responsibilities.

"Dezi, June." Cal steps out of the conference room, his gait easy, relaxed, like it always is. He shakes my father's hand and kisses my mother's cheek. "What a lovely surprise."

"Every word sounds better in that accent of yours, Cal," my mother gushes.

"Yes, everyone loves the accent," I agree, voice flat. "But as great as it is to see you," I lie, "I really need to work."

"Surely the guys can spare you for a day." My dad turns to Cal. "Can't you?"

Desperately, I eye him, silently telegraphing how badly I don't want to be spared.

"Actually," he says without looking my way.

Shit.

"It just so happens that I've got a set of tickets you might find appealing." He pulls a folded piece of paper from his pocket. "There is a ghost tour up the Hudson today."

My mother's face lights up. "Oh, I've always wanted to meet a ghost."

"It's on our bucket list," my father agrees.

"Brilliant. I've got three tickets here."

"Three?" I squeak.

"Oh, hear that buttercup, you can come!" My dad smacks Cals back. "Good man."

He chokes out an uncomfortable laugh. "I-uh-actually, Lola can't go today, but there are three tickets for a reason."

My heart skips. Is this man seriously planning to go in my place? It's a ridiculously kind gesture, but if the three of them spend the day together, they'd probably end up in Timbuktu because it sounds like an adventure.

"We have this ghost," he says. "And I think you'll love him."

I groan.

"Ghost?" Mom side-eyes me, her lips quirking. "You didn't tell me you had a ghost, Lola. How exciting."

"His name's Sebastian and he's a biker. I thought he might be interested in tagging along on your riding tour."

"Well, isn't this a fun turn of events, June," my dad booms.

Mom nods, beaming at Cal, and I breathe out a sigh

"Are you sure you kids don't want to come?"

"Sadly, these were the last three tickets available." Cal shrugs. "But Fuzzy and I will walk you out." He whistles, as if the cat will actually respond.

When he doesn't, I pick up the box of cat treats we keep stashed out here and give it a shake. Five seconds later, the huge creature appears.

"Oh my!" my mother squeaks. "What a beautiful cat. Lola always wanted a cat, you know?"

Hands in his pockets, Cal nods. "That's why I got her the best cat ever."

"This is your cat?" My dad cocks a brow in my direction.

I shrug. Honestly, I don't know anymore. I hound Sully daily ensuring that he feeds Fuzzy, and I remind Brian to walk him every couple of hours. And I make sure he doesn't get out. Though I delegated the cleaning of the litter box to the guys, the task has fallen to me, so I guess, yeah, it's my cat.

My mom drops to her knees, and the cat slinks over, rubbing his head against her cheek.

"What a good boy," my mom coos.

"He does tricks too." Cal stands a little taller. "Let me grab his leash and our ball and we can show you how we play volleyball in the car park."

My mom chatters animatedly, and as they head out, my dad turns back. "We'll swing back later and grab you for dinner, Lola."

Once they're gone, I shuffle back to my desk and drop into my chair with a sigh. That may have been the easiest encounter with my parents in my entire adult life. With a cleansing breath, I turn back to the computer and continue on the certification I need to get to our client before lunch.

"Dammit," Brian curses several minutes later.

"Stop calling him that," Cal says over his shoulder as he appears at the door. Stepping into the room, he shoves his hands into his pockets. "You mad at me?"

I shake my head. "I feel like I should call you my hero. I've never gotten rid of my parents that quickly. Normally when they show up, they bulldoze my day."

He props himself up against the table beside me. "You said you wanted to work today, and what Lola wants..."

I grab his tie and pull him in. When our lips meet, I sigh into his mouth. "Thank you."

"Anything." The single word is a promise.

"I don't suppose you can get me out of dinner too?"

"Not likely." He pecks my lips and pulls back. "But if you don't mind Murphy coming along, we could join you?"

It's tempting, but Murphy will probably be bored out of his mind.

"The guys won't be home tonight?"

"Sully has a meeting with T. J.'s therapist in the city, and Brian has dinner with the Berkshires."

I sigh. I hate the idea of dragging Murphy out, but I can't deny that I'd love their company. "If Murphy's okay with it, then I'd love it if you came."

He gives me a devastating smile before uttering his favorite sentence. "Whatever Lola wants." As the words work their way through me, wrapping firmly around my heart, I find my eyes pricking with tears and my nose stinging.

CHAPTER 39
Cal

I storm into Brian's office, interrupting some phone conference, and nod toward Sully's. "Partner's meeting, now."

I think Brian must sense my pending breakdown because he quickly gets off the phone and slides his chair back. "What's wrong?"

I shake my head not wanting to say anything until we're behind closed doors. Only once we're in Sully's office and the door is shut do I speak freely. "Lola's parents are here."

Brian's eyes dart from me to the door. "And you're hiding because?"

"For fuck's sake I was on with Langfield," my brother mutters, glancing down at the phone he's just hung up.

I press my hands into my knees and try to suck in a breath. I think I might actually be hyperventilating.

"Woah, what's happening?" I hear Brian say. Though the words sound far away as this buzzing sounds loudly in my ears.

"Water," I mumble, grasping at my throat.

"*Shit.*" My brother jumps up and shoves a bottle in my face. I glance at it but finally grab it when I realize it's a fresh one. My hands shake as I tip it back and guzzle it down.

"Shit what?" Brian asks. "Oh fuck, did you already do something to hurt her. I warned you."

Sully chuckles and holds up a hand. "Back off man, this is not that."

"Would someone please tell me what it is then?"

With my tongue in my cheek, I drop my head back and try to relax.

"He's never met a girl's parents before," Sully says, sounding amused.

"Really?" Brian glances at me like this is unbelievable.

"I don't date. I don't—" I fling my arms out wildly. "Do this."

"Okay." The word comes out of Brian's mouth slowly and completely full of judgment.

"It isn't a girl," I tell them both. "It's Lola. She's *the* girl and she invited my son and me to have dinner with her parents."

Brian's eyes widen. "Wait, really? That doesn't seem like Lola. She—" He shakes his head realizing exactly what I did. "Holy shit, you're the guy."

I nod pathetically because yes, I'm *the* guy. Somehow, some fucking way, I got this girl, the one who pushes everyone away, the one who pushed *me* away, to not only agree to be my girlfriend but to turn to me for comfort even when her parents are around. To invite us to dinner. It's not something to be taken lightly. Sure, some people might do those things willy-nilly, but not Lola.

"So, what do I do?"

Sully shrugs, his hands falling to his pockets, as he leans against his desk and studies me. "What do you do about what? You go to dinner. You charm them just like you charm everyone. If anyone can do this, it's you."

Brian nods. "I gotta be honest, this does seem like your forte. I'm not sure what you're worried about. Besides, her parents are easygoing. They've always liked you."

I grind my teeth. That doesn't seem good enough. I want everything to go perfectly.

Sully pushes off his desk and pats me on the back. "You've got this. Hey, even Sloane's parents loved me. You've got this in the bag."

"Too bad Sloane hates her parents. Lot of good that did you."

Sully slumps back against his desk. "I've got no idea what will help anymore. She's shut me out completely it seems."

My swallow is heavy. I don't like that. I don't like that at all. But I can only deal with one family disaster at a time. And right now, my only focus is on making sure Lola has a good time tonight, making sure her family treats her well, and somehow keeping my cool as I do it. I can figure out Sully's problems later.

—

"I really appreciate you doing this," Lola says to Murphy. We're seated at dinner, waiting for her parents to arrive because, of course, they're late.

Murphy shrugs. "Cal said I can order whatever I want and since you haven't stopped talking about the steak in this place, I think I'm going with the big one." He nods toward the platter of steak in the glass case which is right by our table. I made reservations at Berns since Lola and I never did make it back here in person, and because I figured she could use some gluten-free yeast as she likes to call it. My girlfriend's a weird one sometimes. Also, I think this place is appropriate to meet the parents—if they ever actually show up.

"Not even a big steak is worth what my parents put me through," Lola mutters under her breath. Then she looks at Murphy trying to explain herself. "They just aren't exactly like me. They're kind of a lot."

Murphy, the devil he is, smirks and God does he make me proud in the way he looks just like me in this moment. Then he points toward me. "Mine too."

The loud, surprised laugh that comes out of Lola's mouth is the sweetest sound. As is this feeling in my chest over the way the two of them banter back and forth. The way they both tease me. And the way he just referred to me as his parent again. Sure, I'm still Cal, but we're getting there. One day at a time.

Tonight, Lola's hair is down. She's been wearing it more and more like that and I just love it so much. Not because she needed to change, but she just seems happier now. And those damn freckles are dazzling me under the perfectly dim brightness provided by the lamp above us.

Fuck, I'm just obsessed with her.

"Oh dear, I'm so sorry we're late," I hear her mother say from behind us.

I glance at Lola and mouth *you've got this* and wait for her to smile before I stand up. Then I turn and offer my most charming smile to her mother. "You are perfectly on time, June."

Lola's mother, who looks strikingly similar to Lola, but aged from both the sun and lots of laughter it would seem, beams the moment she sees me. "Cal, I didn't know you'd be joining us."

I reach out and greet both her and her husband—who's about two heads shorter than me and currently wearing a leather jacket and the same dark jeans he had on earlier.

Lola comes around to greet her parents as well and then she motions for Murphy to join her. "And this is Cal's son, Murphy."

Murphy holds out his hand like he's a little adult and I almost have to glance away because the pride in my chest is bursting. He's so damn impressive this son of mine. I still don't like that he even knows to act this way, that he's so grown up at the ripe age of six, but I've come to realize that's just who he is and I'm going to embrace it. "It's a pleasure to meet you," he says.

June nudges her husband's arm as she takes Murphy's hand. "You hear that, it's a pleasure to meet us." She looks at Lola and then turns to me, her smile growing. "Wait, are the two of you dating?"

I'm not sure what Lola will say so I allow her to handle this. When she slips her arm around my waist and settles her head on my chest, I just about die on the spot. "Yes. Why don't we order dinner and you can tell us about the tour today," Lola says, reaching for

Murphy now. He takes her hand and they return to their spots at the table.

Not a single one of us can take our eyes off them. Her parents and I all seem enamored by that simple moment. "You're good for her," June says out the side of her mouth as she continues to watch Lola. I pull out June's chair and wait for her to sit, then take the spot between Lola and her mother. Murphy is next to Dezi. We're like her little protectors, keeping Lola sane for the evening. "She's even wearing her hair down. She looks so relaxed." She shakes her head and sighs. "We never quite could get her to loosen up but it looks like you were just what she needed."

Lola is going over the menu with Murphy so she doesn't hear her mother's comments but I feel it's important to address them just the same. "She's good for me. I think she's what we all need. A little way to balance all our chaos, no?"

Dezi chuckles as he leans across his wife. "I wouldn't know, we don't balance one another at all, we just go where the wind blows us. But you may be right. You do also look happy. Keep our baby girl smiling and relaxed like that and we'll all be a little more balanced, yeah?"

Lola huffs. "What are you guys talking about over there? Don't go bartering me for a cow or something, Dad."

Murphy giggles and I wink at her. "Certainly not, you're definitely worth more than a cow, Lola. Perhaps a tiger and some fish."

She rolls her eyes but she's smiling. And fuck does she look pretty when she does that. Her parents aren't wrong. I think I am good for Lola. I think the three of us, Murphy, Lola, and I, are good for one another.

CHAPTER 40
Lola

In what would shock absolutely no one, Cal wooed my parents easily. His patience as they told ghost stories was beyond impressive, and both my mom and my dad were enamored with Murphy.

At the end of the night, my mom swore Murphy reminded her of me when I was his age.

I get it. Though, I'd hope it's not because at only six, even when surrounded by adults, he seemed like the responsible party. It's my greatest hope that Murphy will never have to feel that way again. Not with Cal in his corner.

"Can you read to me tonight, Lola?" Murphy asks as he pads out of his bathroom, already dressed in his PJs.

Warmth blossoms in my chest. "I wouldn't miss it for the world. I can't wait to find out more about the flying shoes."

Murphy's blue eyes sparkle. "Me too."

"Flying shoes?" Cal straightens, leaning forward.

"Yeah. If you put them on your feet, you can soar." Murphy throws his arms out and zooms around the room.

A low chuckle rumbles out of Cal. "That sounds awesome."

"Yeah," the little boy shrugs, "but only Hermes' kid gets to wear them."

Cal's eyes narrow. "Is he the god of thieves?"

"Travelers," I say.

"Both," Murphy corrects, standing a little taller.

"Come on, then, my little traveler, let's get in bed." I drape an arm over his shoulder.

"Wait." He slips out of my hold and darts for Cal. When he throws his arms around him, Cal's eyes go wide. "Goodnight. Even if you can't give me flying shoes, you're a pretty cool dad."

Cal squeezes him tight, blinking rapidly.

My throat tightens, and my own tears threaten as I witness this moment between them. It couldn't have been easy coming into his son's life the way he did, but Cal is excelling at parenthood in every way.

"Let's go." Murphy releases his dad and rushes past me.

Once he's under the covers and I've settled beside him with *The Lightning Thief* in hand, he sighs heavily.

My chest tightens at the sudden sadness wafting off him. "Everything okay?"

"Can I ask you something?"

"Always," I assure him closing the book. "What's up?"

Blue eyes so much like Cal's lower, his focus drifting to the bed, his fingers idly picking at the comforter. "Has my mom called or texted or anything?"

The question guts me. This boy has been here for months, and he hasn't once spoken to the one person he should be able to count on.

I'm almost positive the answer is no, but I can't say for sure, so with an arm around him, I pull him close. "I'd have to ask Cal, but he hasn't said she has."

His little body slumps against mine, cracking my heart in two.

"Even if she hasn't called, that doesn't mean that she doesn't care," I assure him. "My parents love to travel, and when they're gone, they'd love it if I was with them. But like you have to go to school, I have to work. That doesn't mean we don't miss them though."

"I do miss her," he whispers, head tipped back and eyes fierce. "But I like it here."

"We like having you here," I promise him. "I'm sure your mom liked having you with her too. People show love in all kinds of ways. It may not always make sense, but usually, they love us the best they can. That might mean that certain people are ones we have fun with, while others are the ones we can rely on. You know what I mean?"

Murphy studies me, lips turned down. His expression far too knowing for such a young soul.

Two months ago, I never could have imagined saying this, but the words come easy now. "Cal will always be here for you. I can promise that. He may be a total goofball, but he wants to be more than just your fun dad, he wants to be the person you can rely on. Don't discount that." I swallow past the lump in my throat. "I think that by leaving you with your dad, your mom did what's best for you. She knew that this way, you could go to school and that you'd have someone who loves you nearby all the time."

He nods. "Do you think it will hurt Cal's feelings if I tell him I miss her?" His eyes mist over. "If I want to see her when she comes back?"

I shake my head resolutely. "He would never be upset." I hug him tighter to my side. "Cal's got a big heart. He'd never be mad that you inherited that from him. You're free to love whoever you want to love."

CHAPTER 41

Cal

Bollocks. This is bad. So very bad. If I thought earlier I was having a breakdown, it had nothing on this.

I tug at my hair as I pace my bedroom, my heart pounding a feverish rhythm in my chest. I knew I was falling for Lola. These feelings have grown deeper by the day. But tonight? Watching the way she tended to Murphy, how she included him in conversation with her parents? It blew me away. Every part of tonight felt so damn natural. So damn right. Like we're already family. It's all too damn much.

She comforts him when he needs it, makes him laugh when that expression of his gets too serious. Hell, he seeks her out night after night, unafraid to ask her to read to him and tuck him in.

As devastated as I am that I've missed so much of his life already, the way he gravitates toward her doesn't upset me in the least. I'll give him whatever makes him happy if it's in my power. And I understand why she's what lights him up. I just—*fuck*, what if her feelings for me don't match this intensity?

I'm falling in love with this woman. Scratch that. I'm already there. My heart is hers. I'm a pile of mush. Splat on the pavement outside this Jersey flat, desperate for her to reach down and help me up but terrified that she'll walk right on past, eager to get back to New York City.

All I know for certain is that she hasn't fallen with me. And I can't blame her. The sex may be bloody out of this world, but outside that, all I do is make more work for her.

Okay, I make her smile too. I suppose I've got that working in my favor, but it doesn't even come close to comparing to the way she makes me feel. For the first time in my life, I feel like I'm actually living. My heart beats out a steady rhythm when she's around and when she's not, this is what happens. I pace, pulling at my hair, my pulse erratic and my mind spinning out. Because any second now, she'll wise up and drop me like the lousy sack of potatoes I am.

"Cal?"

Jumping a foot off the ground, I let out an embarrassingly high-pitched shriek and whip around, arms flailing.

Lola's eyes are wide, her teeth sunk into her lip, like she's holding back a laugh.

I suck in a breath. "You scared the bejesus out of me."

Her lips twitch, and as she steps into the room, she breaks into a full-fledged smile. "The bejesus, huh?"

Chest heaving and breaths still coming too fast, I yank her to me and press my forehead to hers. "Yes."

"You seemed very deep in thought so I didn't want to interrupt."

I close my eyes and breathe her in. "How long have you been standing there?"

Pulling back, she smiles up at me, her eyes mischievous. "Long enough to hear you say you're splat on the sidewalk."

Cringing, I release her and tug at my hair again. "What else did I say?"

She shrugs, but by the way her eyes dance, she definitely heard more. "Couldn't make out anything else."

I grunt. "How was Murphy? He asleep?"

With a nod, she grasps my hand and guides me toward the bed. The fucking single bed. How could this perfect creature love a man who lives in a shithole flat with his brother and his best friend, sleeps in a twin-size bed, and has no idea how to raise a child?

I settle onto the edge of the mattress beside her. I'd follow her anywhere.

"Thanks for today," she says softly, taking my hand in hers.

I study her, heart in my damn throat, and croak, "It was nothing."

"That couldn't be farther from the truth. You have no idea how badly the day would have gone if you hadn't sent them on that ghost tour. Dinner with them was bad enough."

Head bowed, I squeeze her hand. "They're just vibrant people."

"Who talk over me and refuse to even try to understand that maybe I enjoy hard work and learning. Everything's fun and games to them."

A pit opens up in my gut. "Just like me."

Straightening, she scoffs. "Not even close."

"Yes, they are. This is exactly what you always disliked about me."

"No." She gives her head a violent shake, though the movement slows quickly. Then, with her eyes shut, she nods once. "Okay, yes." She sighs. "But only because I never allowed myself to see the other parts of you. You were charming and far too gorgeous for my well-being. I chose to focus on the qualities that maybe reminded me of my parents so I could push you far, far away."

I'm like putty in her hands. A melted puddle out on that sidewalk once again.

Does this mean she's now looking for the good? A bloke like me can only hope.

With a hand to my cheek, she says, "But over the last few months, I've seen you. The real you. The kind, generous, funny, intelligent man behind that cheeky smile."

She ducks, her cheeks going pink.

"What you did today is the perfect example of just how incredible you are. You understood immediately that I wanted to work, that I had responsibilities that couldn't be ignored, and you made it all better in your own unique way. They never would have recognized that."

She shifts so she's looking at me, her knee bumping mine. "That's why Brian asks you to help with so many cases. You know that?"

I shake my head, ready to argue.

Before I can, she squeezes my thigh, shutting me up. "He does it because you're good, Cal. Better than he is at handling certain things. You have a way with people. You see an emergency, you notice the way a person is melting down, and you don't hesitate to lighten their load with a joke or a smile, you don't belittle their feelings or reaction. You make the situation manageable."

Maybe it's the way she sees me, or the way she always seems to know just what to say. Or maybe it's just that she's her. Lola. My Lola. I don't know much, but right now, staring at this woman, and listening to her once again put me back together, I know without a doubt that I love her.

I'm *in* love her.

The words almost slip out, too. I'm desperate to tell her.

But maybe she's right. I can see that the admission wouldn't lighten her load. It wouldn't make anything more manageable. So I don't.

"Thank you, Lola, you're that for me, too." I press my lips to the top of her head. "You make everything better."

She blows out a breath, her expression going from soft to pensive. "Can I ask you something that you may not want to talk about?"

My gut twists, but I reply, "Anything."

"Have you heard from Brandy?"

I blink as the words register. That isn't at all what I expected her to bring up. "Murphy's mother?"

She nods.

With a shake of my head, I lean to one side and slide my phone from my pocket. "I've called the number he used the night he tried to contact her a couple of times, but I haven't gotten a response." I open the text thread I started the first day of school. I send pictures and updates every couple of days, but she's yet to reply. "I keep reaching out in the event she is receiving them. Or for when she's back so she can look through."

Lola takes the phone and scrolls, roving over line after line.

"I don't know why she kept him from me or how the bloody hell she could leave him like that, but I'd give anything to have this kind of stuff from the years I missed." I shrug and let out a sigh. "So I give her as much information as I can."

Lola blinks and a single tear lands on the screen. Then another. When she looks up at me her green eyes are glassy, her lips wobbly. "Cal, that's really sweet. And so much more than she deserves."

"You're probably right. But he deserves the best things life has to give. And if he wants a relationship with her, I'll never stand in the way of that."

That thought has been swirling in my head since the day I met Judge Espadrilles in her chamber while Brian tracked down his client last month. Neither parent put that kid's best interest above their own, and I'll be damned if I ever make that mistake.

With a sigh, I angle forward, forearms resting on my knees and fingers laced. "Living with my mum in London meant only spending a week with my father every Christmas and two weeks in the summer. For years, I was certain it was because my father didn't want us. That he cared about the firm more than his sons. That he preferred the arrangement the way it was."

Lola shakes her head. "I can't tell you how many times he told me how badly he regrets not fighting harder to have you here."

I nod, swallowing past the lump that's formed in my throat. "Their divorce was brutal. My mother hated him because he cheated, and I can't blame her one bit for that. My father wasn't a good husband, there's no denying that, but that doesn't mean he didn't deserve the opportunity to be a good father."

Lola rests her head on my shoulder. "Divorce is never easy. No one is always right."

I smile down at my feet. "Except for you."

Chuckling, she pushes off my shoulder. "Right. Of course."

With a long breath out, I straighten again. "As soon as I could, I moved to America for University. Not because I don't love my mum, but because I finally realized that my father wanted to have a relationship with me. She'd been the one putting up roadblocks.

He screwed up plenty, sure, but for most of my childhood, she had us convinced that he cared little for us. She allowed us to believe that the issue was that he refused to move to the UK to be with us."

I rub my hands down the fabric of my trousers. "In reality, she insisted on taking us to the UK after the divorce." I eye Lola. "Sully and I were born here. Did you know that? When we left, our father truly thought that it would be best for us if we stayed with her. But he never stopped caring."

Lola sets the phone down on the bed and squeezes my hand. "Of course he didn't."

Thumb gliding over her smooth skin, I focus on our joined hands. "He was right to set up the trust."

She sucks in a shocked breath, stiffening beside me.

With a shrug, I peer over at her. "We were all fucking up our lives. Sully almost lost Sloane."

"He still might," she points out.

Gut clenching, I shake my head. "He'll get it right this time. It may have taken the man too long to see it, but he knows what matters. He'll figure out how to get through to Sloaney."

Lola gives me a lopsided smile. "You have more faith in either of them than I do."

I turn my body so I'm facing her full-on and tip her chin up. "I have faith in us too. In all of us. We'll figure it out. And honestly? I'm glad we're here in Jersey."

She lets out a surprised scoff, but she's smiling. "Seriously?"

"I wouldn't have known what to do with Murphy if not for Sully and Brian. But especially you. Fuck, Lola, I'd be lost without you. And I hope like hell that my dad would think I'm worthy of you."

Eyes softening, she leans in. "Cal, he was your father. Pretty sure he'd be more concerned about whether I was good enough for his baby boy."

This time I'm the one to scoff. "He adored you. If he hadn't sat me down the week he hired you and told me to stay away, I would have been chasing you years ago."

Her jaw drops, but she doesn't speak, like she's at a loss.

With two fingers, I snap it shut. "I wasn't ready. And I think he knew that."

Lips pressed together, she inhales deeply through her nose and scrutinizes me for a long moment, like she's summoning courage. Eventually, she whispers, "But now you are?"

"Yes, Lola," I lean in close, my lips tickling hers. "I'm ready for whatever comes our way."

She grips my shirt with those tiny fingers of hers and pulls me to her, kissing me fiercely.

Electricity arcs through me as I palm her arse and pull her into my lap.

With a moan, she straddles me and as I focus on the woman of my dreams and the reality that she's *mine*, every thought, every worry, every concern, simply melts away.

"Do you think you can be quiet?" I mumble against her lips, already wanting to rip off her clothes and do ungodly things to her.

Lola shrugs innocently. "I don't know, you might need to figure out a way to keep me quiet." She plays with the tie around my neck, rolling the smooth satin back and forth across my cheek. "Then again, maybe we need to figure out if we can keep you quiet. You're the talker."

I chuckle. "You could just sit on my face and that would do the trick."

She shakes her head and I see the devious glint in her eye. "I've got another idea." She looks around my room. "Do you have any more of these?"

"Ties?" I've got at least a hundred. She knows that, though. The little minx is up to something.

She nods. "Show me where?"

I motion over to the drawer. There's not a ton of space in this room so there aren't too many places they could possibly be. Lola jumps off me and then pauses when she gets to my drawer. "Is it okay if I open this?"

I laugh. It's loud, not quiet at all, and she makes a *tsking* sound. "What's mine is yours, darling. Do with me what you will."

She grins as I settle my hands behind my neck, relaxed. "You're going to regret saying that."

I won't. If I know Lola, she's about to take my previous lessons and blow them out of the water, and I'm going to enjoy every second of it.

My girl is still in her dress from dinner and I'm still in my slacks. As she goes through my drawer, pulling one tie out after another, I admire her curves, anticipating the moment she lets me see every pretty inch of her again. When she finally turns to me, five ties in her hand, each a different shade of blue, my brows dance. "Five huh?"

She nods, her smile wicked. "Need you completely naked for this."

"Only if you are."

She tosses the ties onto the bed and then spins, giving me her back so I can unzip her dress. I sit up and do just that, pressing sweet kisses across her neck as I do. With each one I feel her melt beneath my lips just a bit more, and when she spins, I think just maybe I'll be the one using those ties on her. But as I reach for one, she pushes me back. "Stay."

I chuckle. "Whatever Lola wants."

Patiently, I watch as my girl slips her dress over her hips, revealing another dark green lingerie set. This one has little crystals all across the lace. She's a dazzling present that I get to keep. "I like this," I mumble, dragging the back of my fingers across the swell of her breasts.

She sucks in a breath. "I told you to stay. Now I'm going to have to punish you."

"Fuck." The curse is a raspy whisper. "Do your worst."

Lola smirks. "I plan to." Then she begins to undress me. First my shirt, then my slacks. When she finally slides my boxers down I wait as her breath ghosts down my body, my cock begging for her mouth. But she almost ignores it, reaching for one of her ties first. "I thought this bed was ridiculous for such a big man," she says as she wraps the first tie to the post at the end of the bed. "But now," she turns back to me right as she loops the tie around my ankle. "I realize how perfect it is."

Another curse slips out as I realize what she intends to do with those ties. I stare at the four posts on my bed and my stomach tightens. "You're going to tie me up."

She nods, eyes dilated and hungry. "And then I'm going to have my way with you. So do you think you can be quiet or am I using this last tie on your mouth?"

The entire thing is too hot and for some reason I want her to do it. I want her to control every one of my senses. "You can try," I droll.

She laughs, it's a bit raspy and hellishly sexy. "It would be my pleasure." She leans over me, those tits of hers in my face, and I bite at them as she ties both my hands to the top posts. I'm naked and like a starfish, my cock so hard it's beginning to pulse against my stomach.

Lola licks across my chin to my lips and then moans right before wrapping the last of the satin around my mouth, making it impossible for me to speak. "God, you're hot like this."

With my words stolen, I can do nothing but watch as Lola shimmies her sexy body down my own and then when she settles between my thighs, I groan. Fuck yes, she's going to suck my cock.

She licks across the head and makes the hottest fucking sound when she moans in delight right as she sucks me down her throat. Good girl is what I want to tell her. The fucking best girl ever. She takes me all the way to the back and the gagging sound she makes has my balls tightening. Fuck, if she keeps that up I'm going to come. I want to see her naked and riding me but I can't say it. I just have to take whatever she gives me.

Lola continues to lick and suck, she fondles my balls and I whimper and pull at my restraints. The need to touch her is all consuming and when she pulls back and undoes her bra, revealing her perfect tits, and then rubs them all over my cock, teasing me with every inch of her perfect body, a wave rolls through me.

She slides her panties down and grinds her wet pussy against my cock. "Look what you do to me, Mr. Murphy."

Fuck, I'm going to come.

She leans back and with one hand she plays with my balls while she grinds her silky wet clit against my impossibly hard cock. It feels *so fucking good.*

I squeeze my eyes shut and she tuts, "Eyes open, Mr. Murphy. You're not going to want to miss this."

"Holy fuck," I mumble around the tie. It's jumbled but she hears it just the same and it has her smiling.

She sits up just a bit and then takes my cock in her hand, lining me up to take her. The moment she slides me inside of her perfect body I pulse in excitement. This—this woman, this moment, every single bit of it—is perfect. She sets her hands down on my chest and then she pushes all the way down, stealing my fucking breath. Her head lolls to the side. "Fuck yes, you feel so good, Mr. Murphy."

I whimper beneath her as she begins to ride me, making slow waves roll through me with every swivel of her hips. She's chasing her own orgasm, her skin is flushed, her nipples hard pebbles, and her gorgeous hair is a glorious curtain around us. Finally, fucking finally, she leans forward and tugs the satin of the tie with her teeth and presses her lips to mine. I don't get a word in because the moment her tongue tangles with mine, there's not a single thing left to say.

We're doing this, Lola and I. We're in this for the long haul. And as she steals her first orgasm, I know that even without the use of my hands right now, I'm never letting this woman go.

CHAPTER 42

Lola

I pop in the tab for Exhibit Q and add the group of text messages. Although I rarely agree with a word from Amy's mouth, I'll admit that putting together Exhibits is the worst.

With a couple of taps, I even out the stack, then sigh in relief. I miss our paper juggers but at least it's finally done.

Any time now, Sloane will be here. She picked the boys up from school, and when Cal finishes up in court, we're all headed upstairs for a round-robin Ping-Pong tournament before dinner.

I never could have imagined looking forward to something as ordinary as cooking dinner and hanging out with my bosses in the world's shittiest apartment, but here I am. Sitting around the Ping-Pong table laughing with the guys has become my favorite pastime. Helping with homework is a privilege, reading a book with Murphy the best way to wind down. There's no shortage of entertainment in the presence of all these men—big or small. Sully's grumbles and Brian's huffs when Cal attempts to get them to smile—which he does constantly—are amusing. Even doing dishes with one of the guys has become a cherished activity.

"Are you humming?"

Sloane's sharp accusation startles me and I drop the pile of papers. Half land on the table, while the rest flutter to the floor, covering the hideous gold carpet in a blanket of white.

"Fuck." I crouch and snatch up one paper after another.

"That's more like it," Sloane teases, dropping down next to me.

Head bowed as I scramble to pick up the pages, I chuckle. "I'm supposed to be using *fuck* less."

Papers in hand, she narrows her eyes on me.

"What? I figured you'd appreciate it?" I snatch the last three papers from the floor and stand. "Better example for your son too."

"Yeah, less cursing would be great." She hands her stack to me. "But I want to know why you look like that?"

"Like what?" I roll my lips together trying to fight the perma grin Brian has accused me of wearing so much lately.

"All smiley and dopey—" Her eyes widen and she sucks in a hard breath. "Oh my God, tell me you didn't," she hisses.

I set the motion exhibits down and turn to face her fully. "Didn't what?"

Her blue eyes are assessing, full of knowing, as they skate over my face once and then again. "No, no." She sighs. "You fell in love with the manchild!"

"I...*stop*," I whisper-shout, glancing around to make sure no one hears her.

There are definitely a myriad of big feelings trying to burst out of my chest at any given moment, sure, but Cal and I haven't said those words yet. And the first time I say them will be to his face.

"You totally did." Her expression goes stony.

"Shhhh." I swat at her. "Keep your voice down."

She grasps my wrist, her long French manicured nails biting into my skin as she drags me out of the conference room.

As we leave, I assume she's taking me out front but before we get to the door she makes a sharp left and forces me into the supply closet. She follows me in with a huff, and when she slams the door, we're shrouded in a depressing semi-darkness.

Instantly, I flash back to being trapped in here with Cal. It's a good thing I took charge of having the knob replaced instead of leaving it up to Cal like I did with the exterminator.

"Tell me everything," she demands, finally releasing me.

I scan the dusty shelves. "Why are we in here?"

"So the guys can't hear us. We have a problem to address."

I prop myself up against the counter. "It's so weird how all the big conversations keep happening in here."

Sloane crosses her arms. "What are you talking about?"

"Never mind." I shake my head and mimic her stance. "So, what did you drag me in here to talk about?"

"You and Cal."

That gets my hackles up. I'm sick of defending my relationship to people who are supposed to be my friends.

"Why is my happiness such a problem for you?" I snap.

With a sigh, she backs up, leaning against the shelving unit. "I can see that you're in the happy stage, but Lo, come on. You're smart and driven."

"And?" If she tells me Cal isn't serious enough for me, or that we aren't compatible, I might lose it on her.

"You can't date a man you work with. Yes, the two of you are disgustingly cute, but we both know how easily work relationships can go bad."

Her response takes the wind out of my sails. She isn't wrong, per se. Office relationships can be hard to manage. And I'm not prepared to battle this out. I was gearing up to shut her down when I thought she'd tell me Cal wasn't right for me, and that has left me unprepared for this unexpected argument.

Her lips twitch, like she knows she's made her point. "You know I'm right. And I have a solution." She straightens. "Come work with me. Will would take you in a heartbeat."

I swallow, still putting together a response she'll accept.

"Lo, let's be real. I'm not moving in. The firm is going under. It's time for you to think about your job, your future."

I sigh. For years, my career was the single most important thing in my life. I worked hours that left little time for friendships or relationships. Hell, it's why I have few friends other than Sloane. If she and I hadn't worked together for years, I can't imagine we'd be as close as we are.

She cocks a brow, zeroing in on me. "Don't tank your career for a man. I did it and I'm telling you, it's not worth it."

CHAPTER 43
Cal

Lola was wrong about Murphy's case. It didn't take the court two months to issue a no finding and close the case. It took two months, five days, and six hours.

But who's counting?

Oh, right. Me.

I've spent the last week pacing, racking my brain for how to prove that I'm worthy of being Murphy's parent. I've successfully kept all of my plants alive, Bubbles has just celebrated his eighth week of life, and Fuzzy is the prettiest cat to ever strut down a Jersey street. Most importantly, Murphy is happy, healthy, and smarter than any other kid in his class. Not that I can take credit for any of that. The kid essentially takes care of me.

Regardless, he's officially mine and I'm his. Letter in hand, I rush through the office, poking my head in one room after another in search of Lola.

There's not a person in sight but as I pass the cupboard where Lola and I were trapped a couple of weeks ago, I swear I hear Sloaney's voice.

Stopping short, I press my ear to the door.

"I can see that you're in the happy stage, but Lo, come on. You're smart and driven."

"And?" Lola says, her tone a little biting.

My heart pounds in my chest. What are they doing in there? And why does it feel like I shouldn't be listening?

"You can't date a man you work with."

My heart plummets at Sloane's words.

"Yes, the two of you are disgustingly cute, but we both know how easily work relationships can go bad."

But we're different. We have a plan and Post-it notes.

Tell her, Lola.

But my girl doesn't reply.

Fuck, fuck, fuck. I take a step back and tug at my hair.

"You know I'm right. And I have a solution. Come work with me," Sloaney, the traitor, says. "Will would take you in a heartbeat."

Absolutely not. Muscles tensing, I reach for the door. I've heard enough.

Just as I've grasped the knob, Sloane speaks again, her tone softer this time. Though her words are just as painful. "Lo, let's be real. I'm not moving in. The firm is going under. It's time for you to think about your job, your future. Don't tank your career for a man. I did it and I'm telling you, it's not worth it."

Heart lodged in my throat, I wait for Lola to defend what we have. I hold my breath so long my vision blurs, yet she still doesn't speak.

Bloody hell. Is she seriously considering Sloane's suggestion?

She can't leave. Fuck.

In a panic, letter clutched in my hands, I stumble up the steps to our flat, all the while willing my daft brain to come up with a plan to change her mind.

For now, I won't confront her about it. Hell, maybe I never will.

The flat is quiet so I pace, considering every possible outcome of that conversation. If I get it out now, I can move on and forget I ever heard it.

I'm yanking at my hair again, spiraling, suddenly certain I'll lose Lola to another firm when the door opens and Murphy walks in.

"Cal?" Head tilted, he studies me. "Are you okay?"

Shit. I forgot Murphy would be here.

"Where've you been?" I ask him, releasing my hair.

Murphy steps further into the flat, dropping his backpack by the door where Brian will surely pick it up while complaining about how no one puts their shite away, and heads toward the kitchen.

Over his shoulder, he says, "Ran into Madame E. We hung out with Sebastian for a bit. He told us about this bar he used to run back in the day." He scratches his head. "Did you know that it used to be illegal to go to a bar?"

I frown. Why does Sebastian talk to everyone but me?

With a shake of my head, I force the thought away. Now is not the time to be worried about the ghost. "He probably shouldn't be talking to you about that stuff," I tell him.

Murphy shrugs. "Like Madame E says, I just listen to what they say."

I chuckle. "That's funny. You're a funny kid, you know that?"

His lips kick up on one side, though he quickly doffs his usual stoic expression again. "Why do you look like someone died? Did someone die?" The reserved look turns to panic in a heartbeat.

Fuck. He probably thinks something's happened to his mum.

I dart across the room and squat in front of him. "Everyone's fine."

The frown marring his face tells me he doesn't believe me. "Then what's wrong?"

Fucking hell. I can't lie, but I can't talk to my six-year-old about how my girlfriend might leave me and how Sloane won't move in, which means we'll lose this firm and the home he and I have only just settled into together.

When Fuzzy stalks past us, whiskers twitching, heading for Murphy's room, an idea strikes.

I scramble to my feet and follow him. "Fuzzy's sad."

As if mocking my lie, he nuzzles up to Murphy's race car bed and purrs.

Murphy pads into the room behind me. "He looks pretty happy to me."

With a groan, I shake my head. "That's just a façade. Trust me, he's worried."

My little lad inspects the cat, the wheels turning in his head. "The cat is worried?"

Head bowed, I run my hand over the top of Fuzzy's head. As if he's determined to call me out, he balances on his hind legs and paws at my chest, rubbing his head against my stomach. "Yes, very worried."

Murphy flops down on his bed. "What's the cat have to be worried about?"

"He's afraid things will go wrong and then he won't have a job." I paraphrase Sloane's statement as I sit beside him. Not that it's true. I'd never let Lola lose her job. She's the best of us.

Murphy tugs on my shirt sleeve. "Fuzzy doesn't need a job, Dad. You have money and a really good job. You'll take care of him."

The panic that hasn't loosened its hold on me since I overheard that conversation in the cupboard instantly evaporates. "Did you just call me dad?" I gape at my boy. "Wait. Never mind." I rub my sweating palms down my trousers. "The book said not to make this a thing. Back to the topic at hand. What were you saying?"

He gives me a half smile. "We can make it a thing."

A round of fireworks explodes in my chest. "Really?"

He nods. "Just for a minute, though."

I take a deep breath, tempering my words. "I'm really glad you called me dad. As you know, I really like calling you my son."

He ducks a little, gaze averted. "I'm really glad you're my dad..." His tone is barely above a whisper. "Even if you are kind of weird and obsessive about cats working."

Sighing, I drape an arm over his shoulders and rest my chin on his head. "It's not really about the cat."

He hums, as if he already knew that. "So what is it about?"

Sitting up, I steel my spine. It's truth time. "Lola."

"Oh. You're worried that she can't work for you because she's your girlfriend now?"

I clear my throat. "That's a dumb thing to freak out about, right?"

Murphy shrugs. "I don't know. I'm six. But I think maybe what we all really want is to know that we're safe."

I nod. "Right. And she's safe because she has a job."

Slumping, my son lets out a weary sigh. "No, *Dad*, she's safe because you love her."

That word sends a jolt of excitement through me. It's such an easy thing to admit. "I do love her."

He gives me a proud smile, as if he's the parent and I'm the child. "I know you do. And what happens when you love people?"

I grimace. "I don't know. I've never done this before."

"Well, you love me and you gave me a place to stay. So," he prods, "if you love her…"

I jump to my feet. "Oh my God. I've figured it out."

"Finally," he mutters, dropping his head back.

Heart bursting, I point at him. "I'm going to propose."

His eyes bug out of his head. "I wasn't going there."

"No, this is brilliant." I stalk to one end of the room, then turn on my heel. "Then she doesn't have to work."

"No," he groans. "That's not where I was going at all."

I stop in front of him and hold out a hand. "You are the best son ever, I love you."

He lets me pull him to his feet. Then, to my utter shock, he loops his arms around my waist. "Love you too, but I'm not so sure about this whole plan."

My heart triples in size at the gesture. And his words. I smile because not a thing could go wrong now that I know my son loves me and he's officially mine to keep. Now we just need to make sure we can keep Lola too. I wave a hand, completely relaxed. "It's genius. We'll even get Fuzzy involved. Lola will love it."

CHAPTER 44
Lola

"Cal," I call as I get to the top of the stairs.

Please, please, please let all the plants be alive. The fish too.

All was well when I popped up here to check while Cal took Murphy to school. Though I can't imagine the plants would wither this quickly, the same cannot be said about the fish.

He'll be fine one minute, then *bam*, he's belly up at the top of the tank. We're currently on fish number six. Damn Madame E and her prediction. Every day it gets a little harder to doubt the woman.

Though this fish has been hanging on for almost two weeks, I don't dare to hope.

At least I know the cat's okay. Brian and the cat that definitely thinks its name is Damnit returned from their afternoon walk fifteen minutes ago. How he managed to get Fuzzy to come upstairs afterward rather than curl up on the couch in his office is a mystery, but he managed it.

If Brian hadn't been such a dick about Cal and me, I'd feel bad. Instead, I can't help but believe this is karma.

"Cal?" I call again as I turn the doorknob.

Sully insisted I come up here, but from the silence that greets me, I don't think Cal is here.

As the door creaks open, my jaw drops to the floor.

Fuck. Roses are far more difficult to take care of than any of the other plants up here. Just as the thought crosses my mind, I realize that the dozens of them scattered around the room are already cut.

"Cal?" This time my tone is much less *where are you* and much more *what the actual fuck are you doing now.*

Because the man is standing in the middle of the half lit room surrounded by roses with a giant cat at his feet.

Fuzzy, who's chewing on a black cube-shaped object—a new toy, maybe?—blinks at me, but is quickly preoccupied by his find.

"Lola." Cal stands tall, his dark hair neatly combed and his face lit up. "You mean everything to me. You and Murphy. You're my everything."

Closing the door behind me, I survey the space more carefully. The pomp and circumstance with which he's greeting me puts me on alert. God, if this is his way of asking me to move in...

Not that I don't want to, but we haven't been dating long, and this place is already packed full.

"I know you want job security," he says, taking a step closer. "And a future with the firm. And you know what I always say, *whatever Lola wants...*"

"I'm not worried about my job, Cal." After Sloane's argument about my work situation, I sat her down and spelled it all out for her. And I really think I got through to her.

And that gives me hope that this wild year in Jersey might actually be a success.

"Good. You shouldn't be." He takes my hands in his. "I know just how to ensure the firm is always yours. We'll put your name on it, too."

This man is so sweet, but sometimes he's so ridiculous. "Cal," I hedge. Fuck, I hate to crush his spirit, but if I don't stop this now, there's no telling how far he'll take the idea. "That's not how this works. I'm not an attorney, you can't just list my name along with yours and Brian's."

His smile grows, if that's possible. "I don't have to add anything to make it happen. Not if your name is mine."

And then the man drops to his knee in front of me, head tipped back, eyes dancing with excitement.

Panic grips my chest. *Oh no. What is he doing?*

With a tug on his hand, I inhale sharply, but before I can open my mouth to shut him down, he says, "Shhh, you'll ruin it."

What? I'm not the one ruining anything.

"Lola," he says. "All I need is us. You and me and Murphy. Together. Forever. So, will you do me the biggest honor of my life and marry me?"

I stare down at him, unable to breathe.

"Fuzzy." With one hand still holding mine, he pulls a treat out of his pocket.

Instantly, the cat is at his side, the black toy pinched between his teeth, making one side of his mouth bulge.

"Give it to her buddy." Cal holds out the treat.

Instead of dropping what I can now see is a ring box in favor of the treat, the cat swallows it.

"No." Cal lunges at the giant feline, but it's too late, the box is gone. Down his throat.

"No, fuzzy," Cal whines. "You weren't supposed to eat her ring."

He clutches the cat's snout and pulls, trying to pry his jaws open. It's no use. Fuzzy scrambles away, then snatches the treat off the floor and swallows that too.

Well shit.

I press a hand to my forehead. "That's a sign."

Cal glares at his pet. "A sign I shouldn't have bought the cat."

"No. It's a sign that I'm going to have to spend 5k to replace it."

His lips tug down as he peers up at me. "I'm absolutely not that bloody cheap. Your ring cost way more than that."

I sigh. "That's not what I meant."

With a shake of his head, he wipes his hands on his pants, then clutches my wrist. "We'll get a new one. You can have eight rings. Whatever you want. That's not the important part. The important part is that we're together."

I ease myself to my knees and meet his eye. "I agree. That's the most important thing here." Which makes the rest of this sentence hard. "But."

The smile that reappeared on his face even after the cat consumed a ridiculously expensive piece of jewelry fades.

God, I'm an ass. But this is the right thing to do.

"Cal..." I run my thumbs over his knuckles. "I can't marry you."

He sits back on his heels, his chest deflating. "Wow, didn't see it going this way."

"Listen, babe, I love you."

He perks up a bit.

"But—"

He sinks even lower.

"We've been dating a handful of weeks. That's it."

His grin turns devilish. "But you love me."

"Glad you're listening. Way to focus on the positive."

He drops my hand and cups my cheek. "I just don't want you to leave."

I frown. Leave? Where would he get an idea like that? "Why would I leave? And where would I go?"

His face hardens. This kind of serious expression is so foreign for this gregarious man. "To Sloane's stupid firm."

I suck in a breath. Ah. How is it that when I was trapped, not a soul heard me, yet the topic of my private conversation got out so easily?

"Why would I do that?"

"Because..." He tucks his chin and shakes his head. "Actually, I have no idea. It's a terrible place to work. And you'd work for a terrible man. I guarantee he wouldn't buy you coffee every day."

I nod, a rush of relief hitting me. "Right, so why would I leave this firm? Why would I leave my friends, and the man I love?"

Cal beams. "That's a good point. Why would you if you love me?"

I cough out a laugh. "You really like hearing me say that, huh?"

"Yes, Lola." He scoots forward on his knees. "I'd like to hear it a hundred times more. A hundred thousand, actually. Because even if you're not ready to marry me, you're mine and I'm never letting you go."

"Good." I angle in and stroke his smooth cheek. "Because I don't want to be let go."

Cal's eyes widen. "You don't?"

"No. As I told Sloane, not only am I not leaving, but I'm certain it would be a mistake if she didn't move in with us. It'll take all of us to save the firm. It's our family's legacy."

He makes a strangled sound, his body locking up. "Our family?"

I nod. "Yes, I might not be ready to walk down the aisle yet, but I can see it happening someday."

He pulls me to his chest, tucking my head beneath his. We're both still on our knees, making the position awkward, but I'll never complain about receiving a hug from the man I love.

"Does that mean you're moving in?" he whispers against my hair.

Ten minutes ago, the idea was absurd. Now? It feels right.

"Yes, Cal, I'll move into your terrible apartment with you. I love you, but the cat is not sleeping in our room."

"That's okay." He buries his face in my neck and inhales deeply. "He prefers Brian's anyway."

CHAPTER 45

Cal

"Want to take these wine glasses?" I call over my shoulder.

It's official. She's moving in with us.

But how the hell has she accumulated so much shite in the three months she's lived here?

"Um—" Her tone is measured, unsure. She's trying not to be difficult. She's been so good about this move.

"I think you should," I say, taking pity on her. She can bring whatever the bloody hell she wants. "Ours are rubbish. We can toss them." I wrap the first and ease it into the box, humming as I work.

It's hard to believe that Lola is truly mine. It feels like a dream. The best kind. And I never want to wake up.

When my mobile buzzes on the counter, I flip it over to check the incoming message and almost drop the glass I'm wrapping when the sender's name registers.

Brandy: Hi Cal! Thanks for the updates!
Looks like Murphy is loving New York. That
makes this a bit easier…

Who's Your Daddy

My stomach rolls. This can't be real. For three bloody months, we haven't heard a word from her, and now she thinks she can have Murphy back just like that? She didn't respond to a single one of the messages I sent. Fuck. Did she even read them? Unlikely, since she thinks we still live in New York.

How is it possible that this woman could care so little for her own child?

I stomp into Lola's room.

"Okay, you're walking very hard. I can live without the glasses. But I do need a place to put all my shoes."

Lola is in her closet, staring at the dozens of shoes that I've obviously already set a place for in my bedroom.

"You can have whatever you want, but she"—I thrust my mobile out to her—"can't have Murphy."

Lola eyes me over her shoulder, her movements jerky. "What?"

I wiggle the mobile in front of me, too fucking brassed off to speak.

She jumps to her feet and snatches the device from me. As her eyes dart back and forth, her lips move, forming the words of each text silently, her face reddening. "She's got to be kidding," she growls.

I squeeze my eyes closed to stave off tears. "Can she do this? Can she just take him back?"

Lola shakes her head, shoulders pulled back. "No. We'll fight it. She abandoned her child. They won't just hand him back over to her. But it's likely that the court will order some type of visitation eventually."

Heart cracking in two, I pound out a response.

> Me: He's not a zoo animal. You don't get to drop him off and then come back into his life when it's convenient for you. You're either in or out. If you're in, we can work together to find a solution that's best for Murphy, but think long and hard about what you really want because this is the only time I'll grant you that kindness.

I shove it toward Lola, hand shaking, and let her review it. She's better at this than I am. More levelheaded. And I trust her to know what's best for Murphy.

"I would have called her quite a few names and probably blocked her," she mutters, still glaring at my mobile. "Make her make an effort to find him."

Though devastation threatens to pull me under, there's a modicum of comfort in knowing that Lola is so fiercely protective of my son.

With a succinct nod, she jabs the Send icon. Then, eyes closed, she lets out a long, loud sigh.

Her eyes fly open when the mobile beeps a moment later and Brandy's name appears on the screen again.

My heart sinks. Fucking hell. She's going to fight.

> Brandy: I understand. Honestly, I don't have the resources like you do to help him. The kid is smart. He knows I'm not good at this. He'll understand. Please tell him I love him.

I'm tempted to offer her money to even the playing field. To set her up so she has access to the same types of resources I do.

If I did, would she try?

I don't know.

Murphy deserves two parents who put him first.

Then again, I also truly believe this is the right call.

I can't make her choose him. If she's pressured into it, she'll only continue to disappoint him.

Because, resources or not, a parent should put their child first. If I lost everything tomorrow, I'd still do everything I could to take care of Murphy. And so would Lola.

That's true, unselfish love. Love shows up, no matter what. A good parent does too, even when all they have to offer is themselves.

Teeth gritted, I lace my fingers on the top of my head. "What do I do?"

Fuck, I'm at a loss. I don't bloody know what's right here.

Lola presses her hand to my cheek, stroking softly. "For now, we continue packing. Tonight, we go home and show Murphy just how much we love him. We make sure he knows just how important he is, how thankful we are for the chance to know him. We show him every day that we want him in our lives and that we'll always put his needs first."

"And if Brandy does come back?"

She hums, giving me a sad smile. "Then we deal with it. From now until Murphy turns eighteen, there's a chance we'll have to battle it out in court. I wish I could package it up in a pretty bow and promise you that everything will be okay, but the reality is that she could come back at any moment and prove that she's willing to do the work."

Teeth grinding, I tuck my chin to my chest. It fucking hurts, but she's right.

Arms looped around my waist, she holds me tight. "The court won't close the door completely on a parent who is trying."

The ache in my chest morphs into a sharp pain. God fucking dammit. We really might have to battle.

If Brandy never returns, it'll be heartbreaking for Murphy. And if she does, it'll hurt in a completely different way.

But we'll deal with it if the time comes.

"We have the best family law attorneys," she says into my chest. "And they love your son. Every single one of us will help you through it. All we can do is take it day by day."

I blow out a breath, burying my nose in her hair. "You're amazing, you know that?"

Pulling back, she cups my cheeks. "We're amazing. Now"—she presses her lips to mine, then releases me—"let's get this apartment packed up and start our new life with Murphy, together."

I tug her into my chest again. "I love you, you know that? You and Murphy are the greatest things that have ever happened to me."

I don't think I'll ever get over how lucky I am. When Murphy came into my life, I was forced to grow up. Without him, I wouldn't have her and without her, I don't know that I could have figured out how to be the parent he needs. We're a family. Lola may not be Murphy's mum, but she loves him like he's always belonged to her.

Love and affection for this woman consume me, but there's a hint of uncertainty there too. Swallowing thickly, I hold her at arm's length. "We don't have to get rid of the flat, you know? I'd understand if you wanted to hold on to it for a bit. Just in case."

Sloane's warning to her was legitimate, no matter how badly I want to deny it. Engaging in a relationship with a coworker can't be easy. I'd walk away from the firm before I'd let her get away. But she should have options. She deserves to feel safe. No matter what.

"Already worried that I'll hog the covers?" she teases as she slides a perfectly folded set of sheets into what looks like the original packaging. Fucking hell. The woman is ridiculously organized.

I yank the parcel out of her hand and toss it onto the bed, then take a step closer. "No, but I want you to be comfortable. So if holding on to this place would ease your mind, then we should do it."

Fingers creeping up my chest, Lola shakes her head. "I'm all in, Mr. Murphy."

Fuck. That sexy tone alone makes my trousers feel a tad too tight. But I don't want to give in just yet. So with a hand on her waist, I pull her body to mine. "Are you sure?"

Her smile is exquisite. It's beautiful and breathtaking, overtaking her entire face, showing her true joy. "No emergency plan needed. I trust you and even more than that, I trust us. We're it."

Ducking low, I bring my mouth to hers and kiss the ever loving shite out of her. "We are," I murmur, fingers threading through her loose hair. "But"—I nip at her lip—"this is actually a convenient little place to escape to from time to time."

With my hands on her hips, I turn her and drop kiss after kiss against her neck.

She leans back against my chest, head tipped to one side, giving me better access. "Are you trying to convince me to keep this apartment as some sort of love shack?"

I hum against the soft skin behind her ear. "If that would make you happy, then yes."

"I'm trying to make a grand gesture by giving up my apartment for you. Let me be grand gesturey." She tilts her head up and gives me a mock glare.

I press a kiss to her chin. "If you insist. But your willingness to sleep beside me in a twin-size bed every night was grand gesturey enough—"

Her eyes widen. "Shit, I forgot about the bed."

A chuckle rumbles up my throat. "I've got movers lined up to bring this bed over this afternoon."

She whirls around and smacks me. "You must stop teasing me."

"Though I could cancel and have a heart-shaped bed delivered instead. What do you think?"

"*Cal.*"

I lick my lips and lean in close. "Yes, Lola?"

"Shut up and kiss me."

Lips slanted over hers, I do just that. And when we come up for air, I whisper, "Whatever Lola wants."

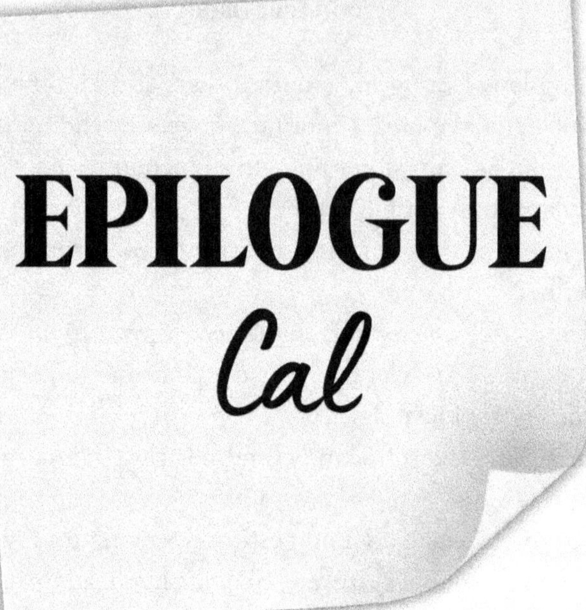

"This seems very unprofessional," Lola says as I tie the satiny fabric over her eyes. "It's the middle of the work day."

Funny how she barely fights me though.

"Everyone is out of the office," I whisper into her ear and smile as a shiver works across her pretty back. "Sully has court and Brian took Amy to lunch."

"Brian and Amy?" Lola squeaks.

I chuckle. "No, Brian is like you. I don't think he could take ten minutes of her outside the office. But he did promise to handle the intern package for her law school mid-term and she said, and I quote, "if we have to fill out this whole thing can we do it with fries and a slushie?"

Lola laughs out loud at my horrible impression of Amy. Lola's is no better, but with my British accent, I suppose mine is worse. I pull on the rolling chair she's seated in and twist her to face me. Then lean down and press a kiss to her lips. I'll never get over the way she melts against me instantly. How she lets me kiss her so freely.

I'll never get over the fact that she's mine.

It's been two weeks since Lola moved in and not to sound like a mushy twat but everything has been fucking perfect since then. Just like before, she and Murphy are my damn world. He now only refers to me as Dad, which is, in my opinion, the greatest word in the English language, and he and Lola are the best of friends.

He did finally have a FaceTime call with Brandy, and though I could tell it was hard for him to see her so bubbly and excited, mostly focusing on all her adventures, I think he seemed a bit more settled knowing she was okay. He asked us afterward if he would be staying in Jersey and I told him he's staying wherever I go. The way the kid tried to hide the big smile by turning toward Fuzzy and nuzzling into his neck was very typical for my son, but I heard him later that night telling Lola he wanted to be wherever we were.

It's going to take time, I know that. But we've got all the time in the world because not one of us is going anywhere.

So long as we can get T. J. to move in. I made an appointment with Madame E to figure out our next steps. She should be here within the hour. Which means my surprise for Lola has to get moving and I have to stop kissing her.

But fuck do I love kissing my girl.

Lola wraps her tiny hands around my neck and I lift her out of her chair. "Are you sure no one is coming back?" She says with a breathy moan as she wraps her legs around my waist and starts grinding against me. Her skirt rides up to her hips and I have to stifle a damn groan to try to keep my cool.

"I'm sure," I promise, hiking her closer and walking her out of the office.

"Cal, we can't do it in Brian's office again. He's been so good with Fuzzy, he'll murder you in your sleep."

I chuckle and peck her lips again. "We're not doing anything in Brian's office. We're doing it in yours."

I walk straight into the last office on the right and then set Lola on the brand new desk that was delivered last evening while she was reading Murphy a story upstairs. Then I pull the tie from her eyes.

"My office?" Lola's face is a mixture of confused elation. Her smile is wide but she also looks like she doesn't believe it.

I nod. "I'm barely here anyway. So you can work in here and stay away from Amy. I'll only need it if I'm meeting with a client."

She snorts. "You never meet with clients."

"Exactly. So it's all yours."

"Cal," Lola breathes my name out. "This is amazing. And this desk. And that filing cabinet." She stands up and walks around the small office which is far less than she deserves but I did try to fill it with all her required things. She spins and sucks in a breath when she spots the picture of her, Murphy and me from Halloween sitting on her desk. There's also a copy of the post-it note framed and a picture of the two of us from our day on the cliff walk—the one where she's kissing me on the cheek. "It's everything I would have ever wanted."

I step closer and push her beautiful red hair behind her ear, then stroke the space beneath it. God, she's so soft. I love touching her. "Well, whatever Lola wants..."

Her eyes light up. Those words are never a taunt anymore. But before I can lean in and take my prize, she presses her finger against my lips, stopping me. "But if I'm in your office, then you'll be in the conference room working with Amy."

I shrug. "Yes."

Her eyes narrow. "I don't like it."

My smile blooms across my face. "Are you jealous, Lola Caruso?"

She rolls her lips and then nods, before wrapping her arms around my neck. "Yes."

"Well, what can I do to make it up to you?"

She bites her lip. "You could work in here with me."

I can't help it, a bark of a laugh sneaks out. "Is Lola actually begging me to stick around?"

She rolls her eyes. "Whatever. You know I like you, this isn't a secret."

I grin. "Good, because I love you."

Lola melts at those words. "I love you too, Cal." This time she doesn't stop me when I lean in to kiss her.

I kick the door shut, because much like my bedroom, there isn't a ton of room and then I settle Lola on the desk prepared to devour her.

"Lo!" My brother's booming voice has Lola pushing back and scrambling to right herself.

"I thought you said no one was here!" she hisses.

I growl as I stare at the door right as my brother swings it open. "No one was supposed to be."

"Lola, I thought I told you I needed the Vishay complaint served," Sully starts, then he covers his eyes like we're naked. "Jesus Christ, can the two of you keep your hands off each other ever!"

Lola huffs in embarrassment and I block her. "We're both dressed you sod! And knock next time. This is Lola's private space."

My brother's hand falls down and he looks about as annoyed as me. You'd think the guy would at least apologize. "And what do you mean she needs to serve a complaint?"

Lola pushes me out of the way. "I did serve the complaint. The guy threw the papers in my face after saying he wasn't Vishay but a court officer was standing right there." Her face gets redder as she explains everything that happened. "So yeah, after all that, the court had no problem calling it served."

I whirl on my brother. "Why did you send my girlfriend to serve divorce papers."

Lola's red hair whips around her shoulders as she stares me down. "I serve people all the time at the courthouse."

"Not assholes who are there for their final restraining order hearing," I growl. I'm ready to rip my brother's head off for putting her in a bad position when I hear another voice.

"Helloooo!"

I straighten at the sound of Madame Esmeralda's greeting. Shockingly, the woman doesn't even need us to call out to her to let her know where we are. Her psychic abilities have her rounding the hallway and peeking into Lola's new office.

"Callahan, we will need to reschedule our session."

Ah, shit. My shoulders slump. I was really hoping we could get her help on the Sloane situation.

"I know, it's disappointing but it's for the best because your path is stable, and there is nothing jumping out to me." Her words have me brightening as I glance at Lola and she gives me a soft smile. For all her anger over me trying to tell her what to do when it comes to our job, I know Lola loves me and appreciates that I care. Or I hope she does. I suppose I'll have to work on that. Madame E continues talking, "Sebastian needs me to take him for a ride. Ever since he went with Lola's parents on that motorcycle tour, he has become obsessed with the rumble of the bike between his thighs."

I grin. "It's so nice he had a good time, June and Dezi still ask about how he is doing."

Lola wraps her arms around my waist and leans against my chest. "It worked out so perfectly for all of us, got Mom and Dad out of my hair, and Sebastian out of yours."

"Enough," Sully barks.

I grab one of the balls I perfectly placed off Lola's desk and nail him in the head. It's like training a dog. Bad behavior deserves a knock in the head.

"Wanker," Sully grumbles, grabbing the ball that's hit the floor. He slips it into his pocket and glares at me. "No more balls."

I smirk. "It seems Mr. Grumpypants hasn't had his happy-nappy."

Madame E chuckles. Lo groans. "No. That one doesn't work."

I shrug. "I like it."

"I'm done," Sully grumbles.

He goes to leave but Madame E steps in front of him. "Sullivan, you need to get ready because the incubator is on the way."

"Incubator?" I try to think what type of animal would require an incubator. I will get the riddle this time. I light up at the idea of a new thing to figure out. "Are we getting chickens next?"

"No." The words fly from Lola's lips. "You promised no more things."

"This is for Sullivan, Callahan. Nothing to concern you," Madame E says to me seriously, then she turns and disappears.

"Wait," I call after her, stalking past my brother. I can hear Lola following. We need more information.

Incubator. Hmm, what the hell would need an incubator?

Madame E is gone before we get to the entryway and I sigh. "Guess we'll find out soon enough," I say to Lola right as the bell over the front door jangles, announcing someone else. I spin hoping Madame E is back only to find my sister-in-law storming in like a woman on a mission.

"Where is he?" she growls. I swear her and Sully are the same person.

"Sloaney!" I say with a smile, trying to calm her down.

"Where is he?" she repeats, not meeting my smile. She doesn't wait for an answer either, she just storms past both Lola and me and heads toward Sully's office.

"What's happening?" I ask Lola.

She shrugs as Sloane reappears, with Sully by her side, dragging him by his burgundy tie down the hall.

"This is the weirdest day," Lola mutters, head tilted as we watch Sloane slam the door to the tiny computer closet.

I slide my hands around her waist. "Want to continue what we started in your office?"

Lola wraps her arms around my neck and leans in to kiss me right when another voice interrupts us.

"For fucks sake, can everyone stop kissing!" We turn to see Brian who has a smudge of red lipstick on his collar.

"Oh my God, did you and Amy—"

He shakes his head wildly. "What? No! Why would you say that?"

Lola points to his collar. "You've got lipstick."

He glances down and growls. "That's ketchup because Amy tried to feed me one of her fries and I refused to play the choo-choo game."

Lola bursts out laughing.

"It's not funny!" Even as he says it, he starts to smile.

"It really is funny," I tell him.

"No!" We hear Sloane yell. "I brought you into this damn closet to say *I'm pregnant.*"

Every single one of us seems to have the same idea as we rush over to the closet door. "Did she just say she's pregnant?" Lola whisper-hisses.

Brian pushes her forward. "Get closer, what are they saying now?"

"Oh shit. You're *the incubator,*" we hear Sully reply.

"No he didn't!" Lola hisses.

"Incubator?" Sloane screeches.

Oh bollocks. I've got to fix this. Sully is fucking this all up. I reach for the door knob without thinking and Lola and Brian fall forward, right at Sloane and Sully's feet.

"Cal!" Lola yells up at me.

Later I'll feel bad that I did that, but right now I've got to save my brother. "Sloaney, you're pregnant?" My arms spread in excitement. Then it dawns on me what this means. "Wait, if you're pregnant, that means you have to move in!"

"Oh shit, he's right," Brian says from the floor next to Lola.

"You've got to be kidding me," Sloane hisses. "Sully, tell them this is ridiculous."

I look to my brother and for the first time in a long time I watch as a smile spreads across his face. He slides his hands into his pockets and nods. "Of course you're moving in, you're the incubator."

Lola sucks in a breath from the floor and curses. "Shh, Sully, you're going to ruin it."

To find out how Sloane reacts to being called the incubator make sure to continue reading *Better Daddy*!

Acknowledgments

A huge thank you to all the readers who loved Mom Coms so much that we knew we had to make Dad Coms happen! Also thank you to Jenni's favorite Jersey family law firm for providing inspiration that made this book so much fun! Orange suits, nerf balls, and interns it all makes our days a never ending adventure.

This book would not have come together without the help of some truly amazing people. Thank you Daphne Elliot for taking on this group project again with us. We keep throwing these ideas at you and you jump in full swing with us. Thank you Tiffany, Sara and Jess, who helped us make this happen. More importantly though, the sincerest of thanks to Tiffany for helping us navigate this multi-cast audio production. To our beta readers, Sara, Jeff, Kayleigh and Kira.

To our lovely editor Beth, thank you for loving these guys and their girls as much as us and making the book better as you always do. To our incredible street teams who help promote our books day in and day out, every release gets better because of you! We are in awe of your friendship and support. A huge thank you to Elin for the gorgeous cover images that brought Cal and Lo to life. And to Melissa for creating the gorgeous covers. Especially thank you for not giving up when we ask for another option and another. You are the best.

Sara thank you for the formatting, graphics, and the million and one other things you did weekly to keep this book on track.

Thank you Alyssa and Jeff for making sure the book was polished with your amazing proofing.

Finally, none of this would be possible without you, our amazing readers. Thank you for all of your messages, your Tiktoks, your dms, your posts and your rants. There is nothing we love more than hearing from each of you how a character affected you, or how a storyline made you laugh. We love your reviews, your anecdotes, and the notes you send. This is only the beginning of Dad Coms so make sure you follow us on Facebook, Instagram, and Tiktok (and join our Patreon, The Bookish Besties) to keep up to date with the rest of this hilarious bunch.

Also by Brittanée Nicole

Bristol Bay Romance

She Likes Piña Coladas

Kisses Sweet Like Wine

Over the Rainbow

Love and Tequila Make Her Crazy

A Very Merry Margarita Mix-Up

Boston Billionaires

Whiskey Lies

Loving Whiskey

Wishing for Champagne Kisses

Dirty Truths

Extra Dirty

Mother Faker

(Mother Faker is Book 1 of the Mom Com Series, but is also a lead in to the Revenge Games alongside Revenge Era. This book can be read as a Standalone, or after Revenge Era and before Pucking Revenge)

Revenge Games

Revenge Era

Pucking Revenge

A Major Puck Up

Boston Bolts Hockey

Hockey Boy

Trouble

War

Playboy

Standalone Romantic Suspense

Deadly Gossip

Irish

Monhegan Summers (Co-Written with Jenni Bara)

Summer People

Also by Jenni Bara

Want more Boston Revs Baseball

Mother Maker - Cortney Miller

The Fall Out - Christian Damiano

Back Together Again - Mason Dumpty

The Fake Out - Emerson Knight

The Foul Out - Kyle Bosco

Finding Out - Coach Wilson

The Freak Out - Asher Price

Curious about the baseball boys from the NY Metros

NY Metros Baseball

More than the Game

More than a Story

Wishing for More

Monhegan Summers (Co-Written with Jenni Bara)

Summer People

www.ingramcontent.com/pod-product-compliance
Lightning Source LLC
Chambersburg PA
CBHW070626300726
48975CB00006B/1934